POKÉMON™

OMEGA RUBY · ALPHA SAPPHIRE

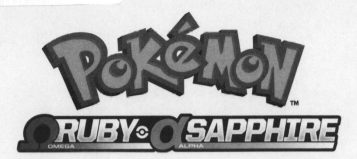

POKÉMON™ ΩRUBY · αSAPPHIRE

OMEGA ALPHA

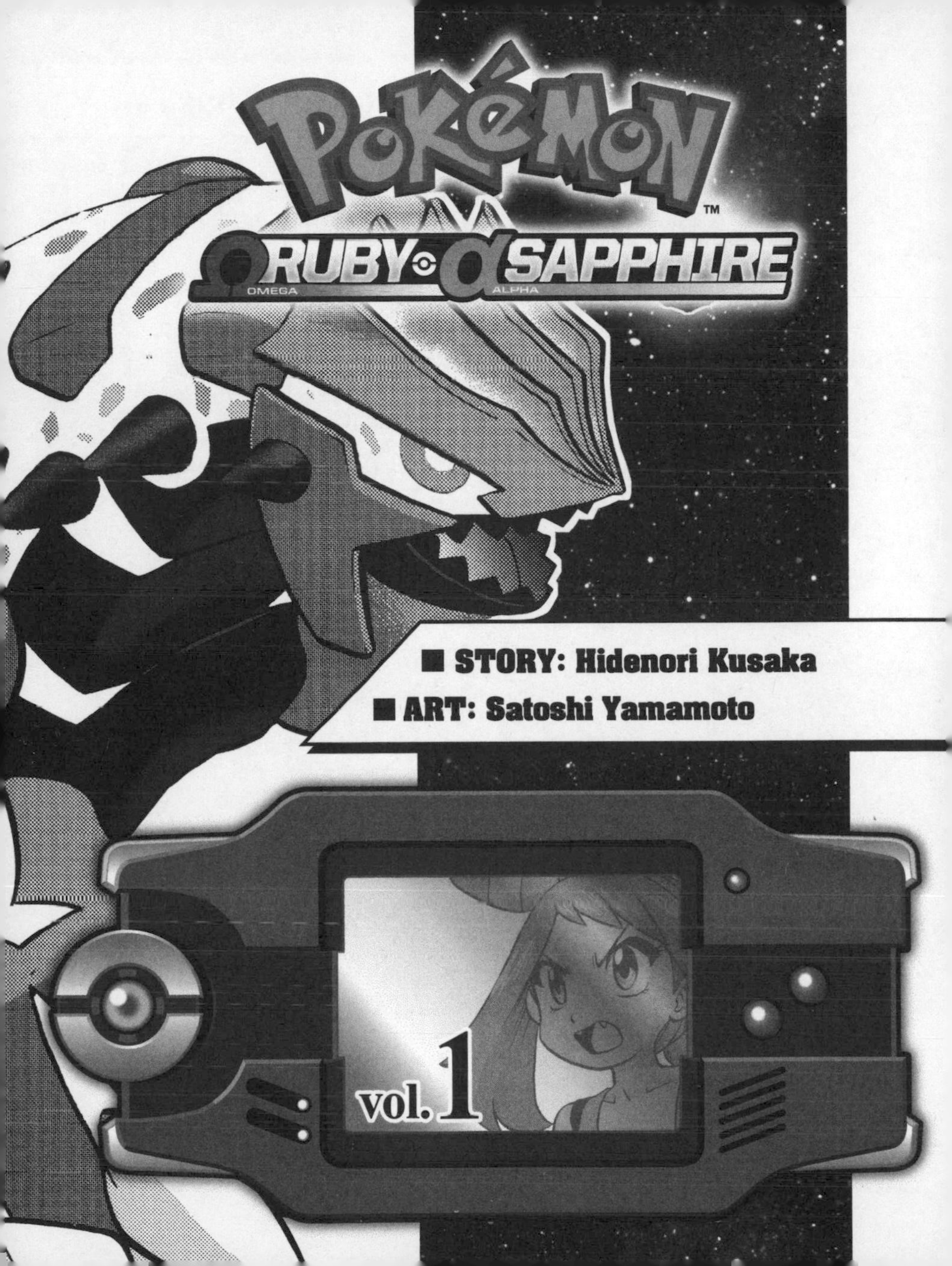

■ STORY: Hidenori Kusaka

■ ART: Satoshi Yamamoto

vol. 1

Our Story Thus Far...

A story about young people entrusted with Pokédexes by the world's leading Pokémon researchers. Together with their Pokémon, they travel, do battle and grow!

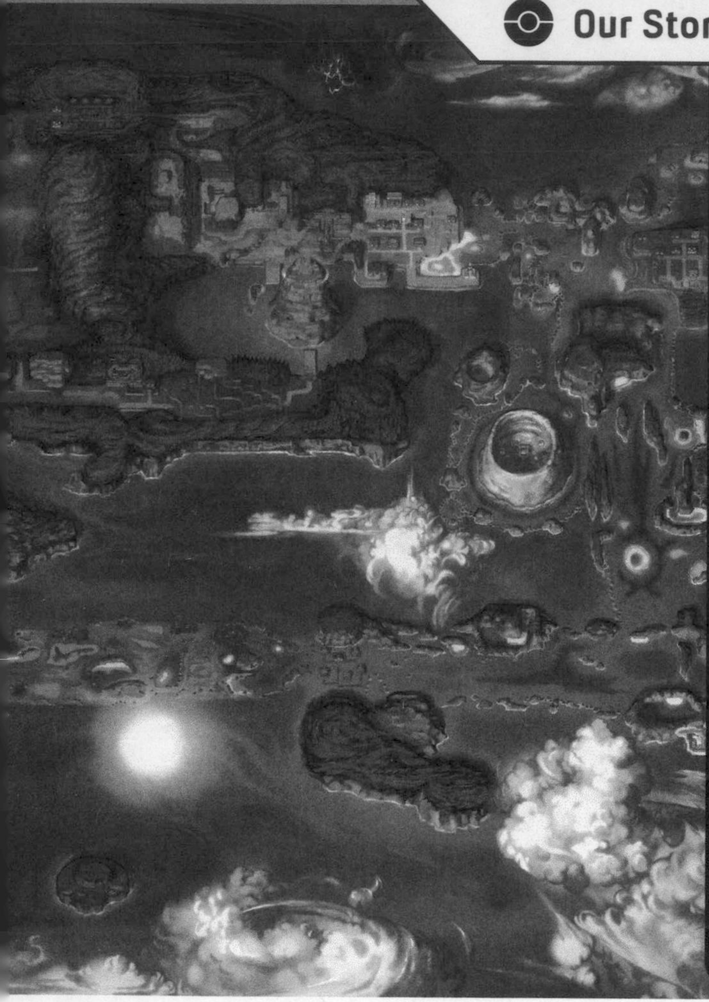

Hoenn Region

Now an area rich in natural resources and unique Pokémon where ancient ruins mingle with modern skyscrapers, in primordial times in this vast region, Legendary Pokémon Kyogre of the Sea and Groudon of the Land battled each other to claim the natural energy of Hoenn for themselves. Kyogre summoned a storm to increase the territory of the sea, and Groudon summoned volcanic magma to increase the territory of the land. They precipitated catastrophic natural disasters, and the inhabitants were powerless to stop them from battling. Finally, both Kyogre and Groudon sunk into hibernation. Time passed... Then one day, two modern world organizations took an interest in these Legendary Pokémon and their powers...

CONTENTS

Omega Alpha Adventure 0 ········ 07

Omega Alpha Adventure 1 ········· 25

Omega Alpha Adventure 2 ········ 41

Omega Alpha Adventure 3 ········ 67

RUBY

SAPPHIRE

EMERALD

Because of their diametrically opposed ideals, at first these two organizations battled against each other—but eventually they joined forces to awaken Kyogre and Groudon, and the two Legendary Pokémon began fighting once more, creating chaos at sea and on land. The Hoenn region settlements and inhabitants were again in danger of being destroyed by natural disasters, just as in ages past...

The crisis was brought to an end by two courageous and determined young Pokémon Trainers, Ruby and Sapphire. Rayquaza, a Legendary Pokémon said to appear out of the sky when Kyogre and Groudon battle, helped them return Kyogre and Groudon to their endless slumber... And so, after many battles, the peace of Hoenn was restored!

But then...we learned of a mysterious mastermind who infiltrated the two organizations to reawaken the Legendary Pokémon. And now we are about to meet someone known as "the Lorekeeper." Will she help or hinder our heroes in saving the world one more time...?

What if you knew
that in ten days' time,
your planet would
be vaporized—
destroyed in the
blink of an eye?

What would
you do for those
ten days and who
would you spend
them with...?

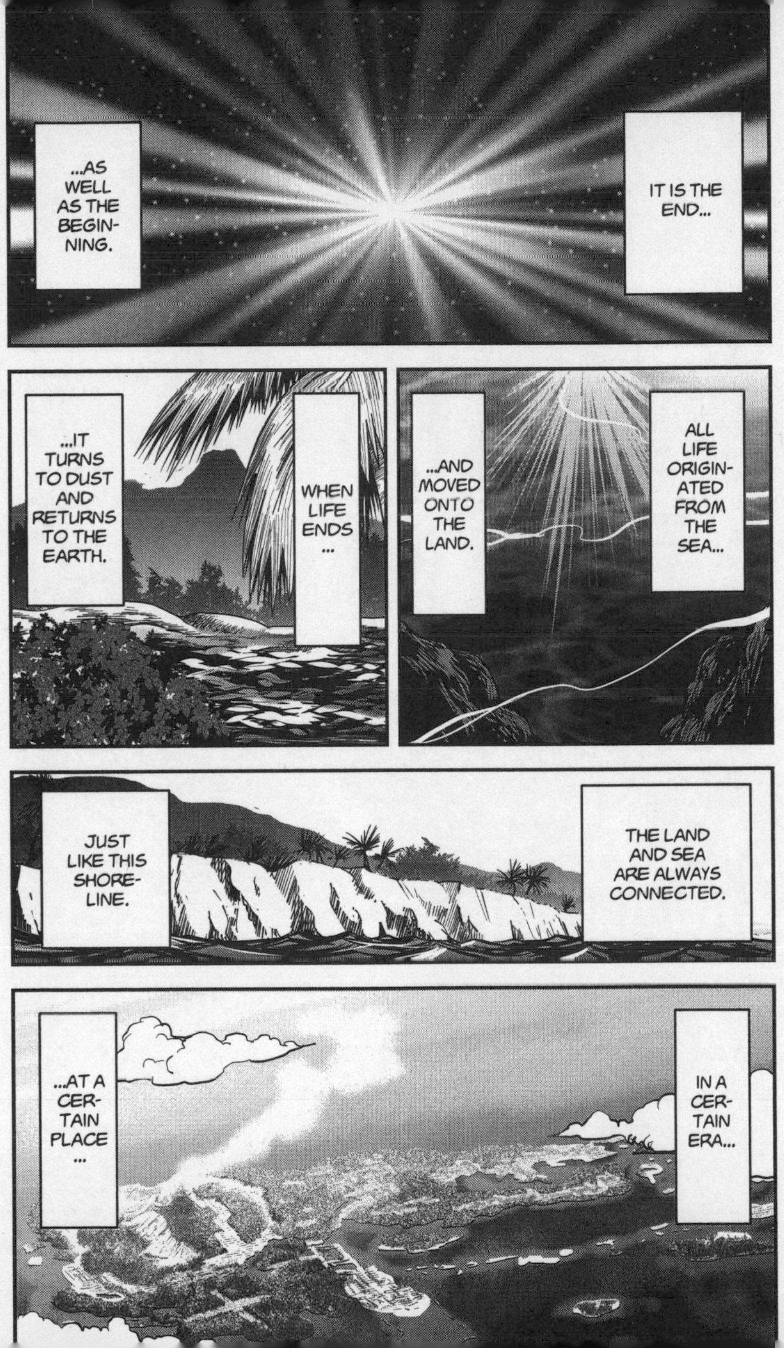
IT IS THE END...
...AS WELL AS THE BEGIN-NING.
ALL LIFE ORIGIN-ATED FROM THE SEA...
...AND MOVED ONTO THE LAND.
WHEN LIFE ENDS...
...IT TURNS TO DUST AND RETURNS TO THE EARTH.
THE LAND AND SEA ARE ALWAYS CONNECTED.
JUST LIKE THIS SHORE-LINE.
IN A CER-TAIN ERA...
...AT A CER-TAIN PLACE...

Omega Alpha Adventure 0

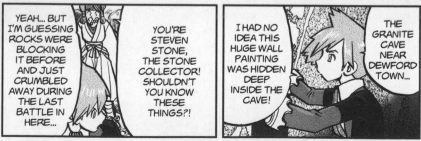

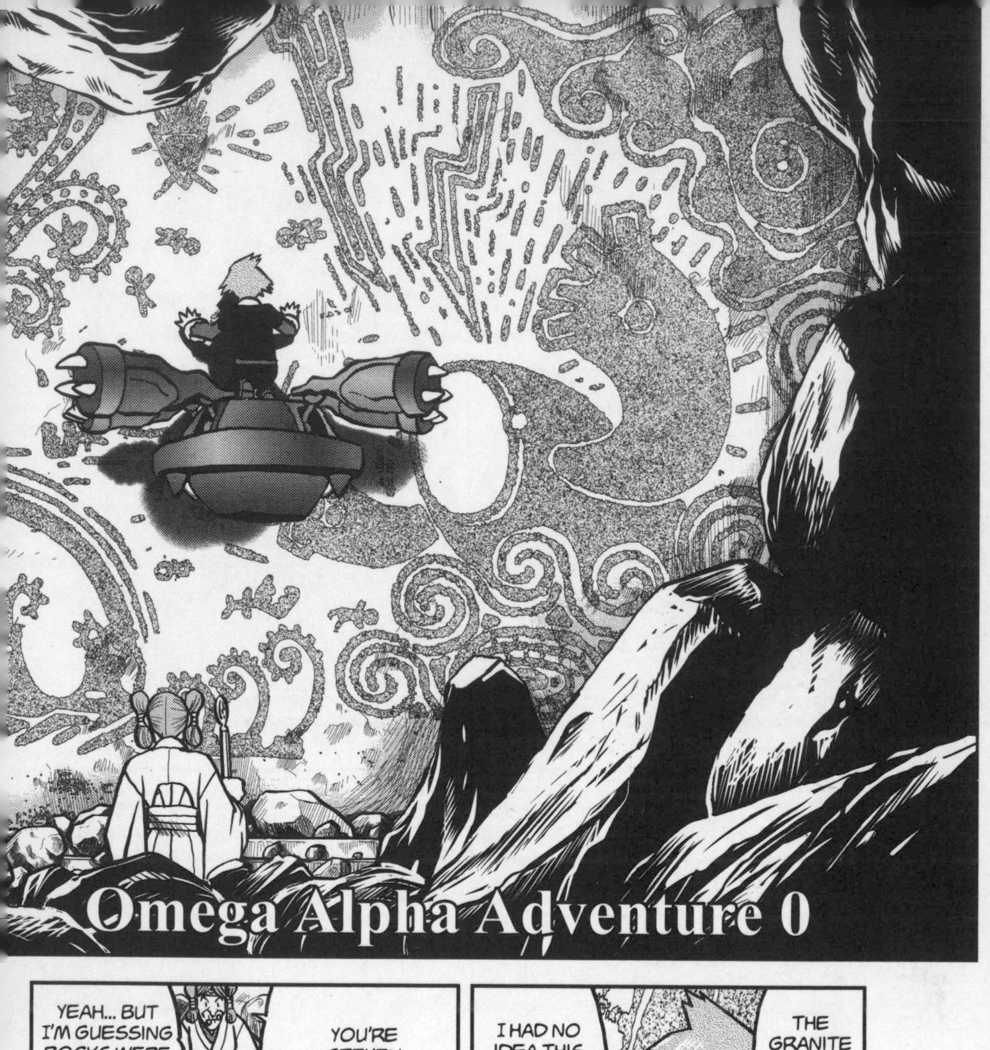
Omega Alpha Adventure 0
THE GRANITE CAVE NEAR DEWFORD TOWN...
I HAD NO IDEA THIS HUGE WALL PAINTING WAS HIDDEN DEEP INSIDE THE CAVE!
YOU'RE STEVEN STONE, THE STONE COLLECTOR! SHOULDN'T YOU KNOW THESE THINGS?!
YEAH... BUT I'M GUESSING ROCKS WERE BLOCKING IT BEFORE AND JUST CRUMBLED AWAY DURING THE LAST BATTLE IN HERE...

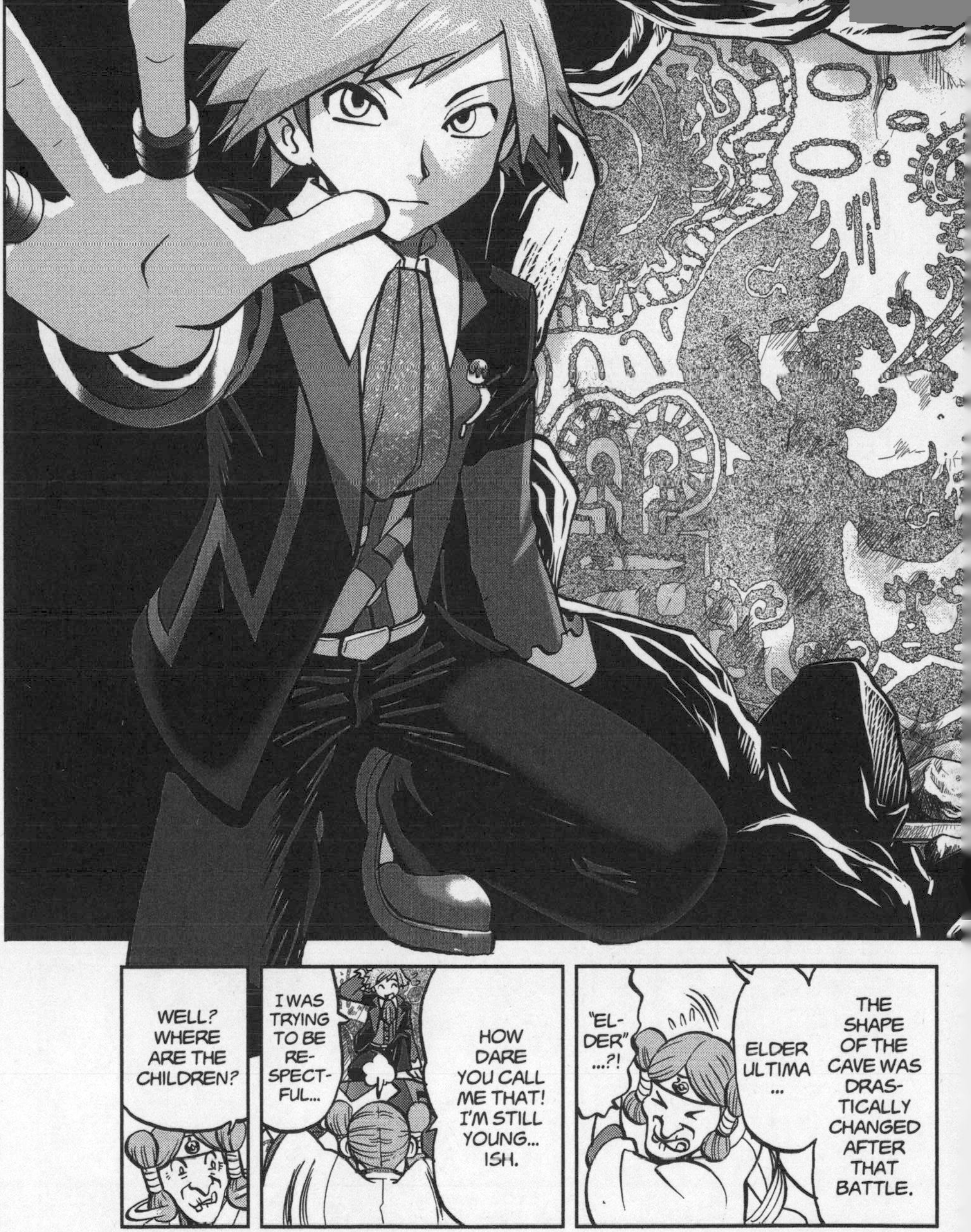
THE SHAPE OF THE CAVE WAS DRASTICALLY CHANGED AFTER THAT BATTLE.
ELDER ULTIMA...
"EL-DER"...?!
HOW DARE YOU CALL ME THAT! I'M STILL YOUNG... ISH.
I WAS TRYING TO BE RESPECTFUL...
WELL? WHERE ARE THE CHILDREN?

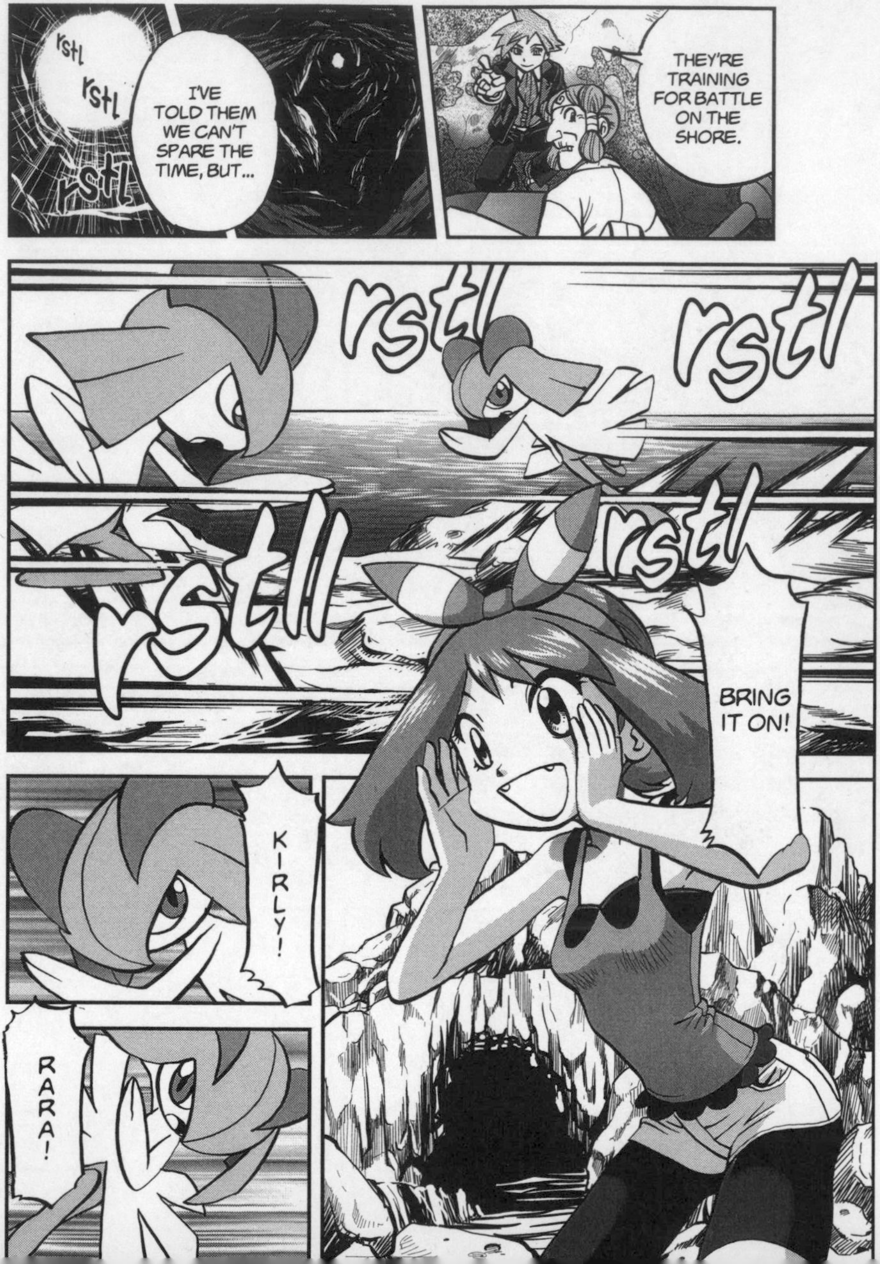
THEY'RE TRAINING FOR BATTLE ON THE SHORE.
I'VE TOLD THEM WE CAN'T SPARE THE TIME, BUT...
rstl
rstl
rstl
rstl
rstl
rstl
rstll
BRING IT ON!
KIRLY!
RARA!

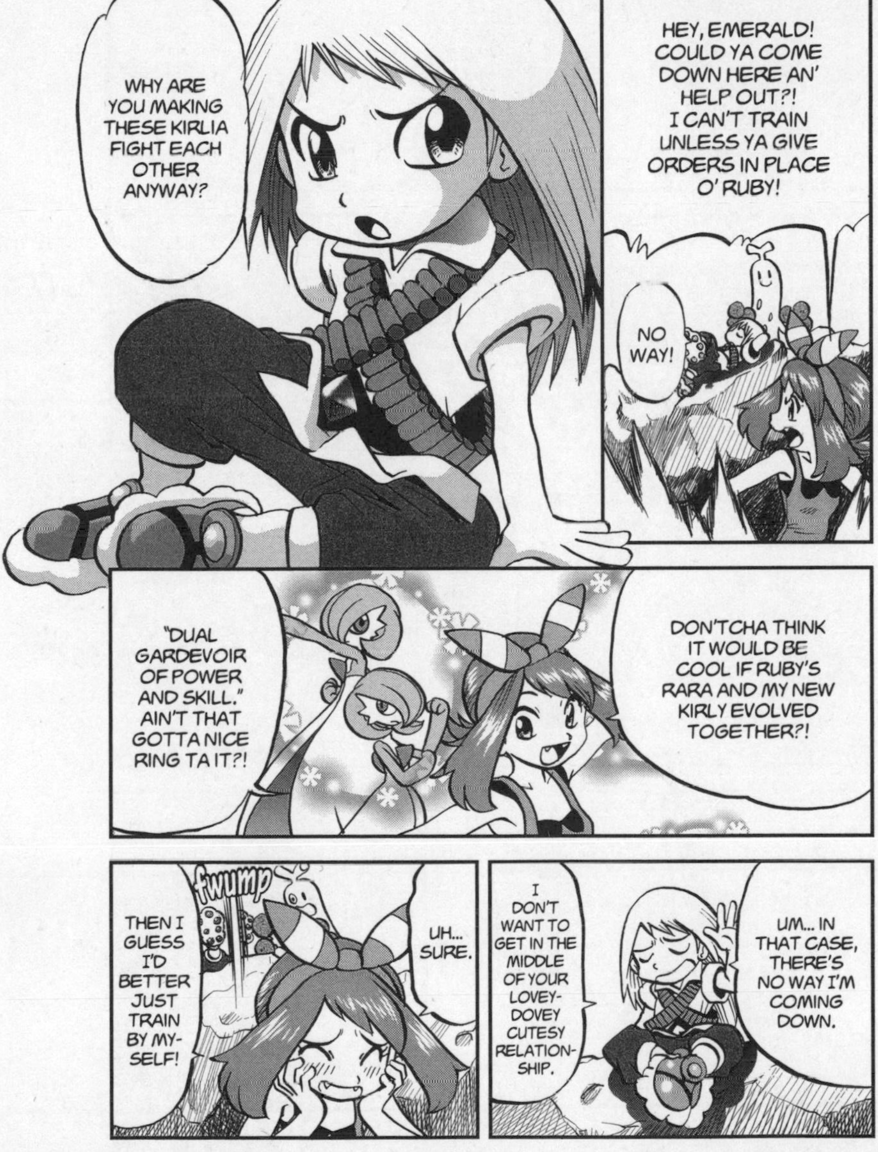
HEY, EMERALD! COULD YA COME DOWN HERE AN' HELP OUT?! I CAN'T TRAIN UNLESS YA GIVE ORDERS IN PLACE O' RUBY!
NO WAY!
WHY ARE YOU MAKING THESE KIRLIA FIGHT EACH OTHER ANYWAY?
DON'TCHA THINK IT WOULD BE COOL IF RUBY'S RARA AND MY NEW KIRLY EVOLVED TOGETHER?!
"DUAL GARDEVOIR OF POWER AND SKILL." AIN'T THAT GOTTA NICE RING TA IT?!
UM... IN THAT CASE, THERE'S NO WAY I'M COMING DOWN.
I DON'T WANT TO GET IN THE MIDDLE OF YOUR LOVEY-DOVEY CUTESY RELATIONSHIP.
UH... SURE.
fwump
THEN I GUESS I'D BETTER JUST TRAIN BY MYSELF!

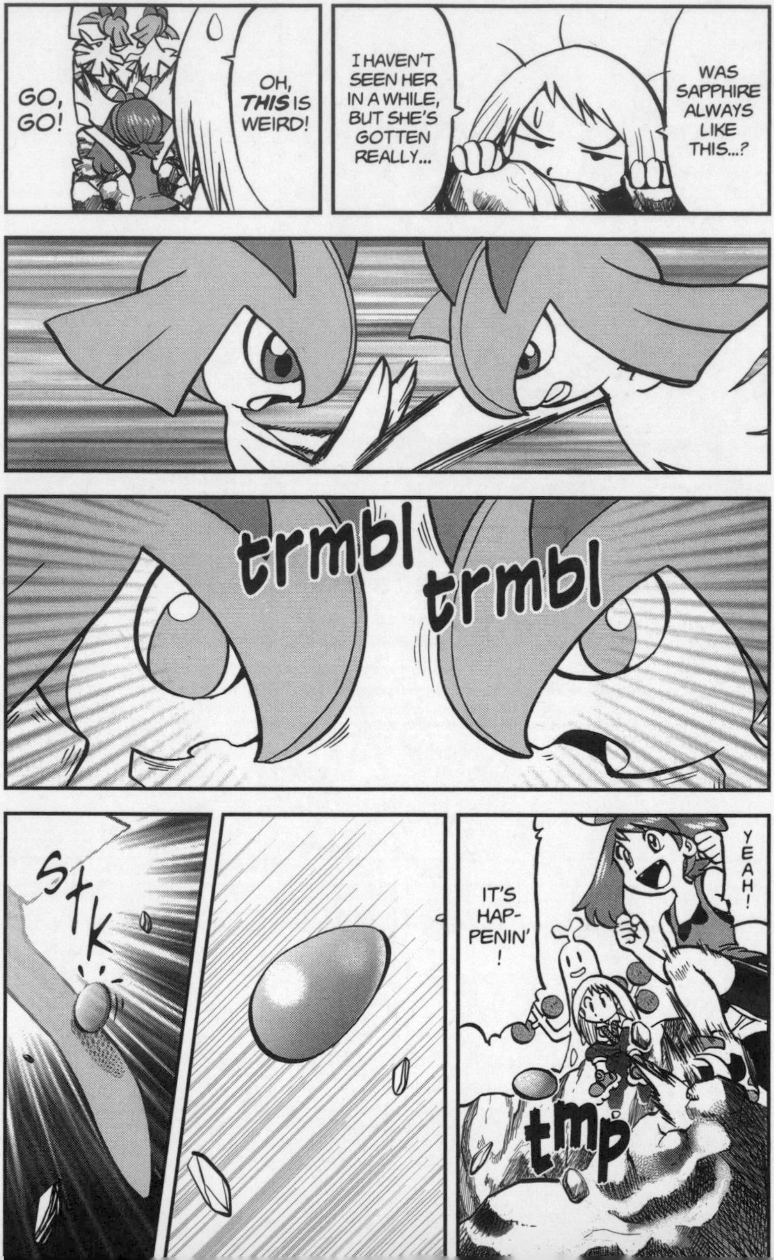
WAS SAPPHIRE ALWAYS LIKE THIS...?
I HAVEN'T SEEN HER IN A WHILE, BUT SHE'S GOTTEN REALLY...
OH, **THIS** IS WEIRD!
GO, GO!
trmbl trmbl
YEAH!
IT'S HAP-PENIN'!
tmp
stk

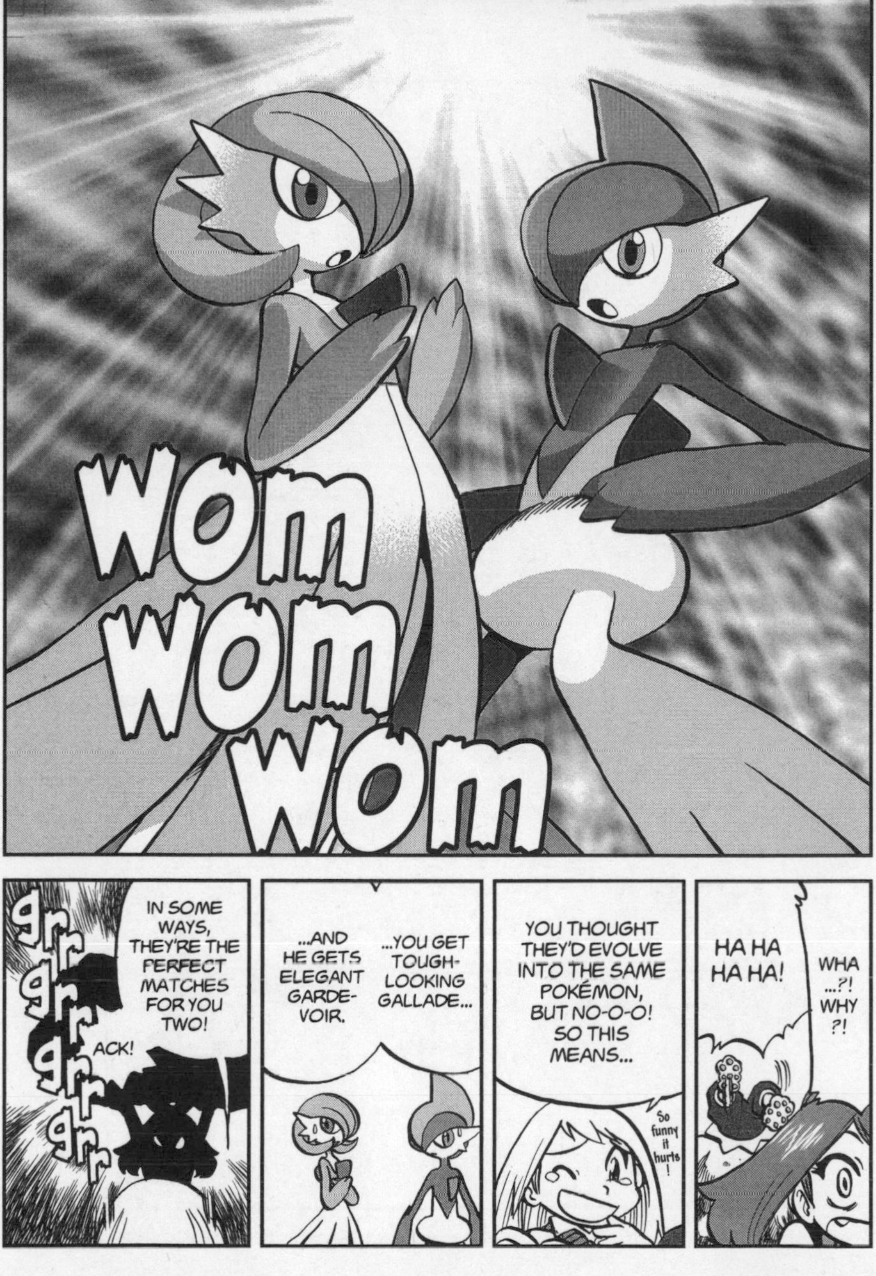
WOM
WOM
WOM
HA HA HA HA!
WHA ...?! WHY ?!
YOU THOUGHT THEY'D EVOLVE INTO THE SAME POKÉMON, BUT NO-O-O! SO THIS MEANS...
So funny it hurts!
...YOU GET TOUGH-LOOKING GALLADE...
...AND HE GETS ELEGANT GARDE-VOIR.
IN SOME WAYS, THEY'RE THE PERFECT MATCHES FOR YOU TWO!
ACK!
grr grr grr grr grr

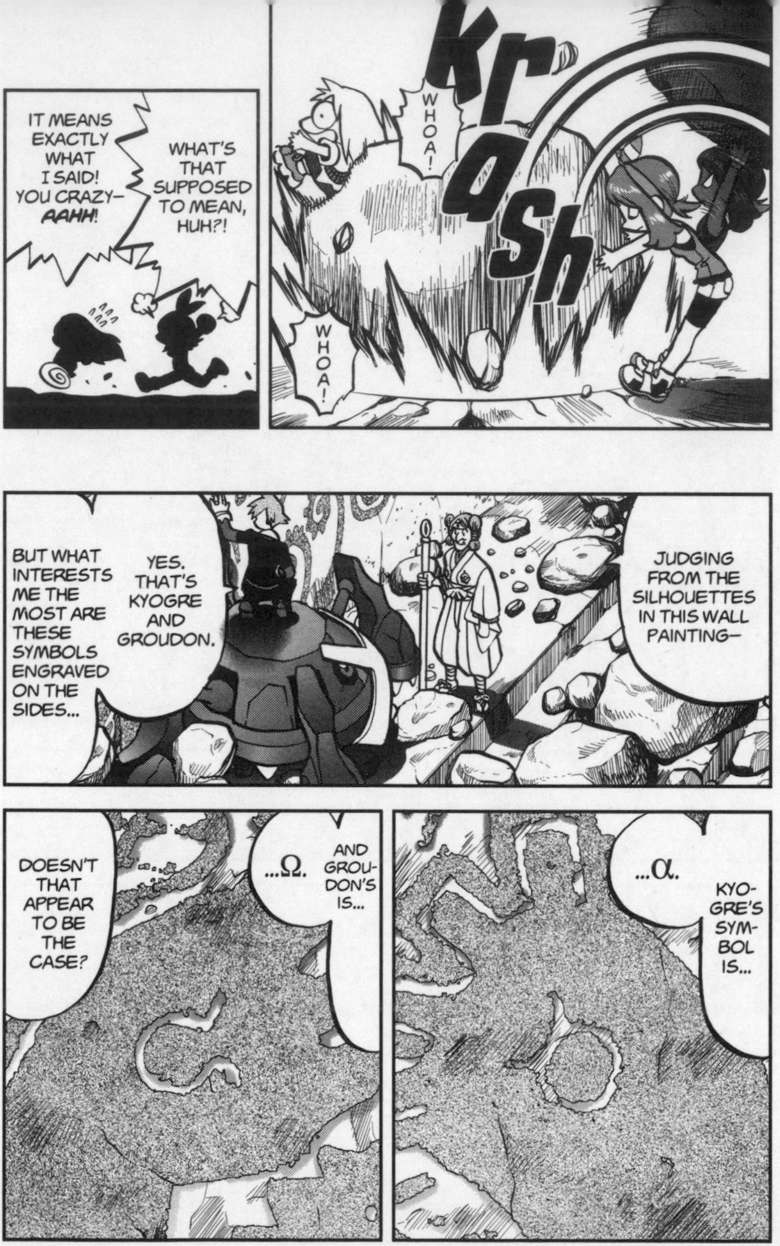
KRASH
WHOA!
WHOA!
WHAT'S THAT SUPPOSED TO MEAN, HUH?!
IT MEANS EXACTLY WHAT I SAID! YOU CRAZY—*AAHH*!
JUDGING FROM THE SILHOUETTES IN THIS WALL PAINTING—
YES. THAT'S KYOGRE AND GROUDON.
BUT WHAT INTERESTS ME THE MOST ARE THESE SYMBOLS ENGRAVED ON THE SIDES...
KYO-GRE'S SYM-BOL IS...
...α.
AND GROU-DON'S IS...
...Ω.
DOESN'T THAT APPEAR TO BE THE CASE?

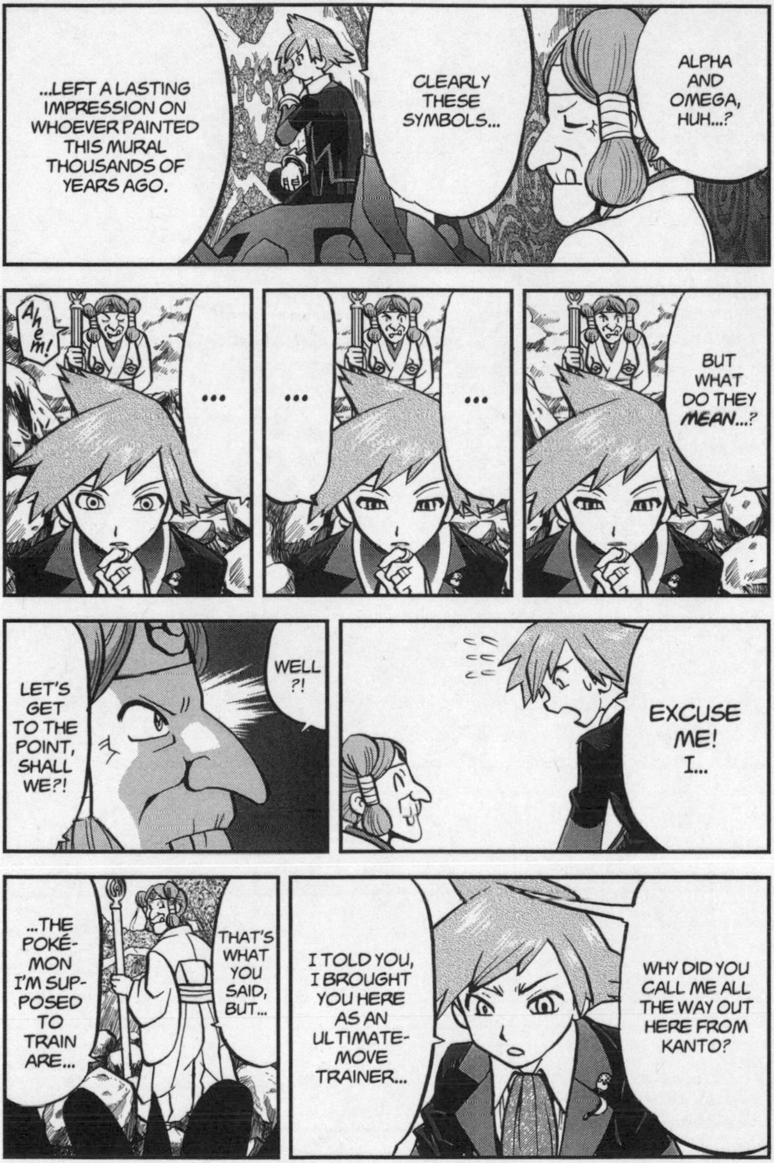
ALPHA AND OMEGA, HUH...?
CLEARLY THESE SYMBOLS...
...LEFT A LASTING IMPRESSION ON WHOEVER PAINTED THIS MURAL THOUSANDS OF YEARS AGO.
BUT WHAT DO THEY *MEAN*...?
...
...
...
Ahem!
EXCUSE ME! I...
WELL?!
LET'S GET TO THE POINT, SHALL WE?!
WHY DID YOU CALL ME ALL THE WAY OUT HERE FROM KANTO?
I TOLD YOU, I BROUGHT YOU HERE AS AN ULTIMATE-MOVE TRAINER...
THAT'S WHAT YOU SAID, BUT...
...THE POKÉMON I'M SUPPOSED TO TRAIN ARE...

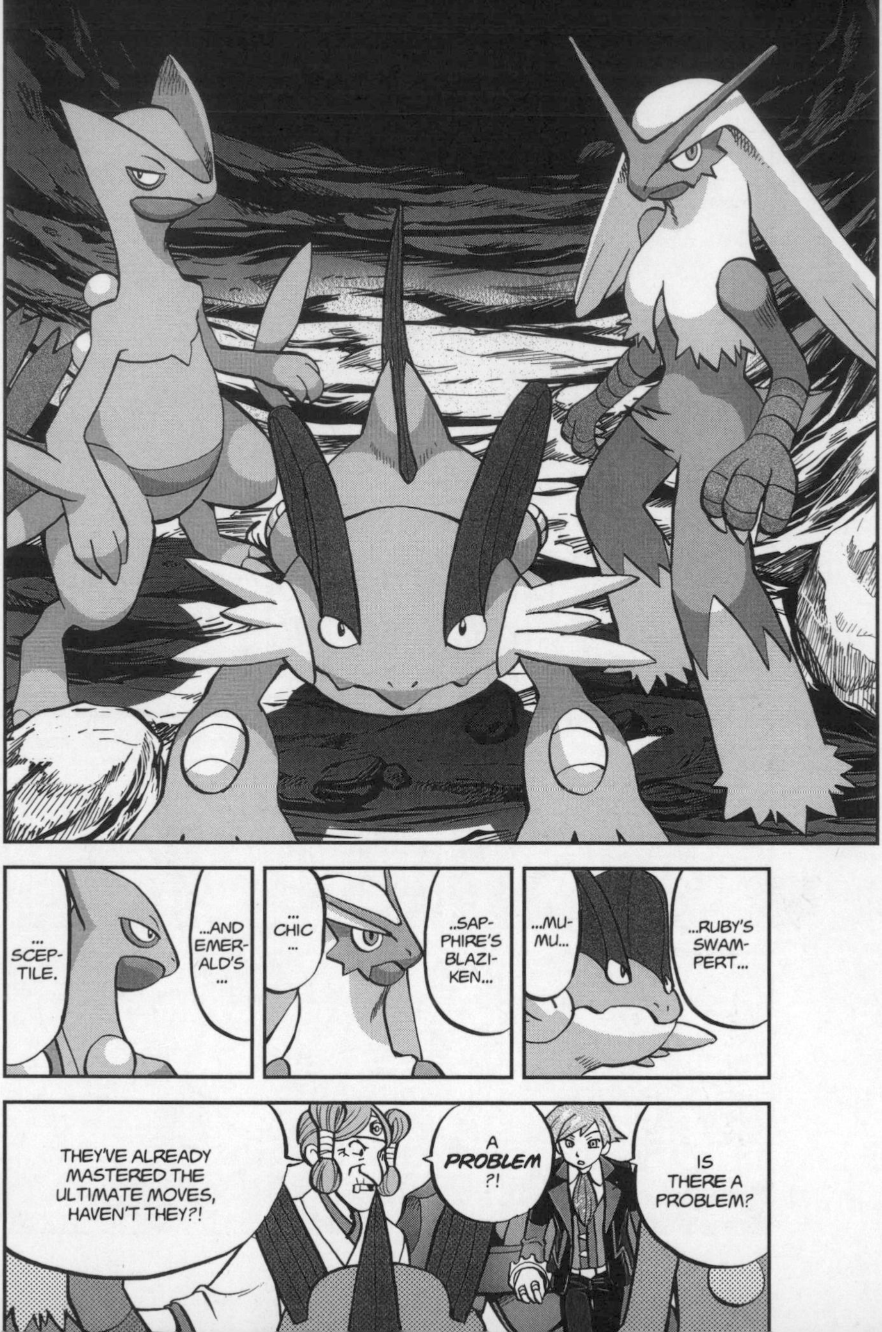
...RUBY'S SWAMPERT...
...MU-MU...
..SAPPHIRE'S BLAZIKEN...
... CHIC ...
...AND EMERALD'S ...
... SCEPTILE.
IS THERE A PROBLEM?
A PROBLEM ?!
THEY'VE ALREADY MASTERED THE ULTIMATE MOVES, HAVEN'T THEY?!

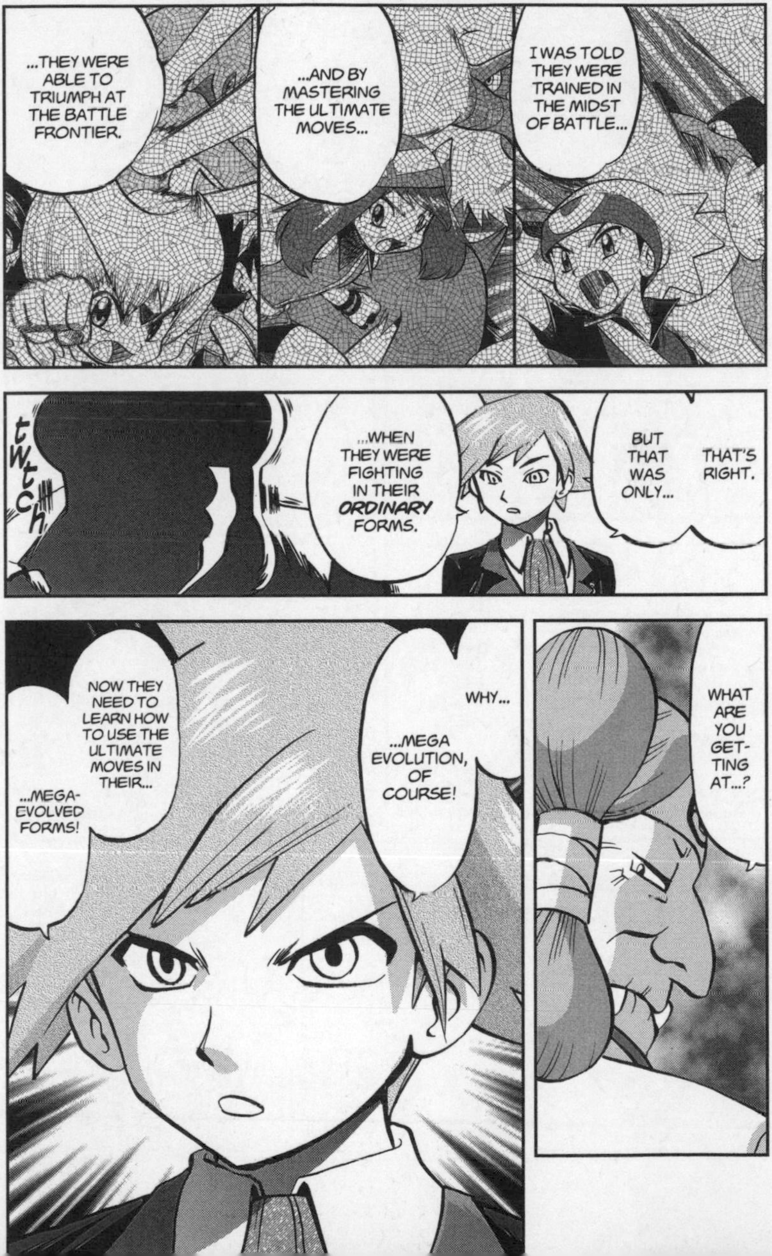
I WAS TOLD THEY WERE TRAINED IN THE MIDST OF BATTLE...
...AND BY MASTERING THE ULTIMATE MOVES...
...THEY WERE ABLE TO TRIUMPH AT THE BATTLE FRONTIER.
THAT'S RIGHT.
BUT THAT WAS ONLY...
...WHEN THEY WERE FIGHTING IN THEIR ORDINARY FORMS.
twtch
WHAT ARE YOU GET-TING AT...?
WHY...
...MEGA EVOLUTION, OF COURSE!
NOW THEY NEED TO LEARN HOW TO USE THE ULTIMATE MOVES IN THEIR...
...MEGA-EVOLVED FORMS!

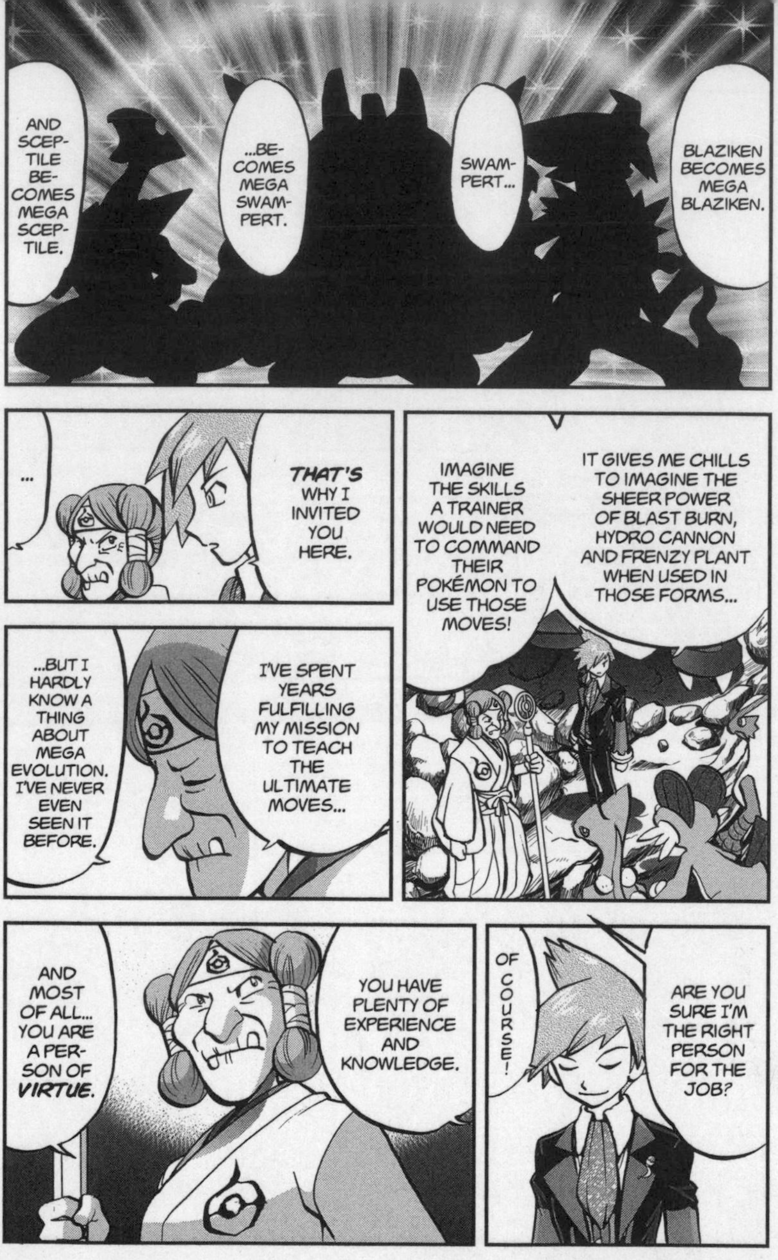

BLAZIKEN BECOMES MEGA BLAZIKEN.
SWAMPERT...
...BECOMES MEGA SWAMPERT.
AND SCEPTILE BECOMES MEGA SCEPTILE.
IT GIVES ME CHILLS TO IMAGINE THE SHEER POWER OF BLAST BURN, HYDRO CANNON AND FRENZY PLANT WHEN USED IN THOSE FORMS...
IMAGINE THE SKILLS A TRAINER WOULD NEED TO COMMAND THEIR POKÉMON TO USE THOSE MOVES!
THAT'S WHY I INVITED YOU HERE.
...
I'VE SPENT YEARS FULFILLING MY MISSION TO TEACH THE ULTIMATE MOVES...
...BUT I HARDLY KNOW A THING ABOUT MEGA EVOLUTION. I'VE NEVER EVEN SEEN IT BEFORE.
ARE YOU SURE I'M THE RIGHT PERSON FOR THE JOB?
OF COURSE!
YOU HAVE PLENTY OF EXPERIENCE AND KNOWLEDGE.
AND MOST OF ALL... YOU ARE A PERSON OF *VIRTUE*.

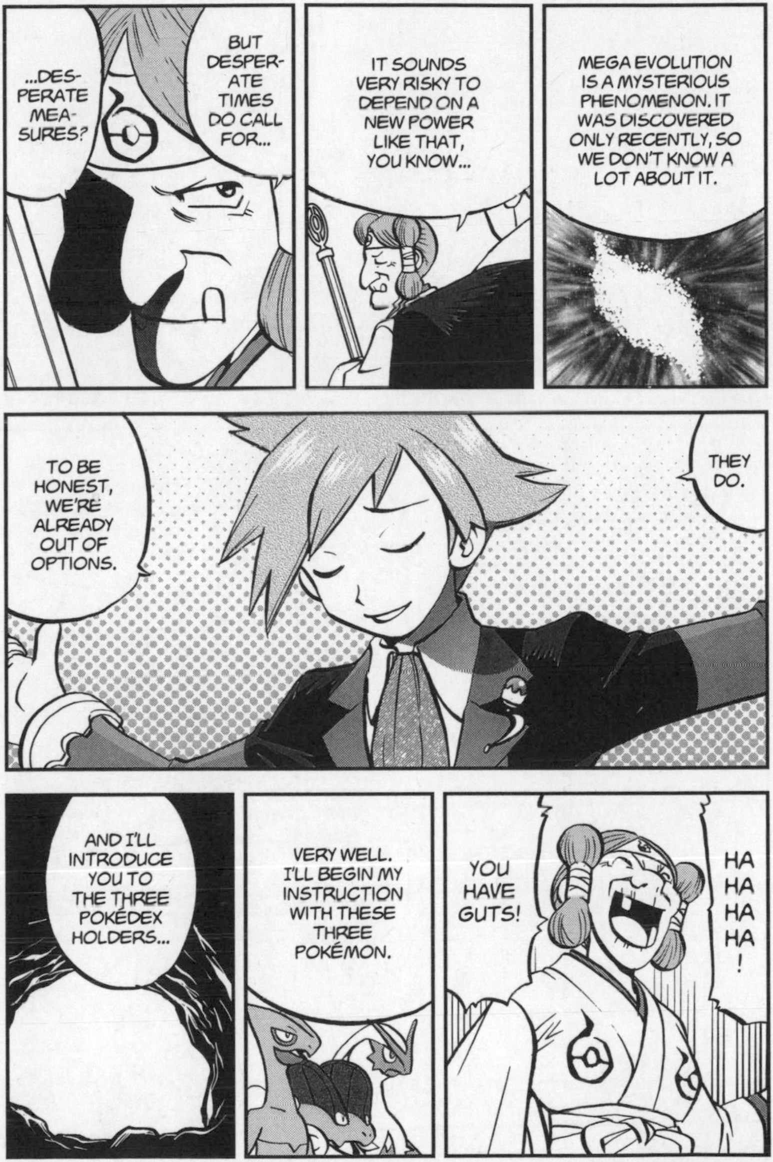
MEGA EVOLUTION IS A MYSTERIOUS PHENOMENON. IT WAS DISCOVERED ONLY RECENTLY, SO WE DON'T KNOW A LOT ABOUT IT.
IT SOUNDS VERY RISKY TO DEPEND ON A NEW POWER LIKE THAT, YOU KNOW...
BUT DESPERATE TIMES DO CALL FOR...
...DESPERATE MEASURES?
THEY DO.
TO BE HONEST, WE'RE ALREADY OUT OF OPTIONS.
HA HA HA HA!
YOU HAVE GUTS!
VERY WELL. I'LL BEGIN MY INSTRUCTION WITH THESE THREE POKÉMON.
AND I'LL INTRODUCE YOU TO THE THREE POKÉDEX HOLDERS...

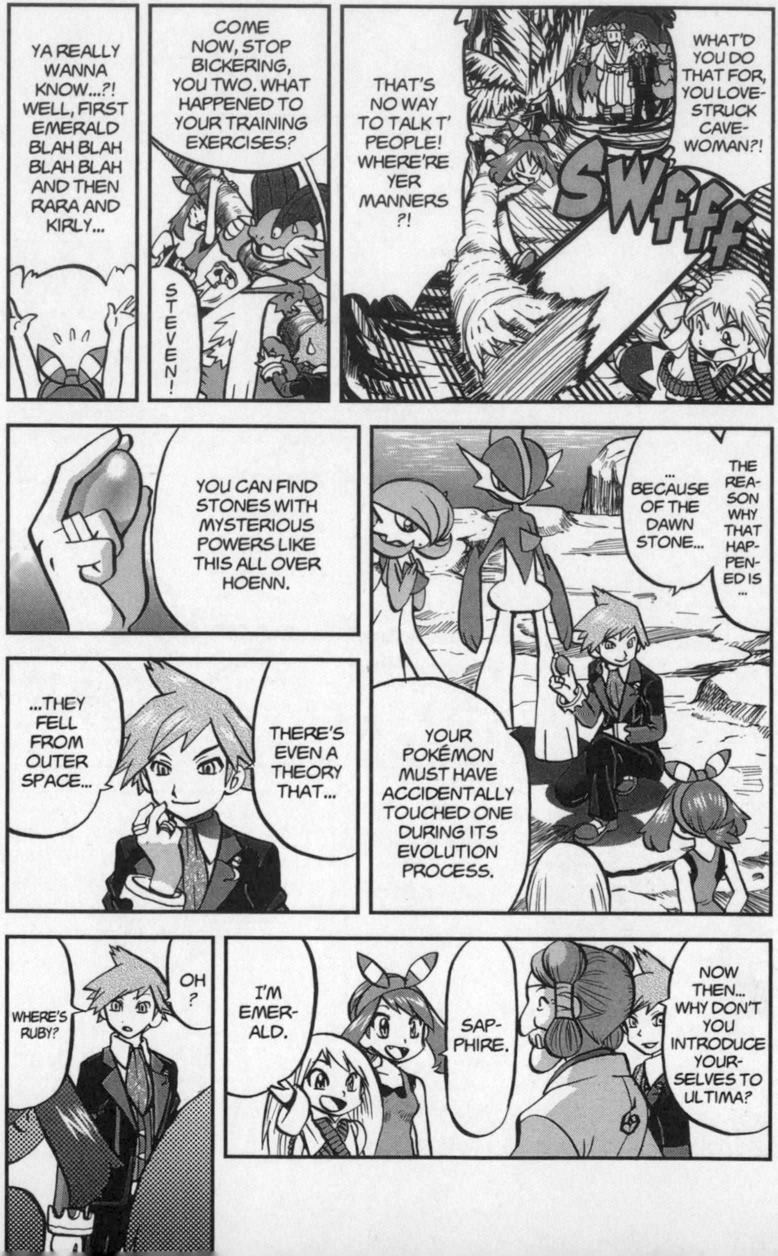
WHAT'D YOU DO THAT FOR, YOU LOVE-STRUCK CAVE-WOMAN?!
THAT'S NO WAY TO TALK T' PEOPLE! WHERE'RE YER MANNERS?!
SWFFF
COME NOW, STOP BICKERING, YOU TWO. WHAT HAPPENED TO YOUR TRAINING EXERCISES?
STEVEN!
YA REALLY WANNA KNOW...?! WELL, FIRST EMERALD BLAH BLAH BLAH BLAH AND THEN RARA AND KIRLY...
THE REA-SON WHY THAT HAP-PEN-ED IS...
...BECAUSE OF THE DAWN STONE...
YOUR POKÉMON MUST HAVE ACCIDENTALLY TOUCHED ONE DURING ITS EVOLUTION PROCESS.
YOU CAN FIND STONES WITH MYSTERIOUS POWERS LIKE THIS ALL OVER HOENN.
THERE'S EVEN A THEORY THAT...
...THEY FELL FROM OUTER SPACE...
NOW THEN... WHY DON'T YOU INTRODUCE YOUR-SELVES TO ULTIMA?
SAP-PHIRE.
I'M EMER-ALD.
OH?
WHERE'S RUBY?

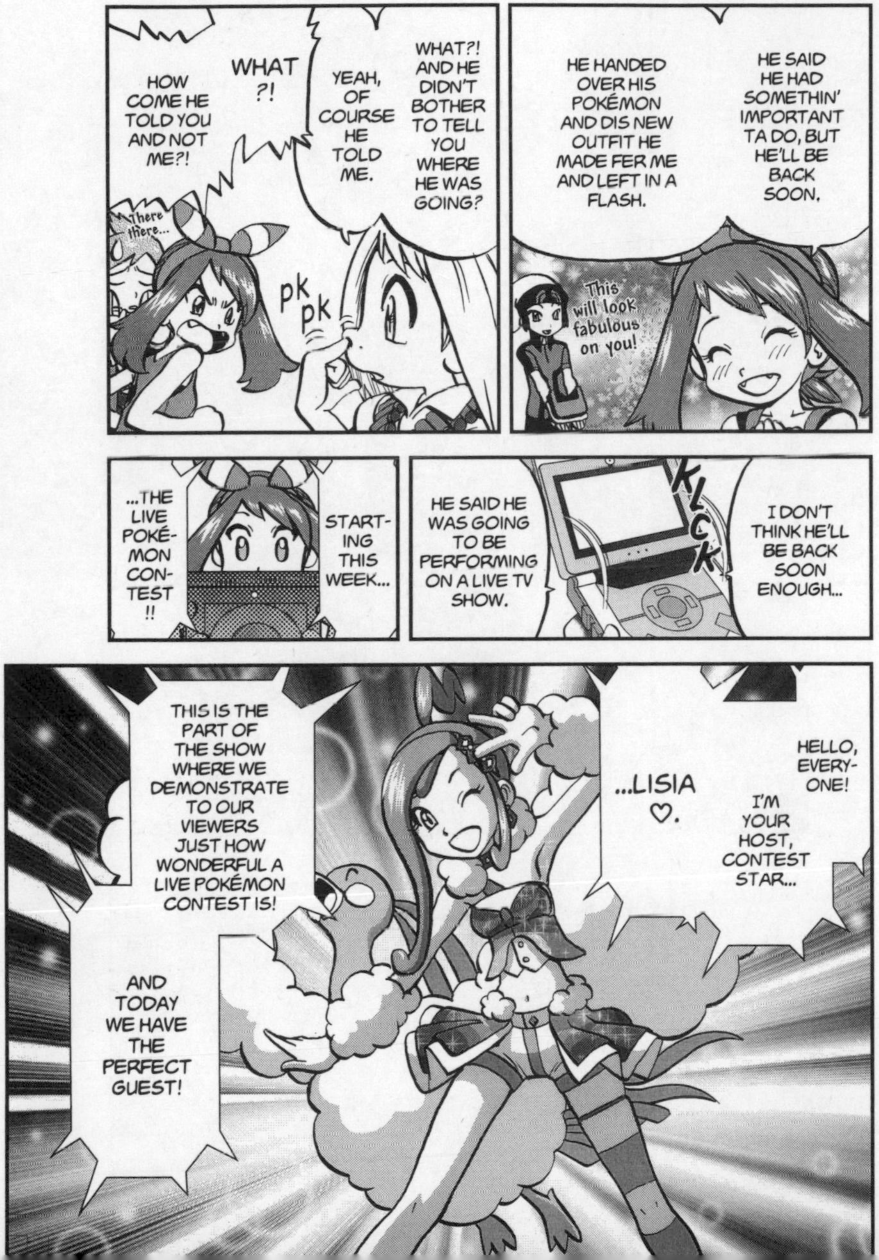
HE SAID HE HAD SOMETHIN' IMPORTANT TA DO, BUT HE'LL BE BACK SOON.
HE HANDED OVER HIS POKÉMON AND DIS NEW OUTFIT HE MADE FER ME AND LEFT IN A FLASH.
This will look fabulous on you!
WHAT?! AND HE DIDN'T BOTHER TO TELL YOU WHERE HE WAS GOING?
YEAH, OF COURSE HE TOLD ME.
WHAT ?!
HOW COME HE TOLD YOU AND NOT ME?!
There there...
pk pk
I DON'T THINK HE'LL BE BACK SOON ENOUGH...
KLCK
HE SAID HE WAS GOING TO BE PERFORMING ON A LIVE TV SHOW.
STARTING THIS WEEK...
...THE LIVE POKÉMON CONTEST !!
HELLO, EVERYONE!
I'M YOUR HOST, CONTEST STAR...
...LISIA ♡.
THIS IS THE PART OF THE SHOW WHERE WE DEMONSTRATE TO OUR VIEWERS JUST HOW WONDERFUL A LIVE POKÉMON CONTEST IS!
AND TODAY WE HAVE THE PERFECT GUEST!

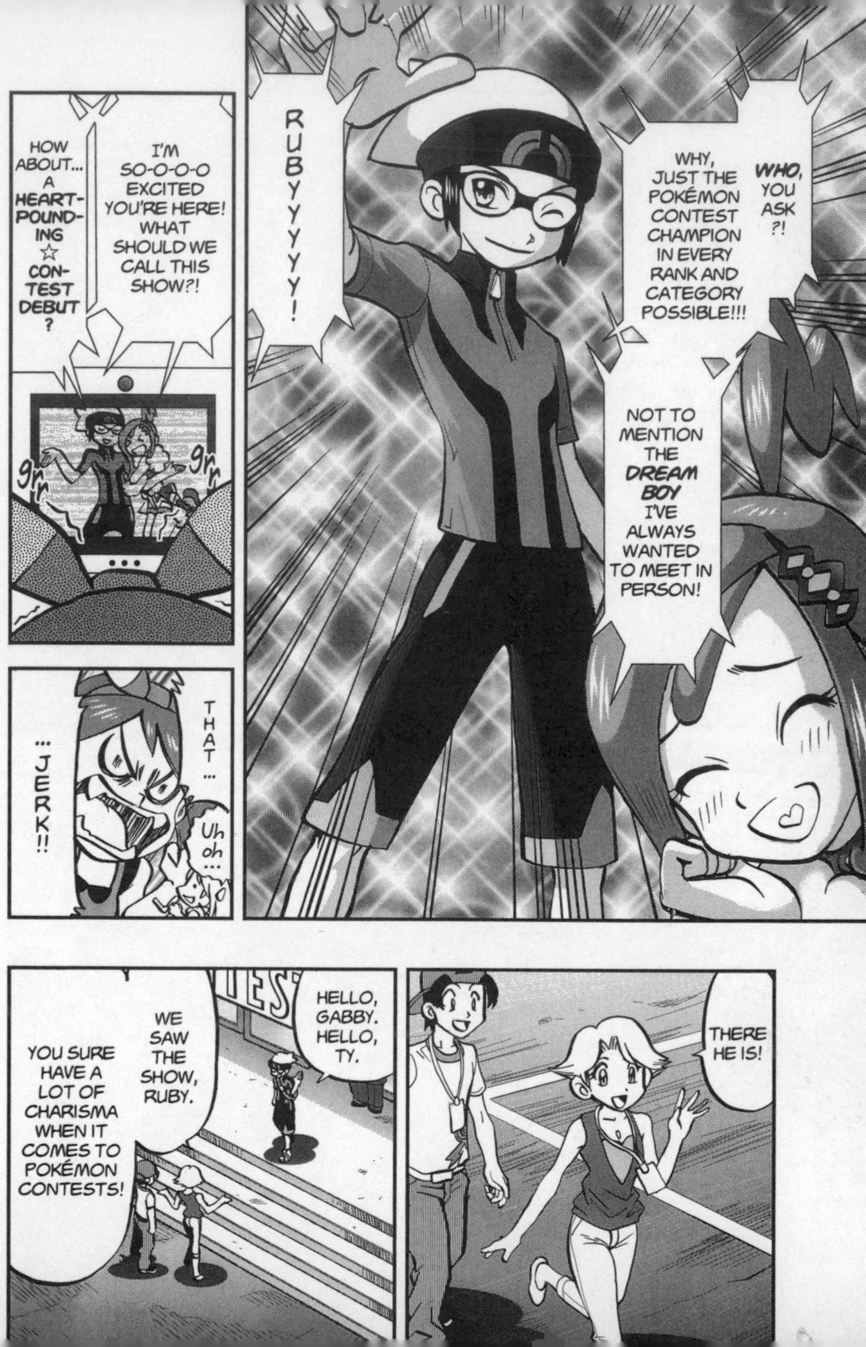
WHO, YOU ASK?!
WHY, JUST THE POKÉMON CONTEST CHAMPION IN EVERY RANK AND CATEGORY POSSIBLE!!!
RUBYYYYY!
NOT TO MENTION THE DREAM BOY I'VE ALWAYS WANTED TO MEET IN PERSON!
I'M SO-O-O-O EXCITED YOU'RE HERE! WHAT SHOULD WE CALL THIS SHOW?!
HOW ABOUT... A HEART-POUNDING ☆ CONTEST DEBUT?
grr
grr
...
THAT...
...JERK!!
Uh oh...
THERE HE IS!
HELLO, GABBY. HELLO, TY.
WE SAW THE SHOW, RUBY.
YOU SURE HAVE A LOT OF CHARISMA WHEN IT COMES TO POKÉMON CONTESTS!

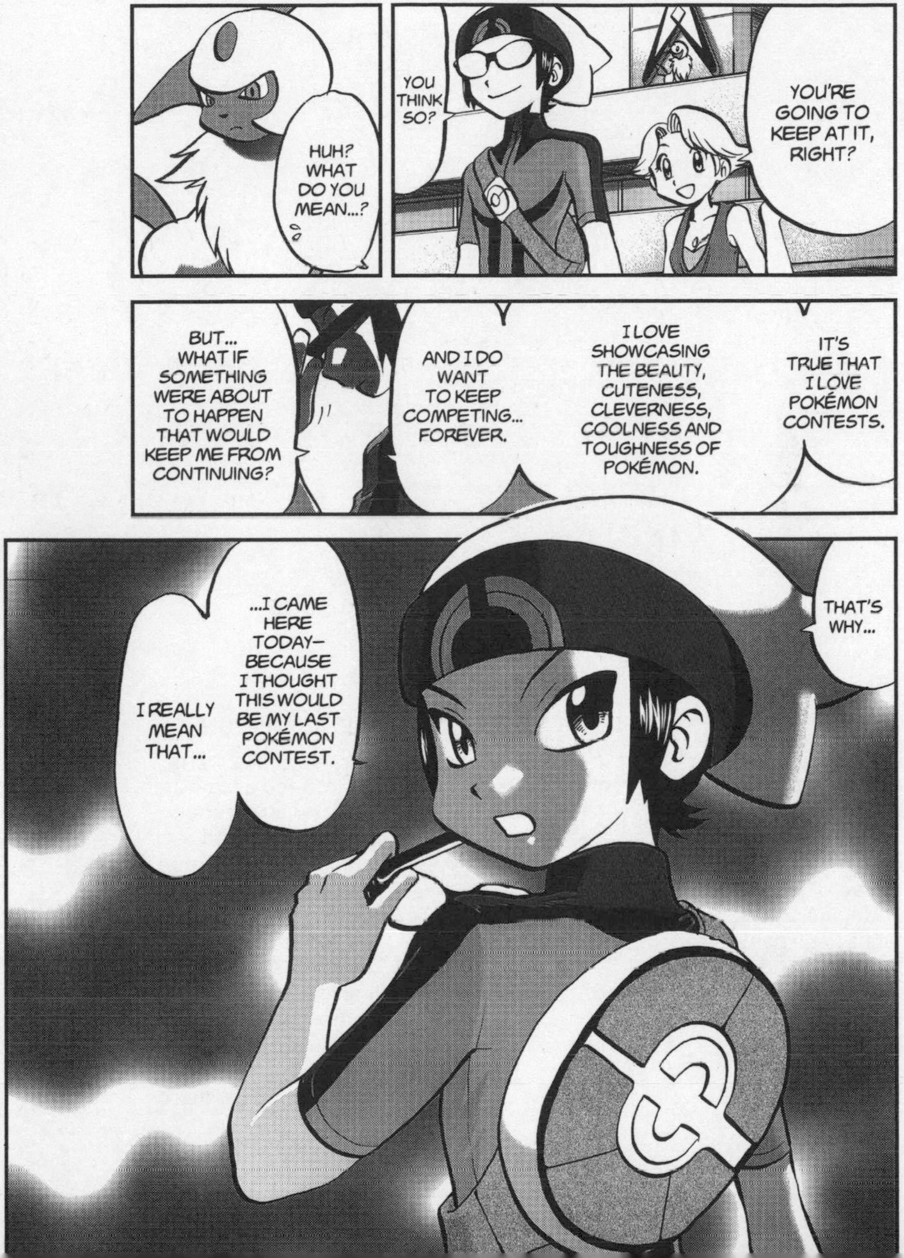
YOU'RE GOING TO KEEP AT IT, RIGHT?
YOU THINK SO?
HUH? WHAT DO YOU MEAN...?
IT'S TRUE THAT I LOVE POKÉMON CONTESTS.
I LOVE SHOWCASING THE BEAUTY, CUTENESS, CLEVERNESS, COOLNESS AND TOUGHNESS OF POKÉMON.
AND I DO WANT TO KEEP COMPETING... FOREVER.
BUT... WHAT IF SOMETHING WERE ABOUT TO HAPPEN THAT WOULD KEEP ME FROM CONTINUING?
THAT'S WHY...
...I CAME HERE TODAY—BECAUSE I THOUGHT THIS WOULD BE MY LAST POKÉMON CONTEST.
I REALLY MEAN THAT...

STONE COLLECTOR

Stones that contain special energy can be found all over Hoenn. Some of those stones have the power to evolve a Pokémon and some are used in technology developed by people. The people who collect these rare stones are known as Stone Collectors. At times they head out to other regions in hopes of discovering new stones.

DEWFORD TOWN

A town in the Hoenn region located on a small island. If you travel along Route 106, you will get to the mazelike Granite Cave.

HOENN REGION

A region with a warm climate and a large area. It has a rich natural environment with a large forest, a volcano that rises more than 4,900 feet into the air and a Seafloor Cavern at the bottom of the ocean. It also has many ruins from ancient times that have come to the attention of many Pokémon researchers.

Omega Alpha Adventure 1

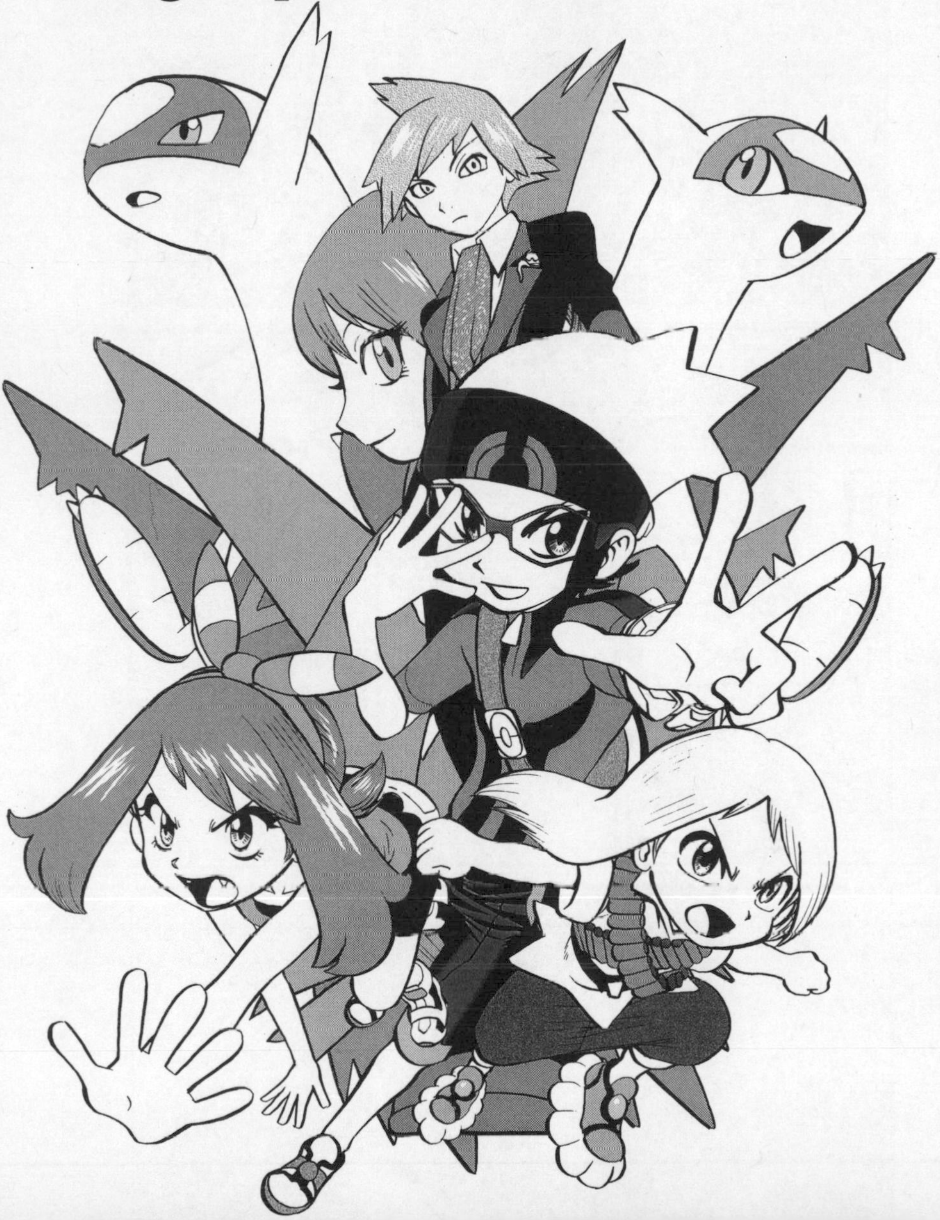

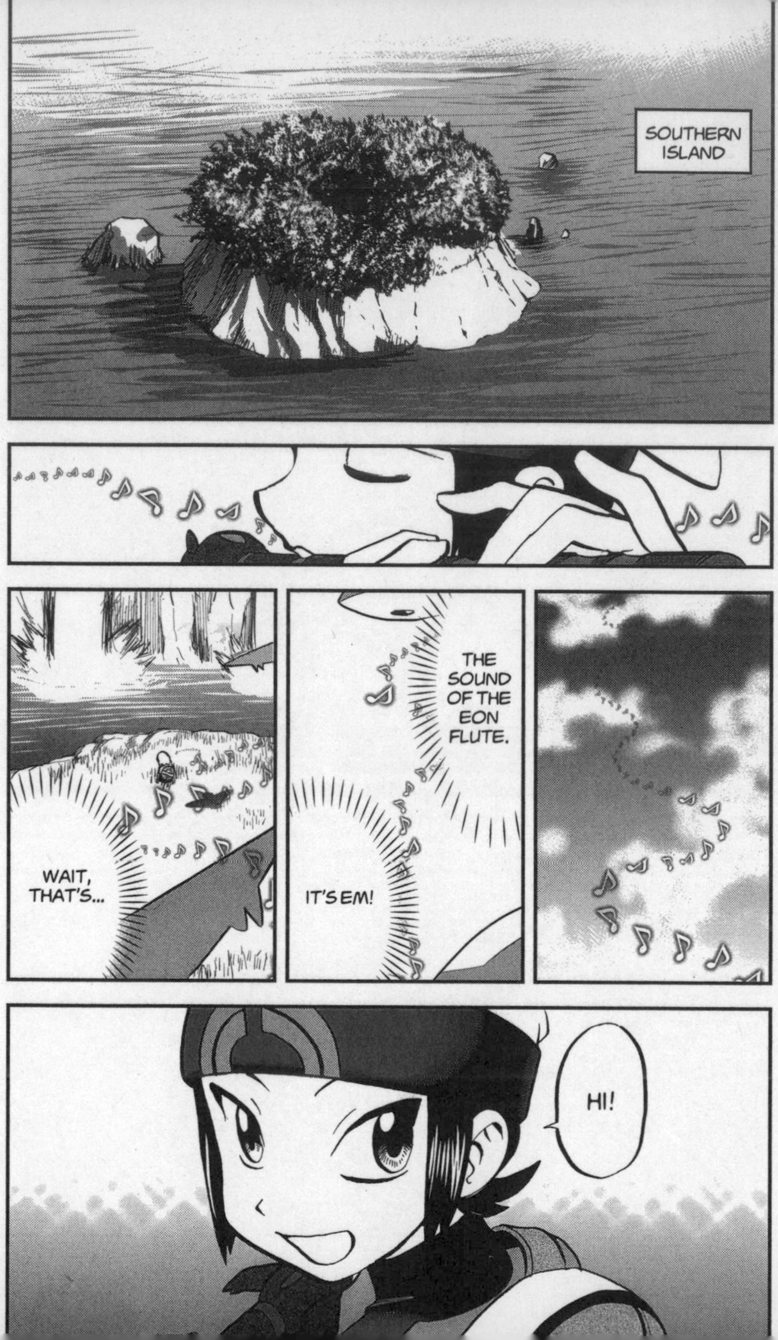
SOUTHERN ISLAND
THE SOUND OF THE EON FLUTE.
IT'S EM!
WAIT, THAT'S...
HI!

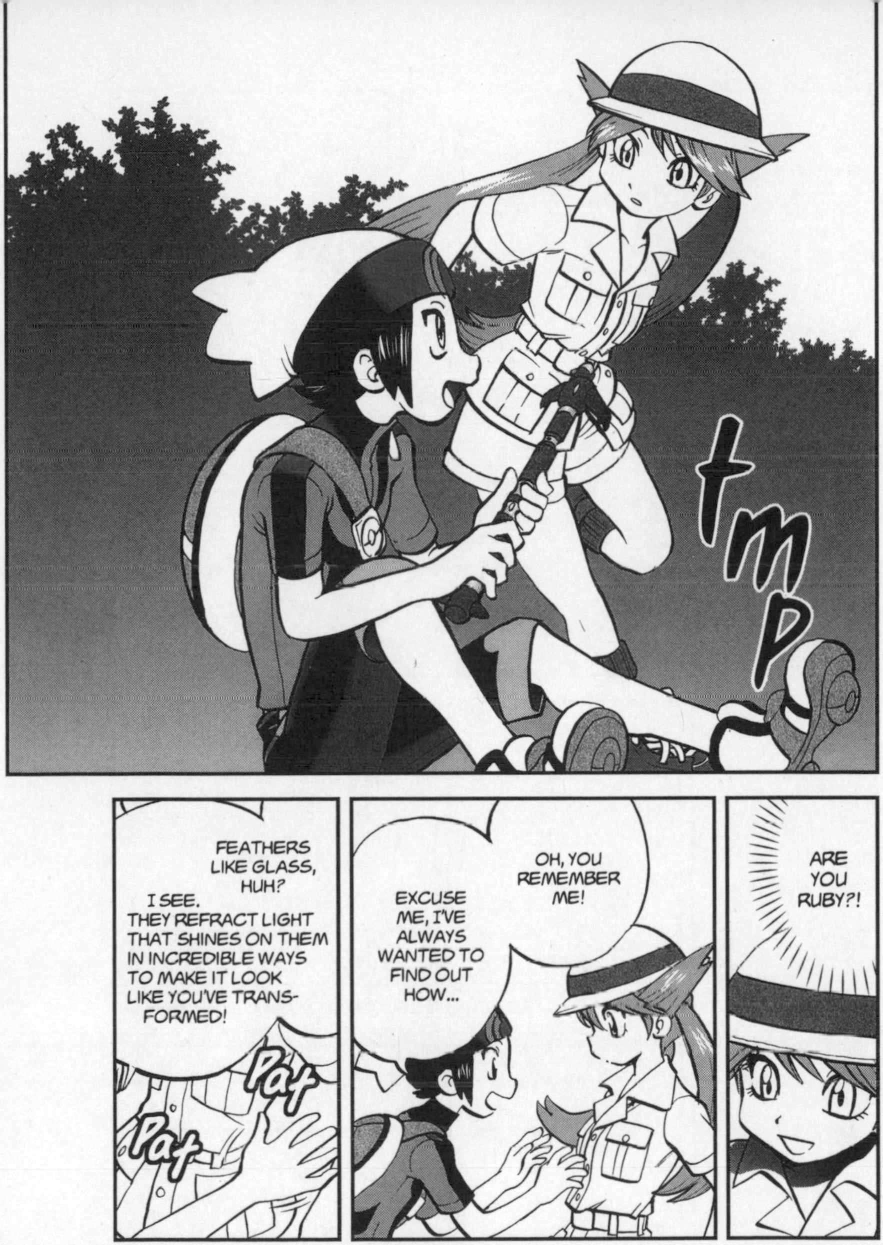
tmp
ARE YOU RUBY?!
OH, YOU REMEMBER ME!
EXCUSE ME, I'VE ALWAYS WANTED TO FIND OUT HOW...
FEATHERS LIKE GLASS, HUH?
I SEE. THEY REFRACT LIGHT THAT SHINES ON THEM IN INCREDIBLE WAYS TO MAKE IT LOOK LIKE YOU'VE TRANS-FORMED!
Pat
Pat

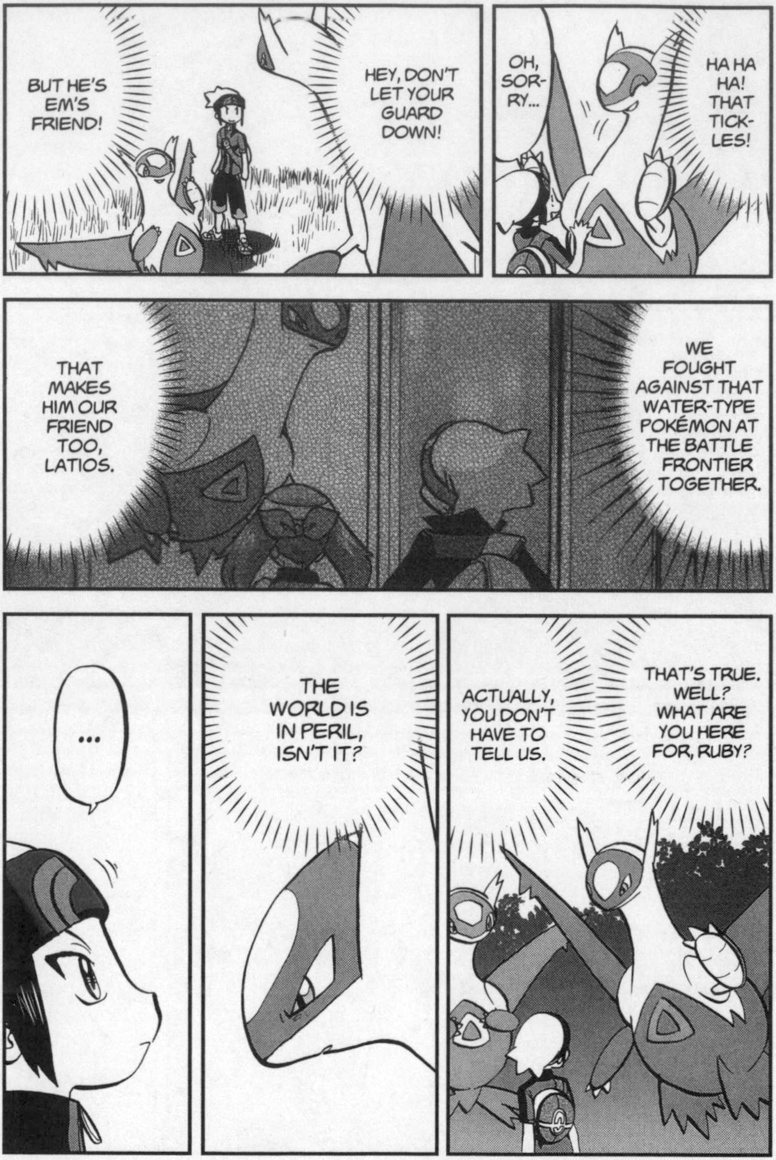
HA HA HA! THAT TICKLES!
OH, SORRY...
HEY, DON'T LET YOUR GUARD DOWN!
BUT HE'S EM'S FRIEND!
WE FOUGHT AGAINST THAT WATER-TYPE POKÉMON AT THE BATTLE FRONTIER TOGETHER.
THAT MAKES HIM OUR FRIEND TOO, LATIOS.
THAT'S TRUE. WELL? WHAT ARE YOU HERE FOR, RUBY?
ACTUALLY, YOU DON'T HAVE TO TELL US.
THE WORLD IS IN PERIL, ISN'T IT?
...

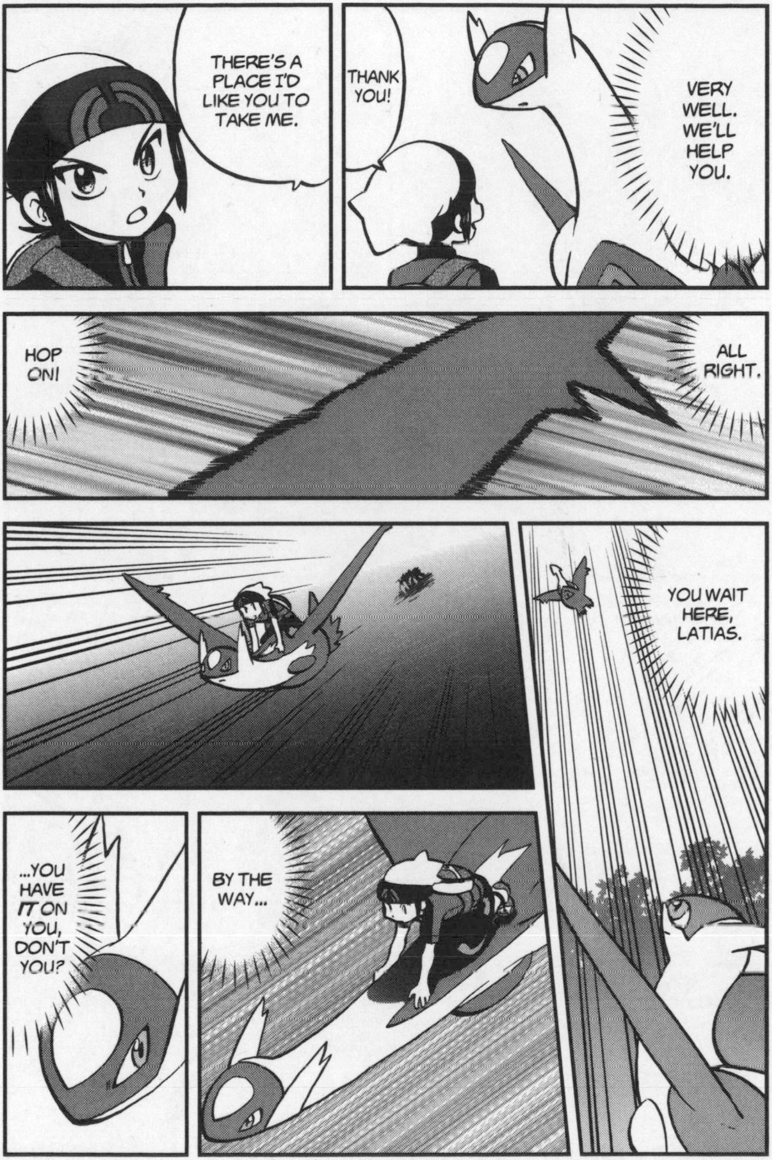
VERY WELL. WE'LL HELP YOU.
THANK YOU!
THERE'S A PLACE I'D LIKE YOU TO TAKE ME.
ALL RIGHT.
HOP ON!
YOU WAIT HERE, LATIAS.
BY THE WAY...
...YOU HAVE *IT* ON YOU, DON'T YOU?

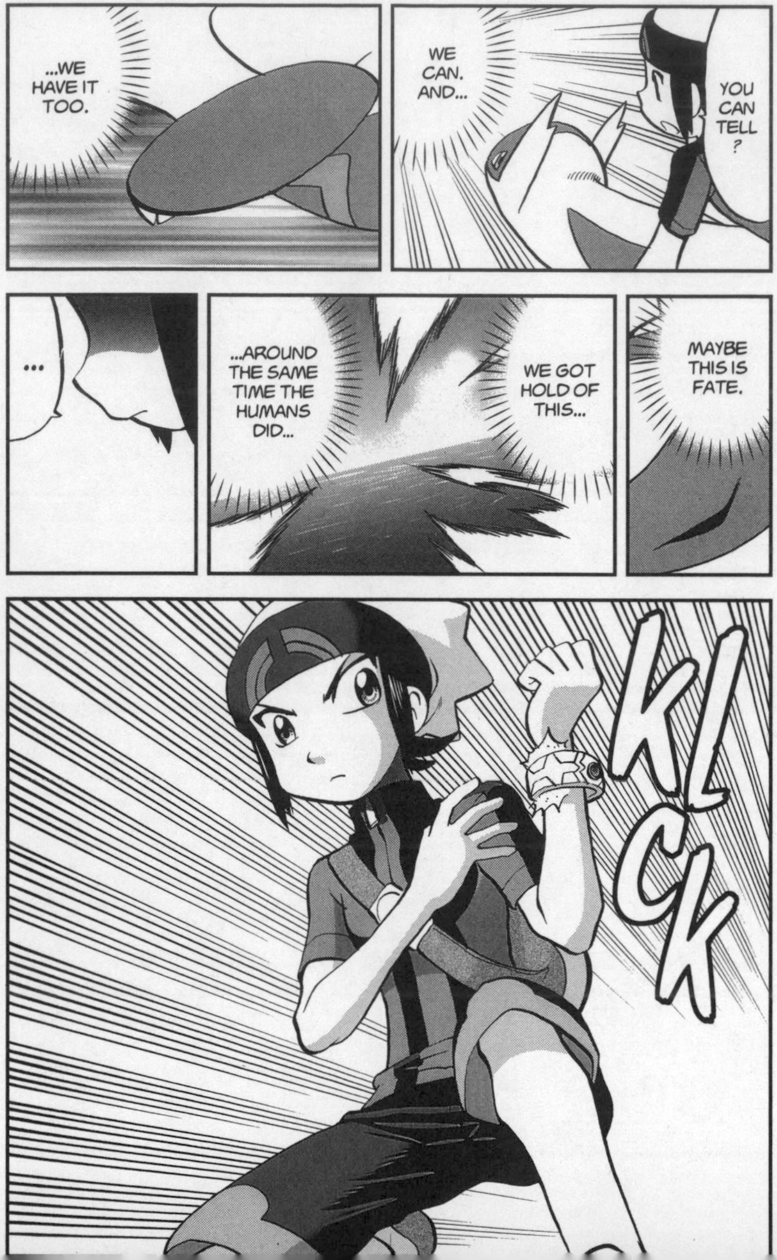
YOU CAN TELL?
WE CAN. AND...
...WE HAVE IT TOO.
MAYBE THIS IS FATE.
WE GOT HOLD OF THIS...
...AROUND THE SAME TIME THE HUMANS DID...
...
KLICK

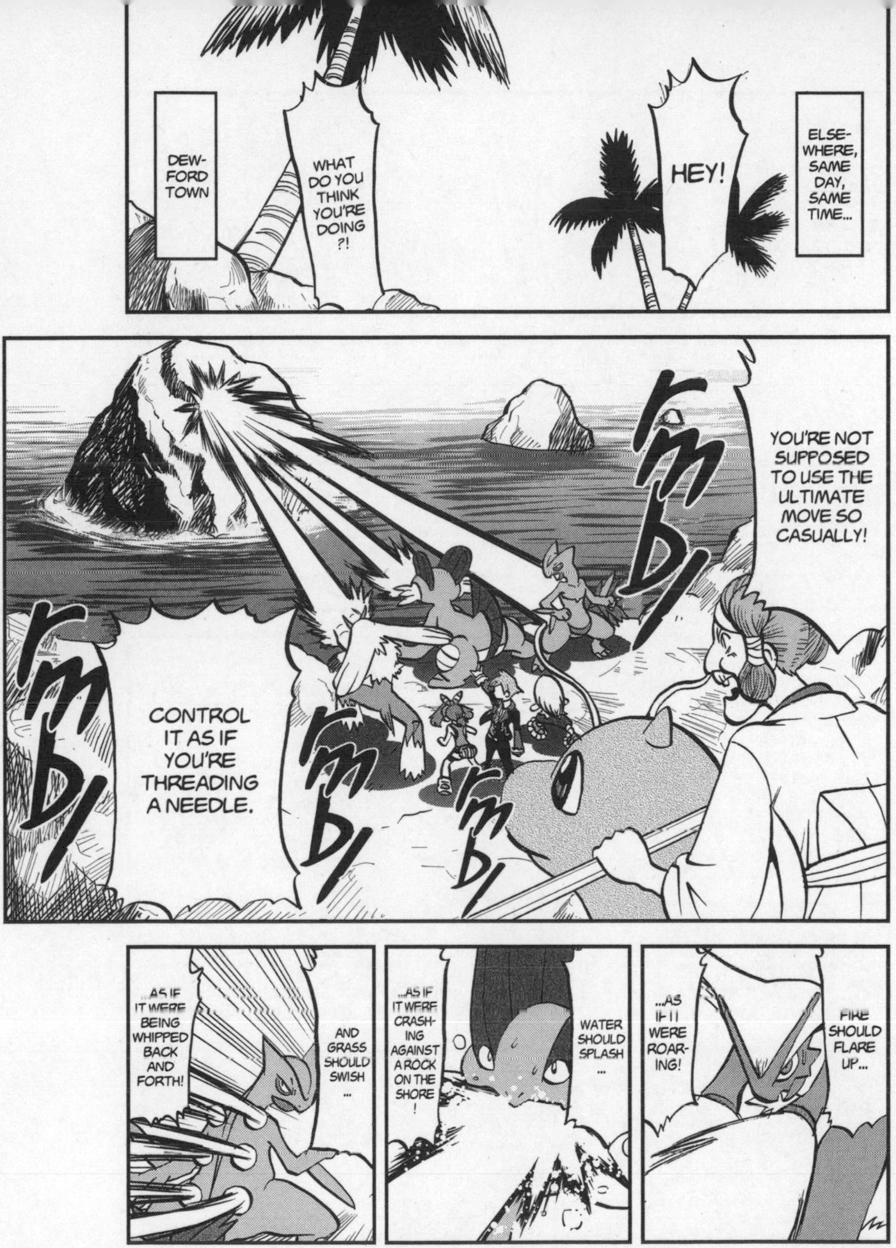
ELSEWHERE, SAME DAY, SAME TIME...
HEY!
WHAT DO YOU THINK YOU'RE DOING?!
DEWFORD TOWN
RMBL
YOU'RE NOT SUPPOSED TO USE THE ULTIMATE MOVE SO CASUALLY!
RMBL
RMBL
RMBL
CONTROL IT AS IF YOU'RE THREADING A NEEDLE.
FIRE SHOULD FLARE UP...
...AS IF IT WERE ROARING!
WATER SHOULD SPLASH...
...AS IF IT WERE CRASHING AGAINST A ROCK ON THE SHORE!
AND GRASS SHOULD SWISH...
...AS IF IT WERE BEING WHIPPED BACK AND FORTH!

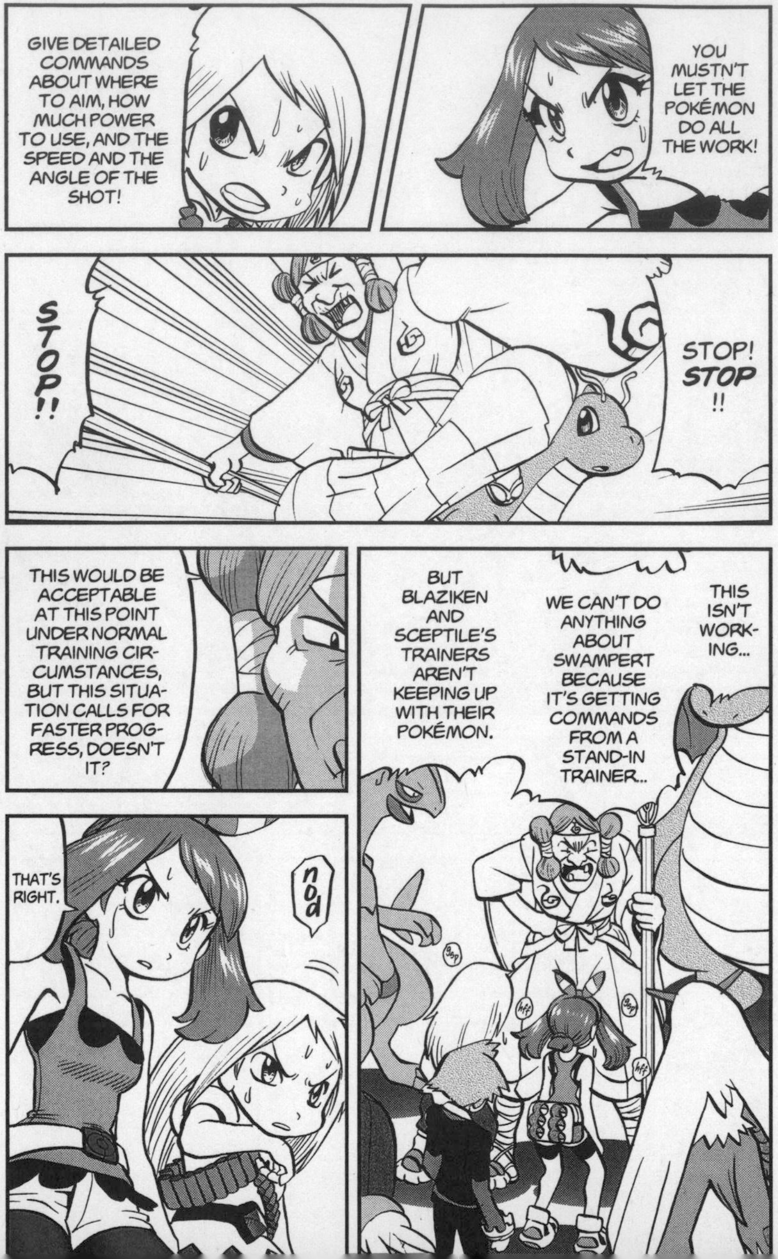
YOU MUSTN'T LET THE POKÉMON DO ALL THE WORK!
GIVE DETAILED COMMANDS ABOUT WHERE TO AIM, HOW MUCH POWER TO USE, AND THE SPEED AND THE ANGLE OF THE SHOT!
STOP! STOP !!
STOP!!
THIS ISN'T WORK-ING...
WE CAN'T DO ANYTHING ABOUT SWAMPERT BECAUSE IT'S GETTING COMMANDS FROM A STAND-IN TRAINER...
BUT BLAZIKEN AND SCEPTILE'S TRAINERS AREN'T KEEPING UP WITH THEIR POKÉMON.
THIS WOULD BE ACCEPTABLE AT THIS POINT UNDER NORMAL TRAINING CIR-CUMSTANCES, BUT THIS SITUA-TION CALLS FOR FASTER PROG-RESS, DOESN'T IT?
nod
THAT'S RIGHT.

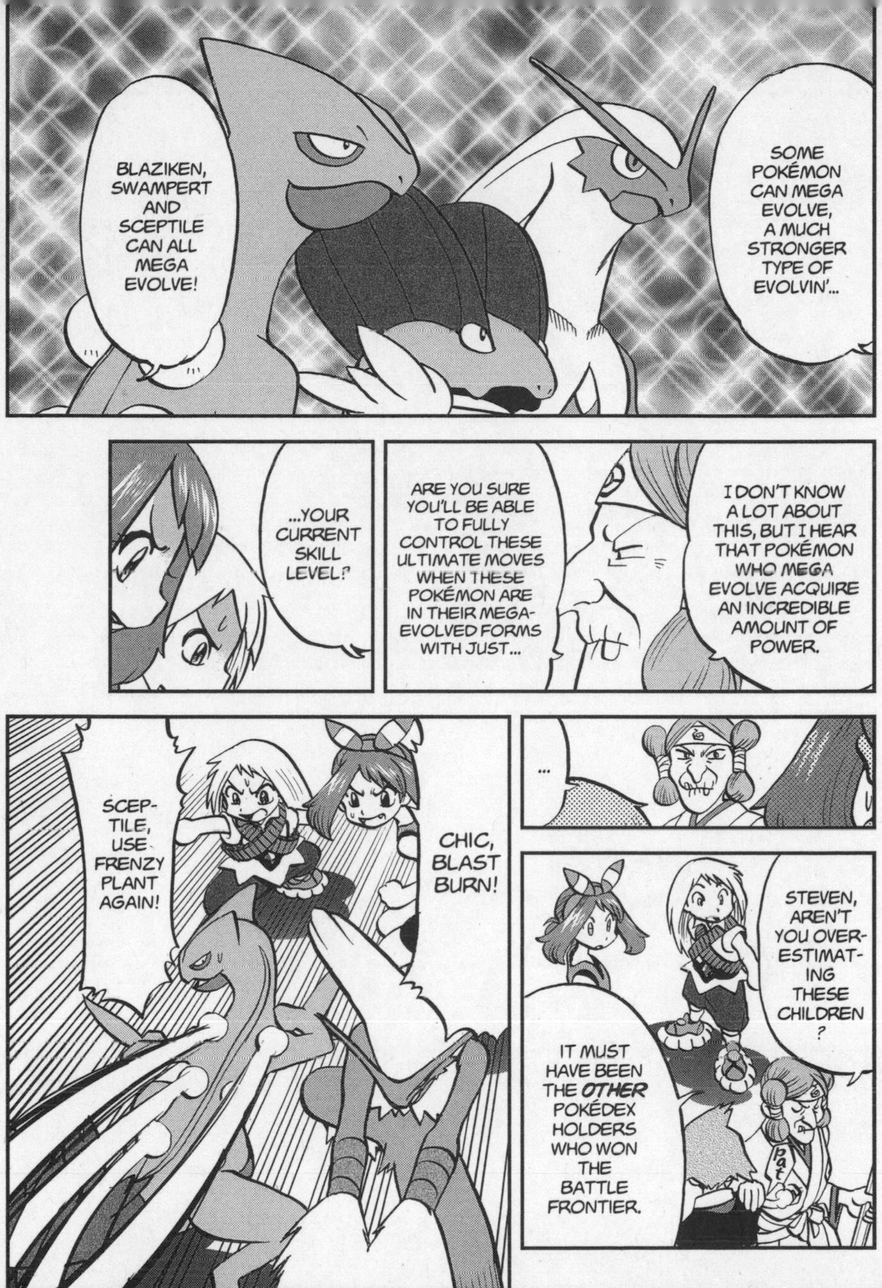
SOME POKÉMON CAN MEGA EVOLVE, A MUCH STRONGER TYPE OF EVOLVIN'...
BLAZIKEN, SWAMPERT AND SCEPTILE CAN ALL MEGA EVOLVE!
I DON'T KNOW A LOT ABOUT THIS, BUT I HEAR THAT POKÉMON WHO MEGA EVOLVE ACQUIRE AN INCREDIBLE AMOUNT OF POWER.
ARE YOU SURE YOU'LL BE ABLE TO FULLY CONTROL THESE ULTIMATE MOVES WHEN THESE POKÉMON ARE IN THEIR MEGA-EVOLVED FORMS WITH JUST...
...YOUR CURRENT SKILL LEVEL?
...
STEVEN, AREN'T YOU OVERESTIMATING THESE CHILDREN?
IT MUST HAVE BEEN THE ***OTHER*** POKÉDEX HOLDERS WHO WON THE BATTLE FRONTIER.
pat
CHIC, BLAST BURN!
SCEPTILE, USE FRENZY PLANT AGAIN!

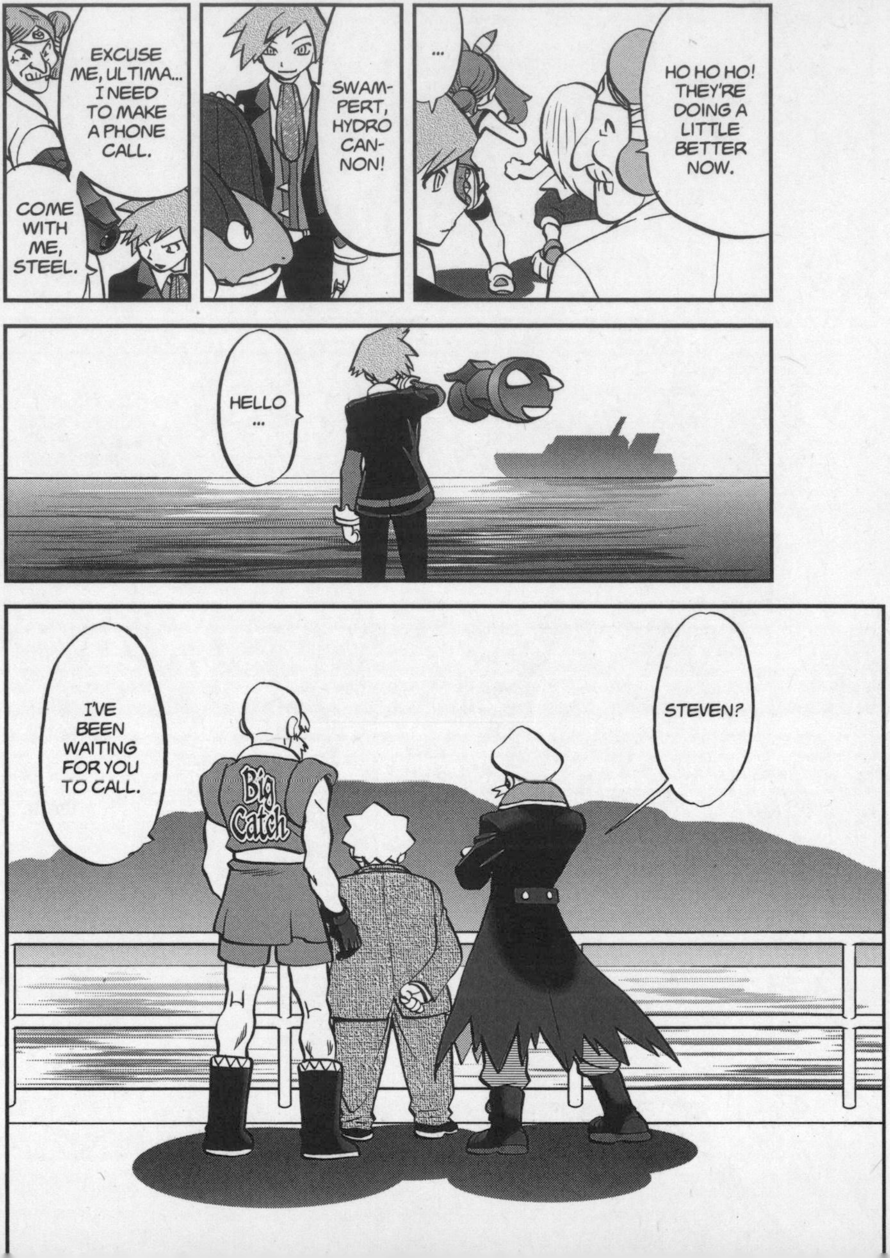
HO HO HO! THEY'RE DOING A LITTLE BETTER NOW.
...
SWAMPERT, HYDRO CANNON!
EXCUSE ME, ULTIMA... I NEED TO MAKE A PHONE CALL.
COME WITH ME, STEEL.
HELLO ...
STEVEN?
I'VE BEEN WAITING FOR YOU TO CALL.
Big Catch

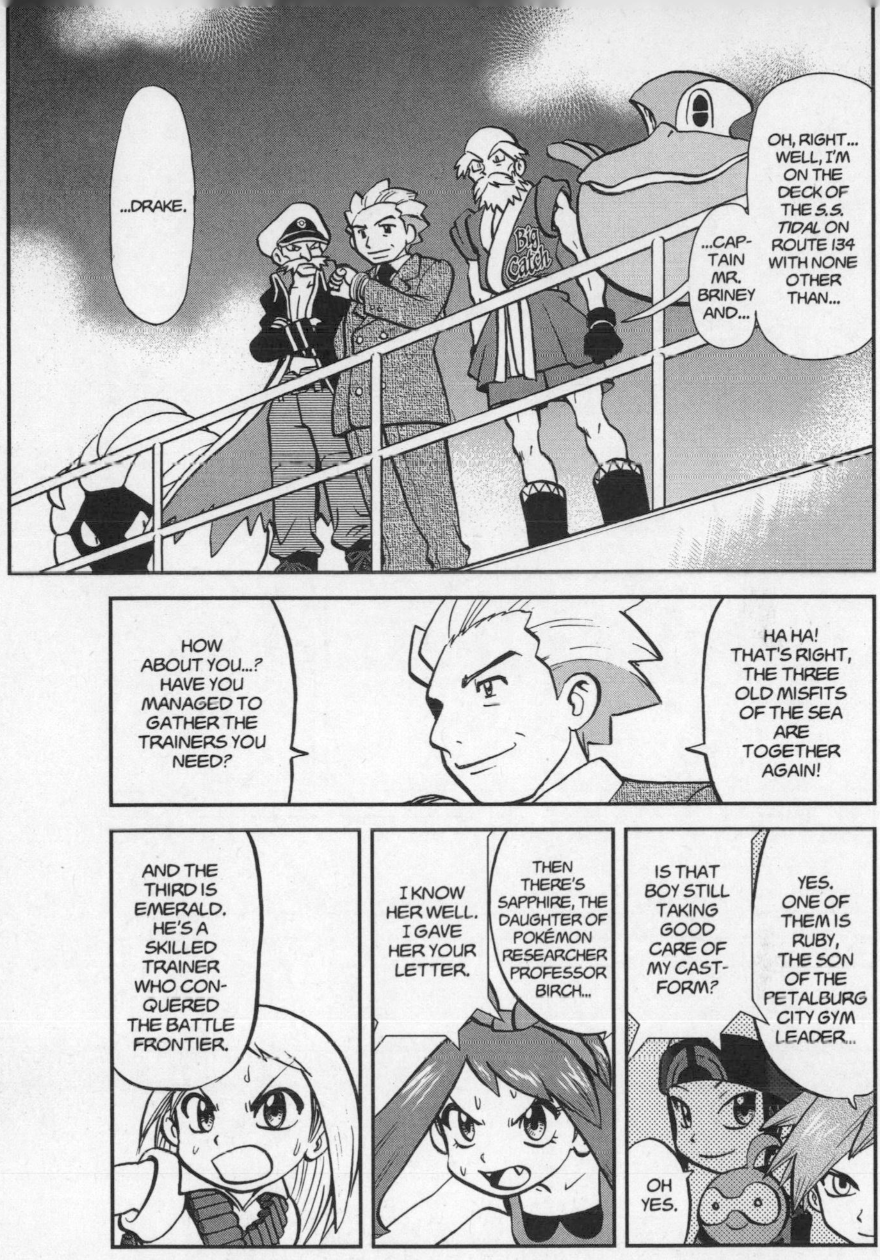
OH, RIGHT... WELL, I'M ON THE DECK OF THE *S.S. TIDAL* ON ROUTE 134 WITH NONE OTHER THAN...
...CAPTAIN MR. BRINEY AND...
...DRAKE.
Big Catch
HA HA! THAT'S RIGHT, THE THREE OLD MISFITS OF THE SEA ARE TOGETHER AGAIN!
HOW ABOUT YOU...? HAVE YOU MANAGED TO GATHER THE TRAINERS YOU NEED?
YES. ONE OF THEM IS RUBY, THE SON OF THE PETALBURG CITY GYM LEADER...
IS THAT BOY STILL TAKING GOOD CARE OF MY CASTFORM?
OH YES.
THEN THERE'S SAPPHIRE, THE DAUGHTER OF POKÉMON RESEARCHER PROFESSOR BIRCH...
I KNOW HER WELL. I GAVE HER YOUR LETTER.
AND THE THIRD IS EMERALD. HE'S A SKILLED TRAINER WHO CONQUERED THE BATTLE FRONTIER.

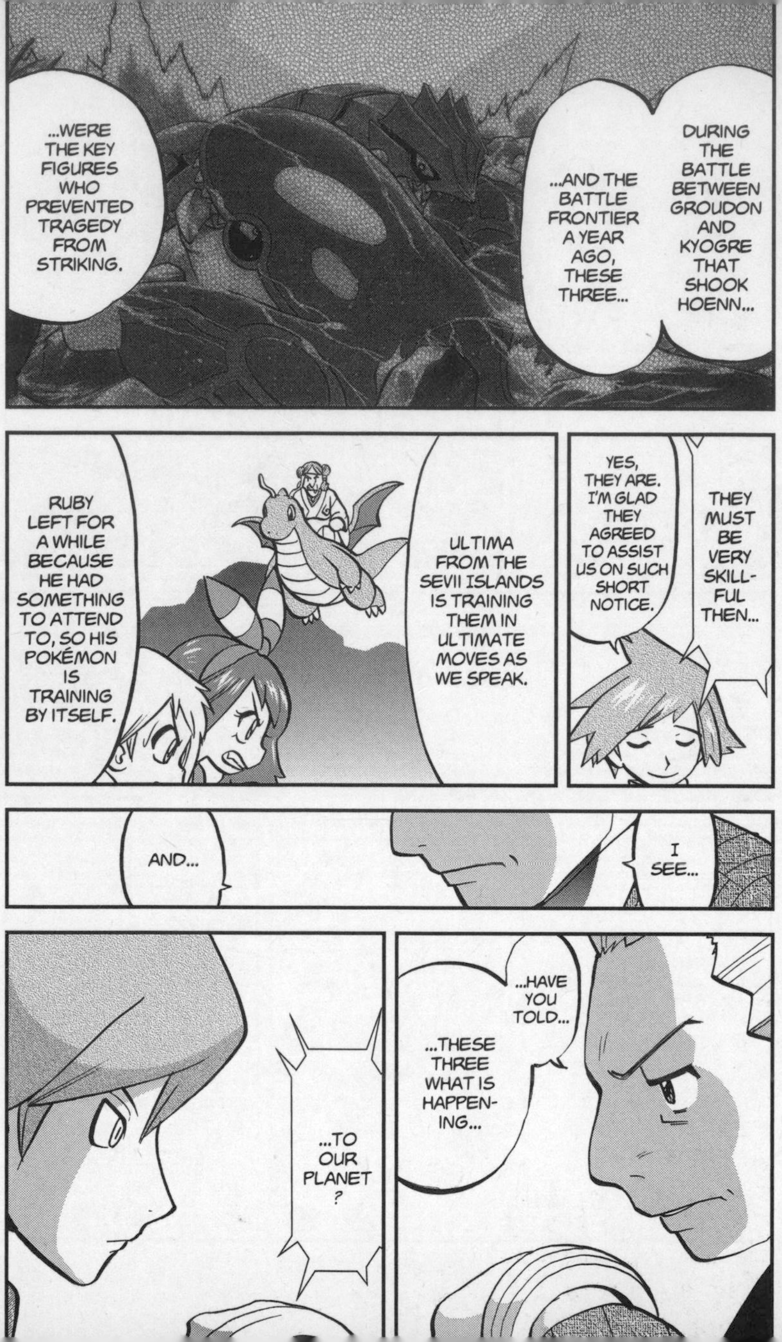
DURING THE BATTLE BETWEEN GROUDON AND KYOGRE THAT SHOOK HOENN...
...AND THE BATTLE FRONTIER A YEAR AGO, THESE THREE...
...WERE THE KEY FIGURES WHO PREVENTED TRAGEDY FROM STRIKING.
THEY MUST BE VERY SKILL-FUL THEN...
YES, THEY ARE. I'M GLAD THEY AGREED TO ASSIST US ON SUCH SHORT NOTICE.
ULTIMA FROM THE SEVII ISLANDS IS TRAINING THEM IN ULTIMATE MOVES AS WE SPEAK.
RUBY LEFT FOR A WHILE BECAUSE HE HAD SOMETHING TO ATTEND TO, SO HIS POKÉMON IS TRAINING BY ITSELF.
I SEE...
AND...
...HAVE YOU TOLD...
...THESE THREE WHAT IS HAPPEN-ING...
...TO OUR PLANET ?

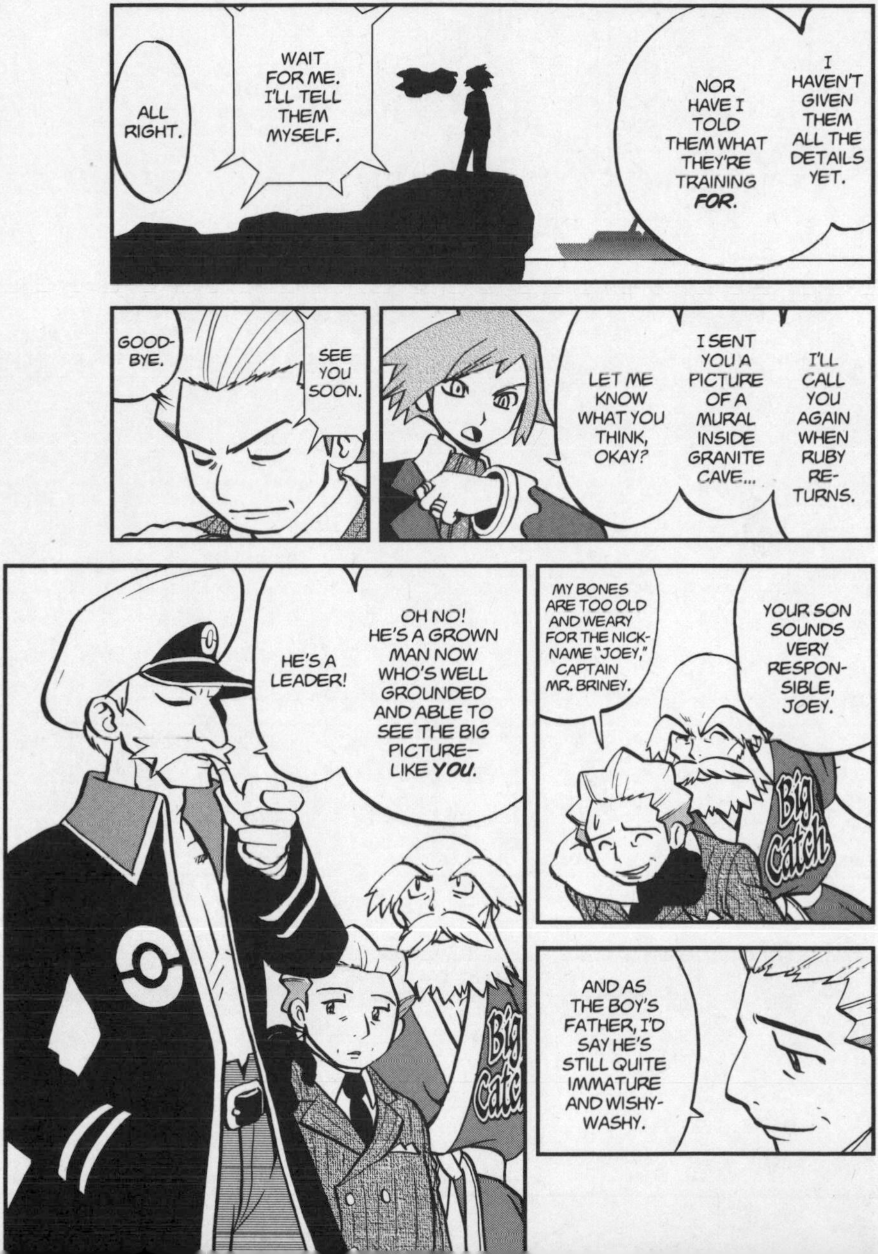
I HAVEN'T GIVEN THEM ALL THE DETAILS YET.
NOR HAVE I TOLD THEM WHAT THEY'RE TRAINING *FOR*.
WAIT FOR ME. I'LL TELL THEM MYSELF.
ALL RIGHT.
I'LL CALL YOU AGAIN WHEN RUBY RE-TURNS.
I SENT YOU A PICTURE OF A MURAL INSIDE GRANITE CAVE...
LET ME KNOW WHAT YOU THINK, OKAY?
SEE YOU SOON.
GOOD-BYE.
YOUR SON SOUNDS VERY RESPON-SIBLE, JOEY.
MY BONES ARE TOO OLD AND WEARY FOR THE NICK-NAME "JOEY," CAPTAIN MR. BRINEY.
Big Catch
AND AS THE BOY'S FATHER, I'D SAY HE'S STILL QUITE IMMATURE AND WISHY-WASHY.
OH NO! HE'S A GROWN MAN NOW WHO'S WELL GROUNDED AND ABLE TO SEE THE BIG PICTURE—LIKE *YOU*.
HE'S A LEADER!
Big Catch

WHY, THIS IS...

OH...!

HUH?

I OUGHT TO TAKE A LOOK AT THE IMAGE HE SENT ME.

HUH. WELL...

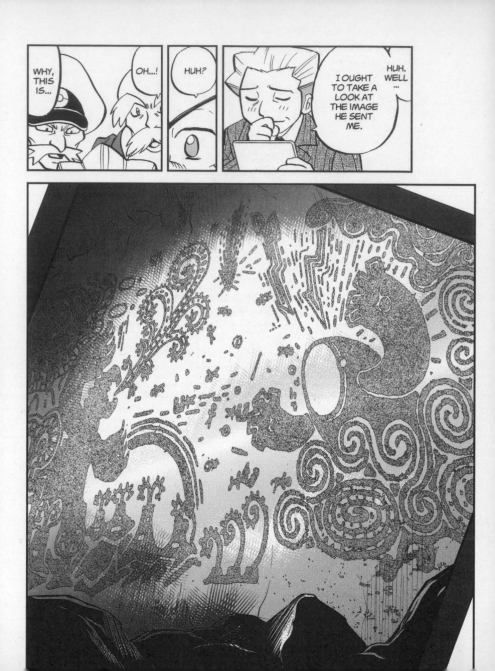

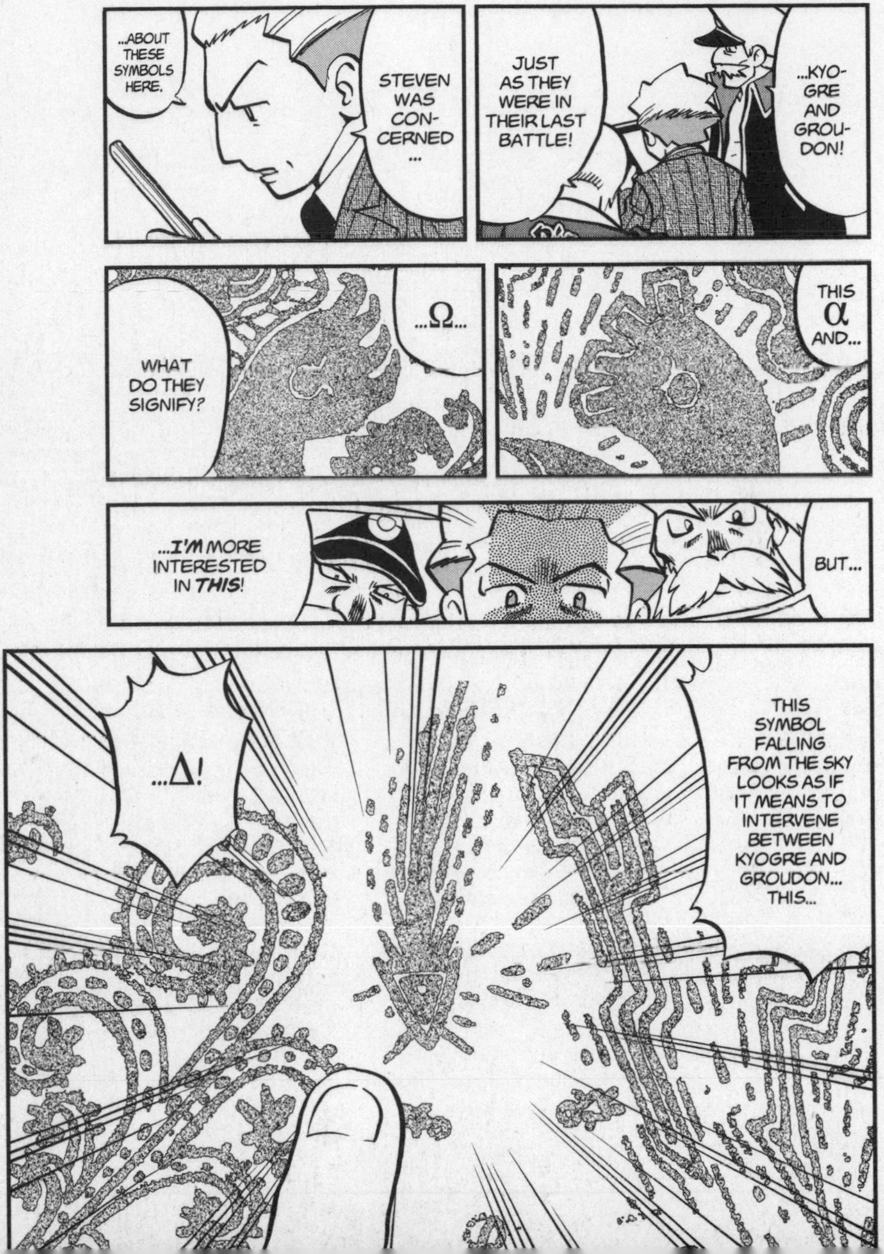
...KYO-GRE AND GROU-DON!
JUST AS THEY WERE IN THEIR LAST BATTLE!
STEVEN WAS CON-CERNED ...
...ABOUT THESE SYMBOLS HERE.
THIS α AND...
...Ω...
WHAT DO THEY SIGNIFY?
BUT...
...*I'M* MORE INTERESTED IN ***THIS***!
THIS SYMBOL FALLING FROM THE SKY LOOKS AS IF IT MEANS TO INTERVENE BETWEEN KYOGRE AND GROUDON... THIS...
...Δ!

S.S. TIDAL

A ferry that connects Lilycove City and Slateport City.

DEVON CORPORATION

An industrial company in Hoenn. It started out as a firm that hewed rocks from mines and manufactured steel from iron ore. But it eventually extended its business to daily commodities, medicines, and Trainer equipment as well as specialized Poké Balls. Their latest popular inventions are their Running Shoes and PokéNav Plus. Their office building is located in Rustboro City.

ULTIMATE MOVE

A unique move which is the strongest of its kind. The existence of three types—Grass, Water and Fire (Frenzy Plant, Hydro Cannon, Blast Burn)—have been confirmed so far. These ultimate moves are protected by a guardian who bestows the moves upon only a carefully chosen handful of trainers.

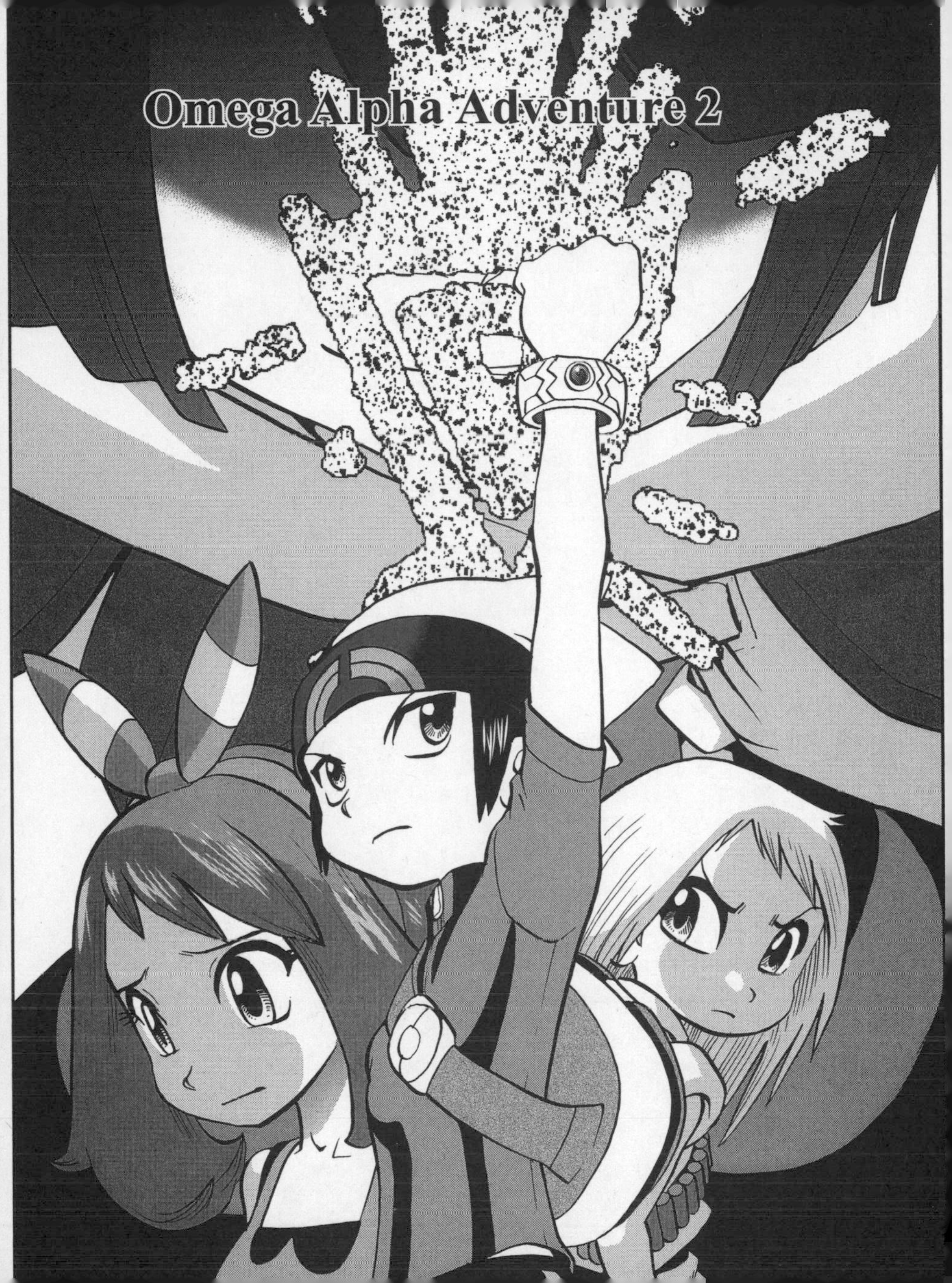
Omega Alpha Adventure 2

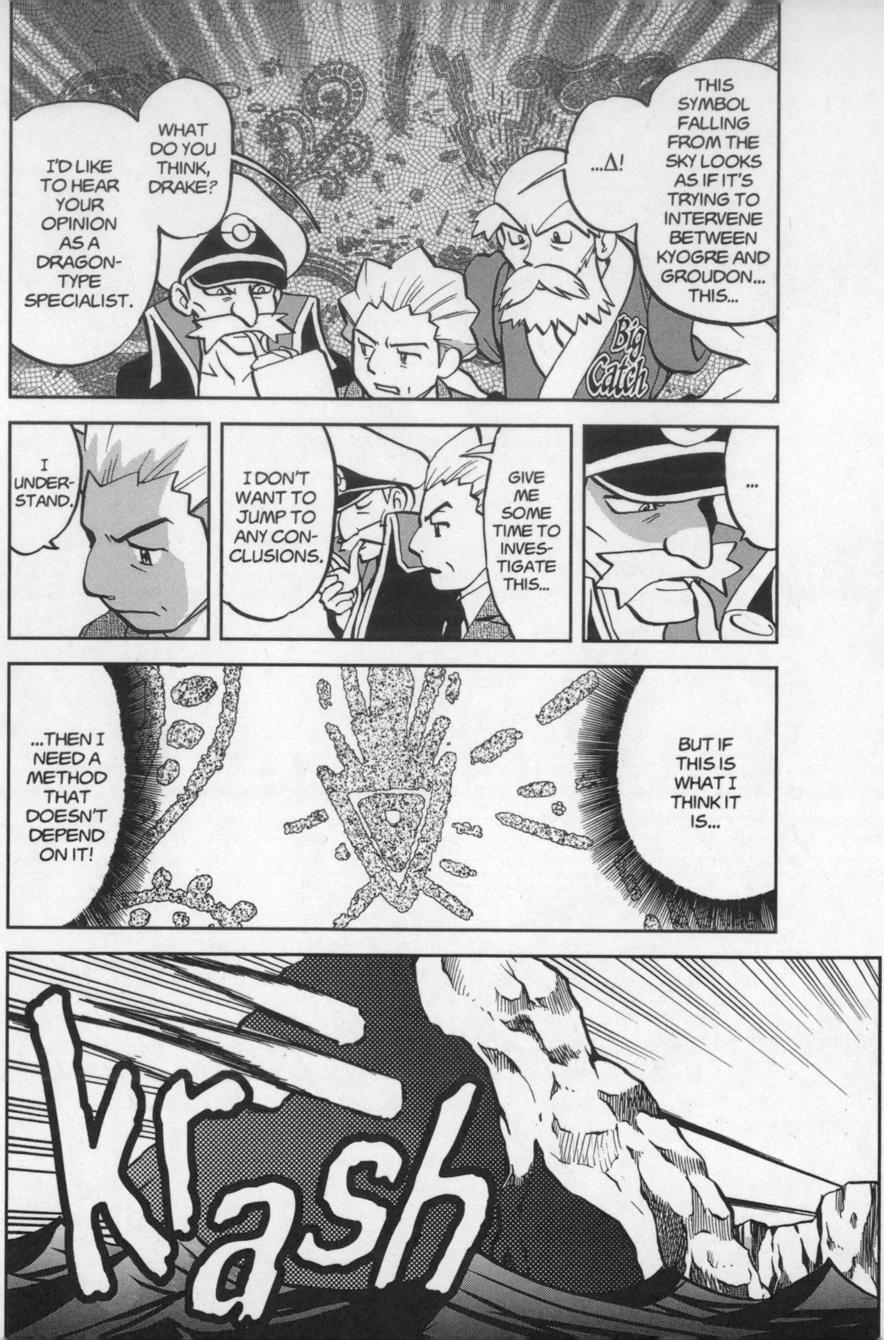
THIS SYMBOL FALLING FROM THE SKY LOOKS AS IF IT'S TRYING TO INTERVENE BETWEEN KYOGRE AND GROUDON... THIS...
...Δ!
WHAT DO YOU THINK, DRAKE?
I'D LIKE TO HEAR YOUR OPINION AS A DRAGON-TYPE SPECIALIST.
Big Catch
...
GIVE ME SOME TIME TO INVESTIGATE THIS...
I DON'T WANT TO JUMP TO ANY CONCLUSIONS.
I UNDERSTAND.
BUT IF THIS IS WHAT I THINK IT IS...
...THEN I NEED A METHOD THAT DOESN'T DEPEND ON IT!
Krash

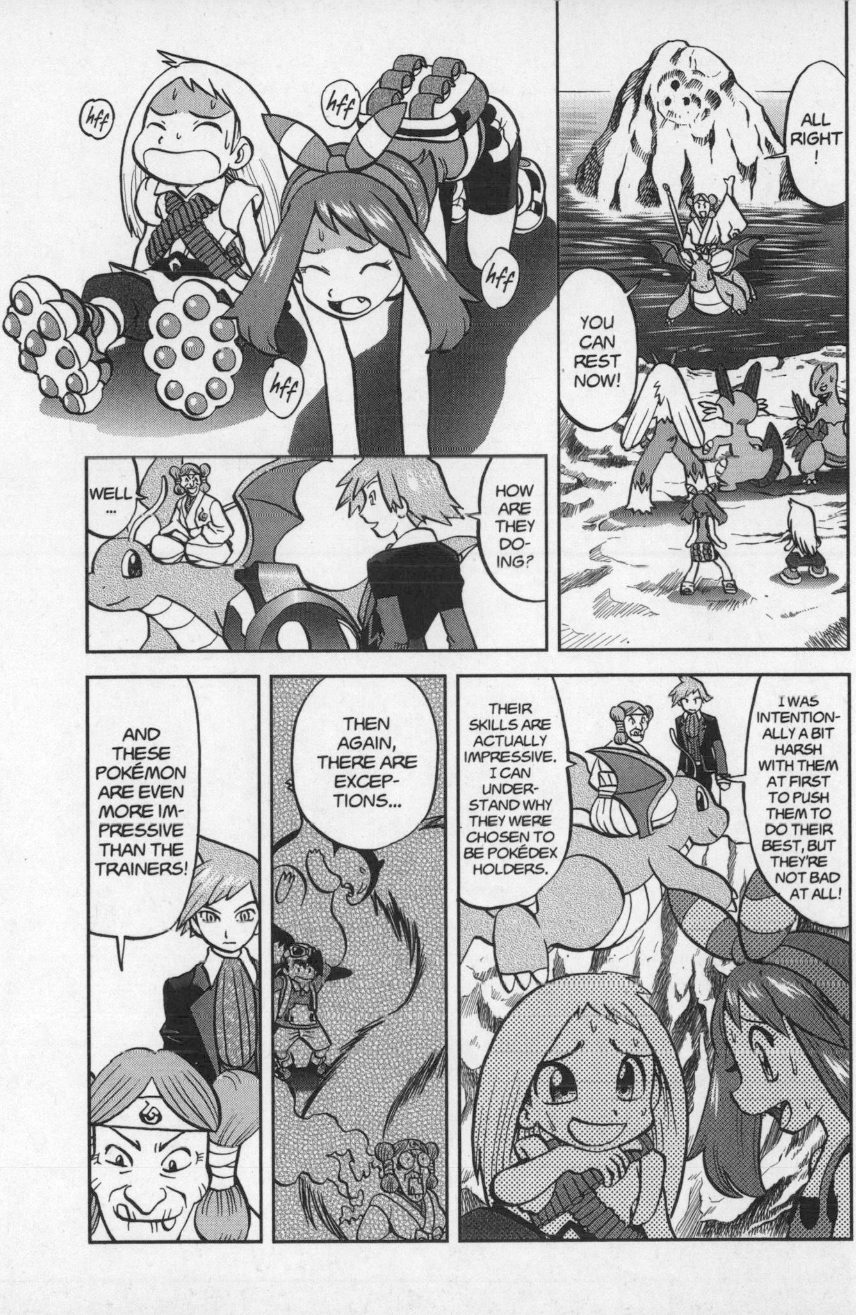
ALL RIGHT!
YOU CAN REST NOW!
hff
hff
hff
hff
HOW ARE THEY DOING?
WELL ...
I WAS INTENTIONALLY A BIT HARSH WITH THEM AT FIRST TO PUSH THEM TO DO THEIR BEST, BUT THEY'RE NOT BAD AT ALL!
THEIR SKILLS ARE ACTUALLY IMPRESSIVE. I CAN UNDERSTAND WHY THEY WERE CHOSEN TO BE POKÉDEX HOLDERS.
THEN AGAIN, THERE ARE EXCEPTIONS...
AND THESE POKÉMON ARE EVEN MORE IMPRESSIVE THAN THE TRAINERS!

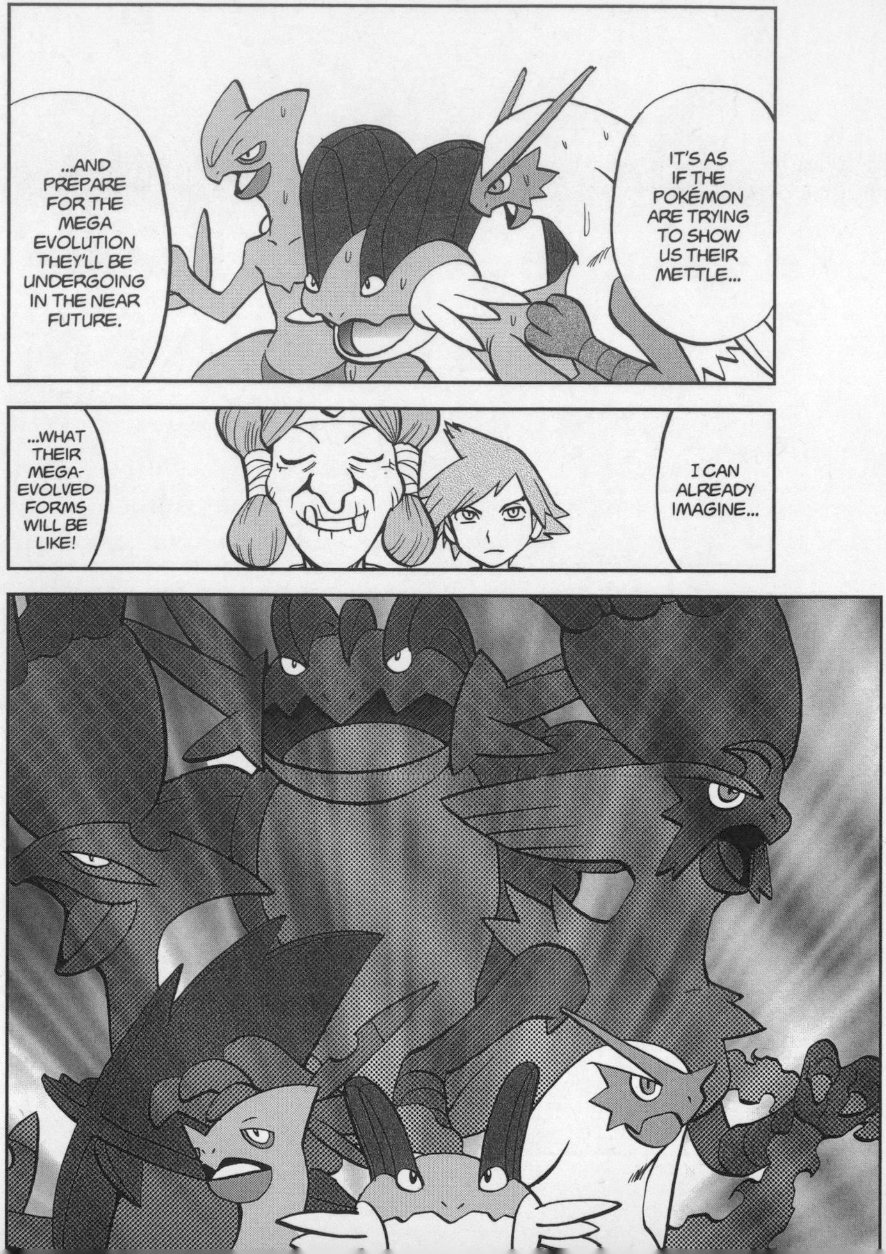
IT'S AS IF THE POKÉMON ARE TRYING TO SHOW US THEIR METTLE...
...AND PREPARE FOR THE MEGA EVOLUTION THEY'LL BE UNDERGOING IN THE NEAR FUTURE.
I CAN ALREADY IMAGINE...
...WHAT THEIR MEGA-EVOLVED FORMS WILL BE LIKE!

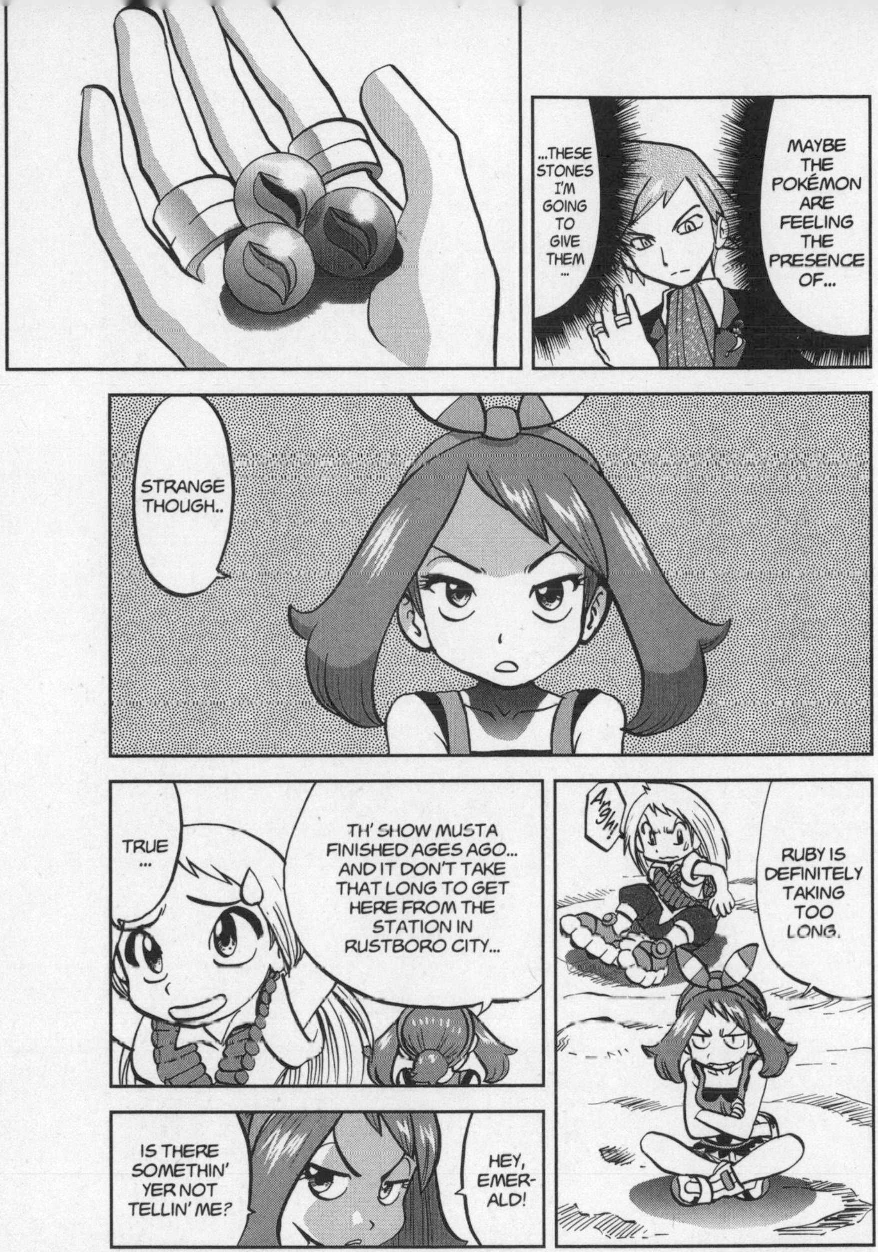
MAYBE THE POKÉMON ARE FEELING THE PRESENCE OF...
...THESE STONES I'M GOING TO GIVE THEM ...
STRANGE THOUGH..
Argh!
RUBY IS DEFINITELY TAKING TOO LONG.
TH' SHOW MUSTA FINISHED AGES AGO... AND IT DON'T TAKE THAT LONG TO GET HERE FROM THE STATION IN RUSTBORO CITY...
TRUE ...
HEY, EMER-ALD!
IS THERE SOMETHIN' YER NOT TELLIN' ME?

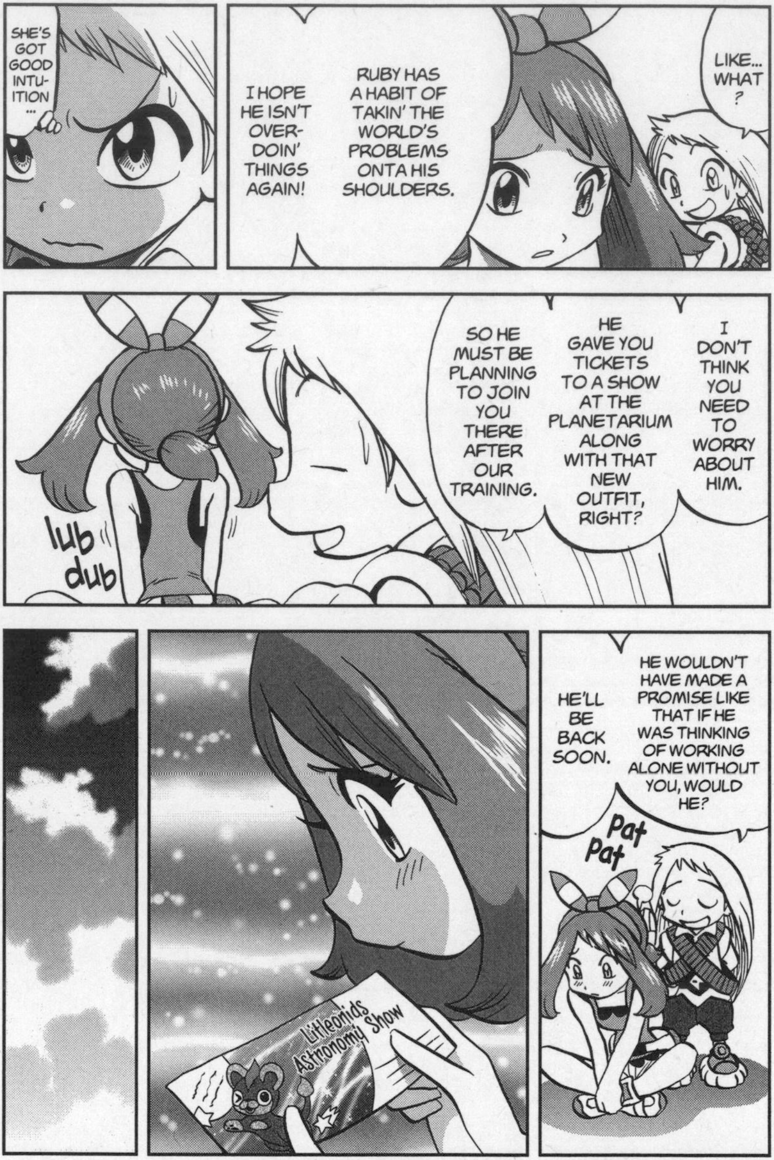
LIKE... WHAT?
RUBY HAS A HABIT OF TAKIN' THE WORLD'S PROBLEMS ONTA HIS SHOULDERS.
I HOPE HE ISN'T OVER-DOIN' THINGS AGAIN!
SHE'S GOT GOOD INTU-ITION...
I DON'T THINK YOU NEED TO WORRY ABOUT HIM.
HE GAVE YOU TICKETS TO A SHOW AT THE PLANETARIUM ALONG WITH THAT NEW OUTFIT, RIGHT?
SO HE MUST BE PLANNING TO JOIN YOU THERE AFTER OUR TRAINING.
lub dub
HE WOULDN'T HAVE MADE A PROMISE LIKE THAT IF HE WAS THINKING OF WORKING ALONE WITHOUT YOU, WOULD HE?
HE'LL BE BACK SOON.
Pat Pat
Litleonids Astronomy Show

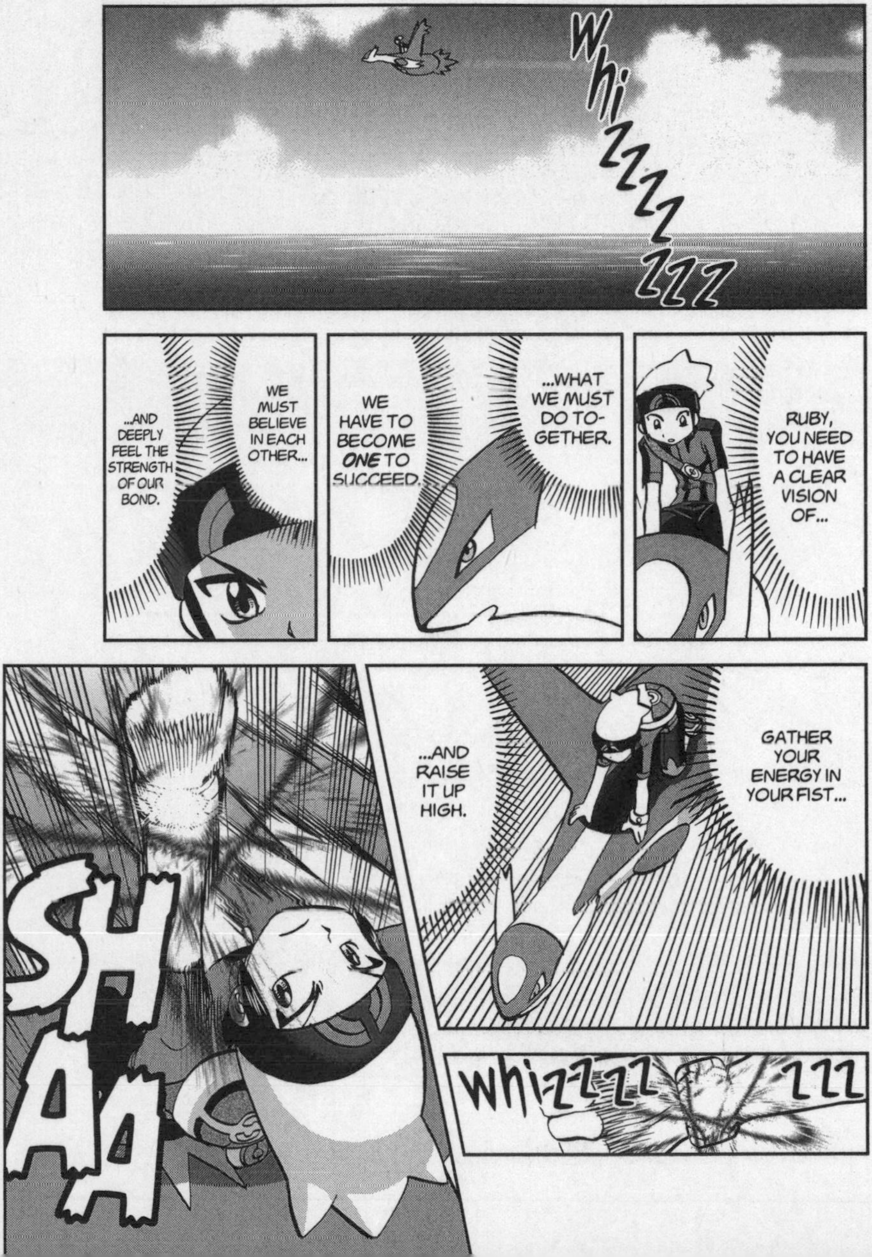

Whizzzzzzzzz
RUBY, YOU NEED TO HAVE A CLEAR VISION OF...
...WHAT WE MUST DO TO-GETHER.
WE HAVE TO BECOME ONE TO SUCCEED.
WE MUST BELIEVE IN EACH OTHER...
...AND DEEPLY FEEL THE STRENGTH OF OUR BOND.
GATHER YOUR ENERGY IN YOUR FIST...
...AND RAISE IT UP HIGH.
whizzzzzzzz
SHAA

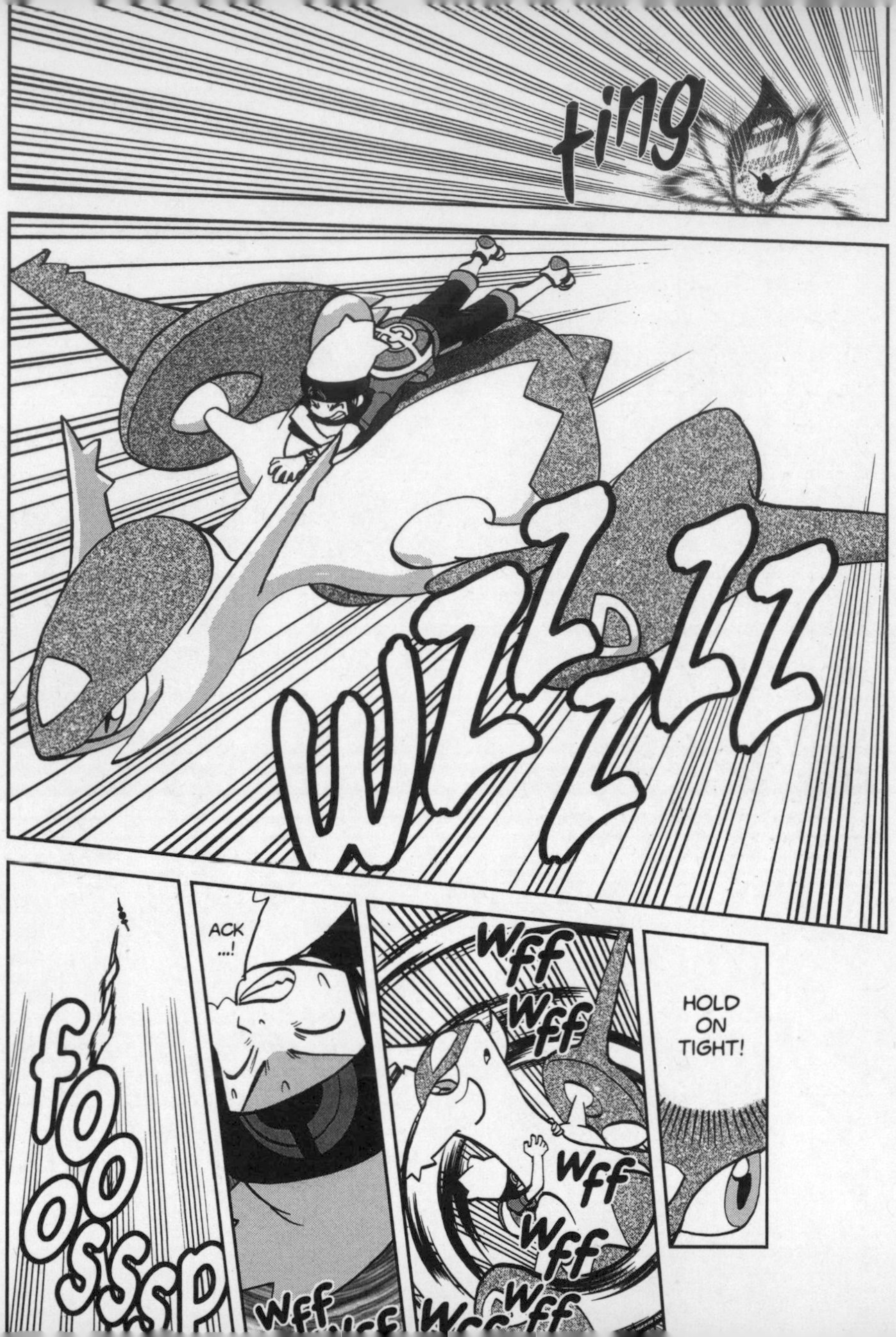
ting
WZZZZZ
HOLD ON TIGHT!
Wff
Wff
Wff
Wff
Wff
Wff
ACK ...!
fooossp
Wff

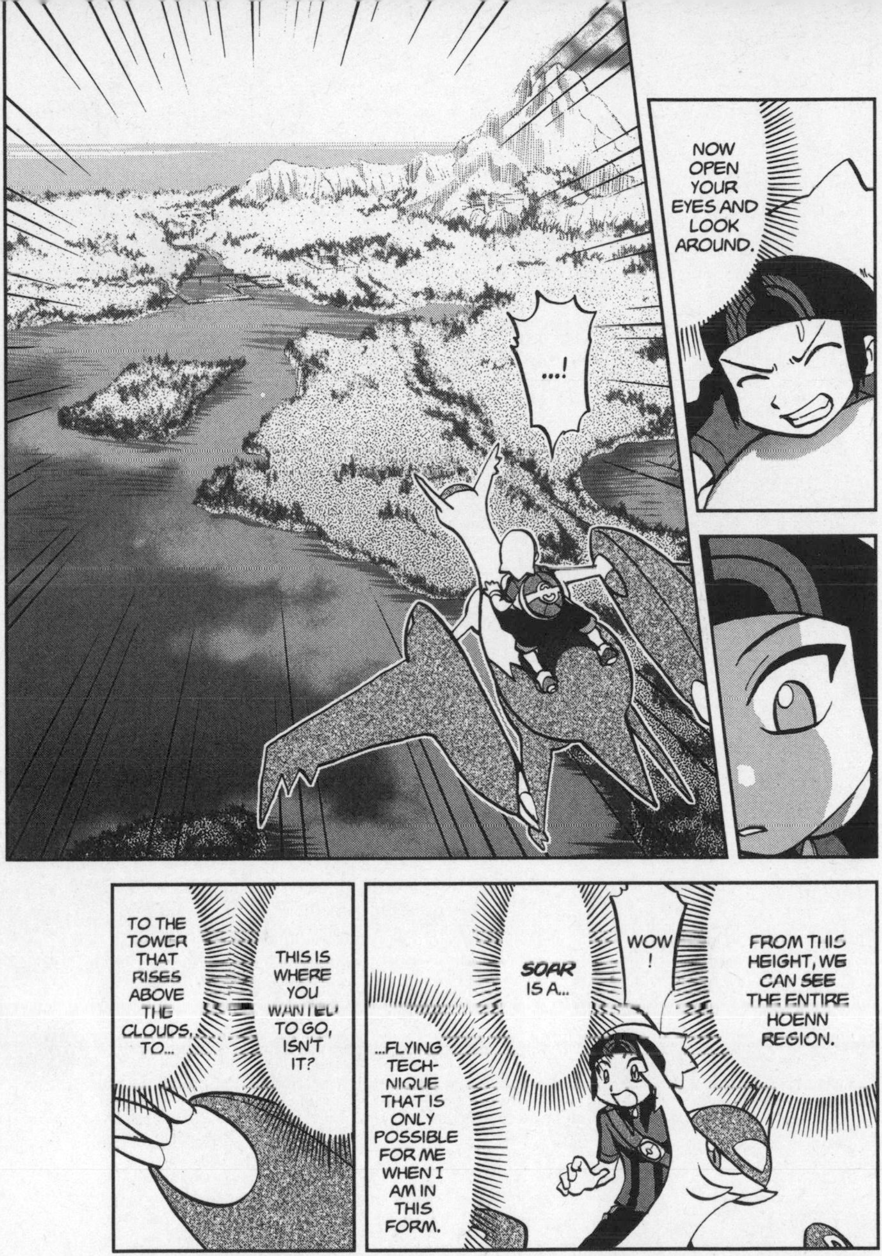
NOW OPEN YOUR EYES AND LOOK AROUND.
...!
FROM THIS HEIGHT, WE CAN SEE THE ENTIRE HOENN REGION.
WOW!
SOAR IS A...
...FLYING TECH-NIQUE THAT IS ONLY POSSIBLE FOR ME WHEN I AM IN THIS FORM.
THIS IS WHERE YOU WANTED TO GO, ISN'T IT?
TO THE TOWER THAT RISES ABOVE THE CLOUDS, TO...

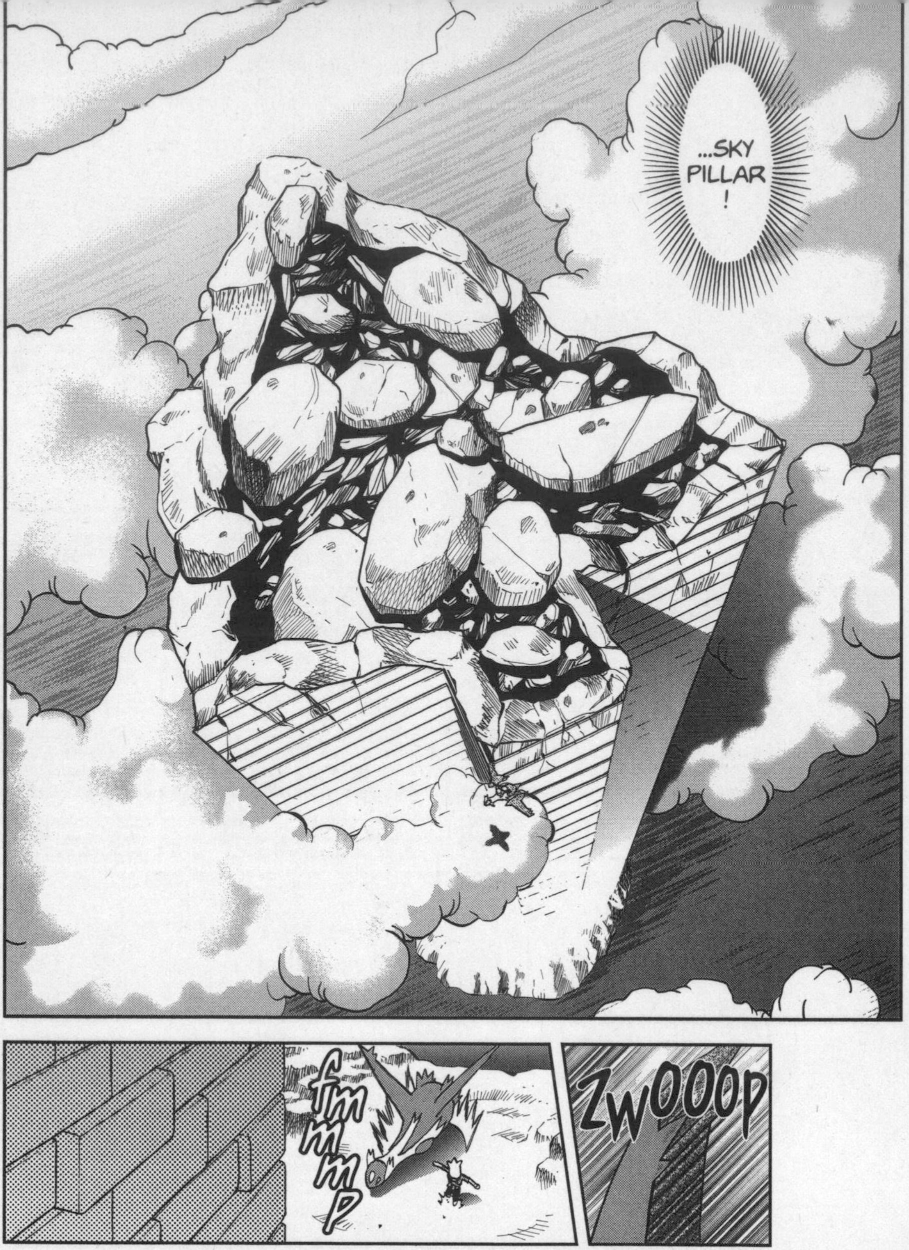
...SKY PILLAR !
ZWOOOP
fmmmp

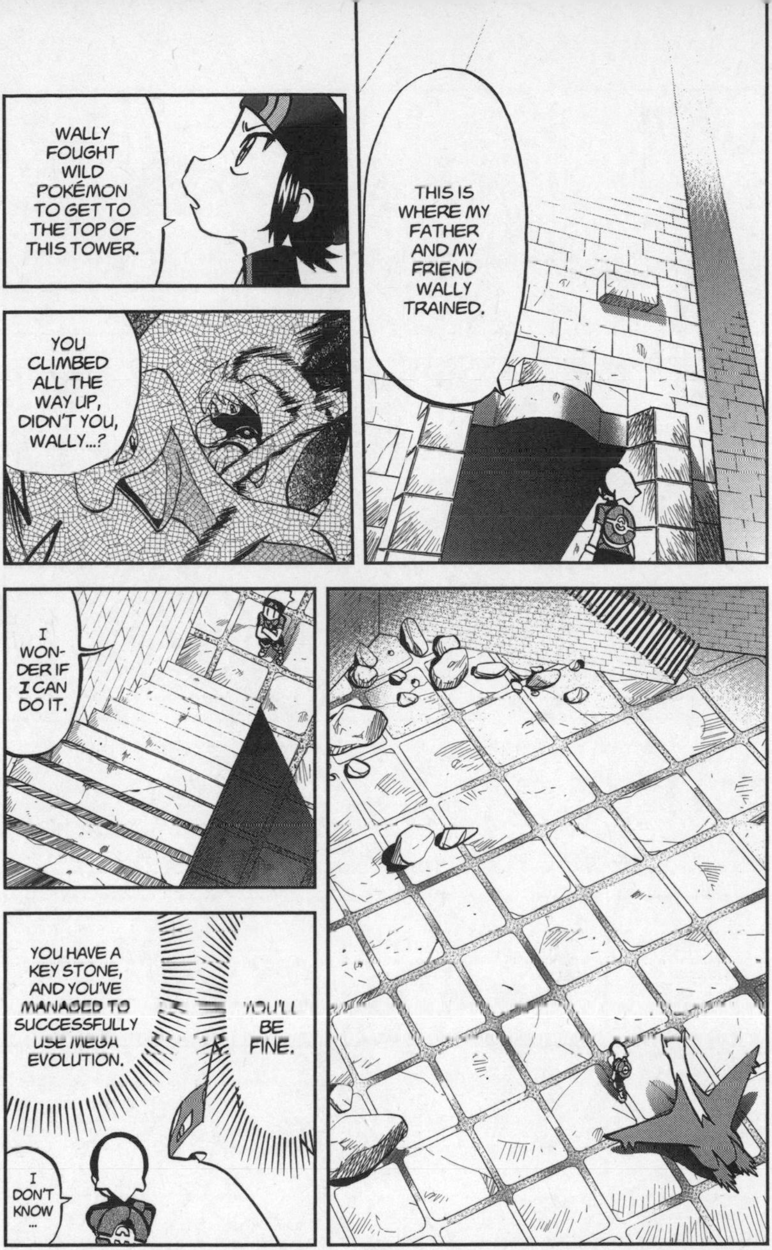
THIS IS WHERE MY FATHER AND MY FRIEND WALLY TRAINED.
WALLY FOUGHT WILD POKÉMON TO GET TO THE TOP OF THIS TOWER.
YOU CLIMBED ALL THE WAY UP, DIDN'T YOU, WALLY...?
I WONDER IF I CAN DO IT.
YOU HAVE A KEY STONE, AND YOU'VE MANAGED TO SUCCESSFULLY USE MEGA EVOLUTION.
YOU'LL BE FINE.
I DON'T KNOW...

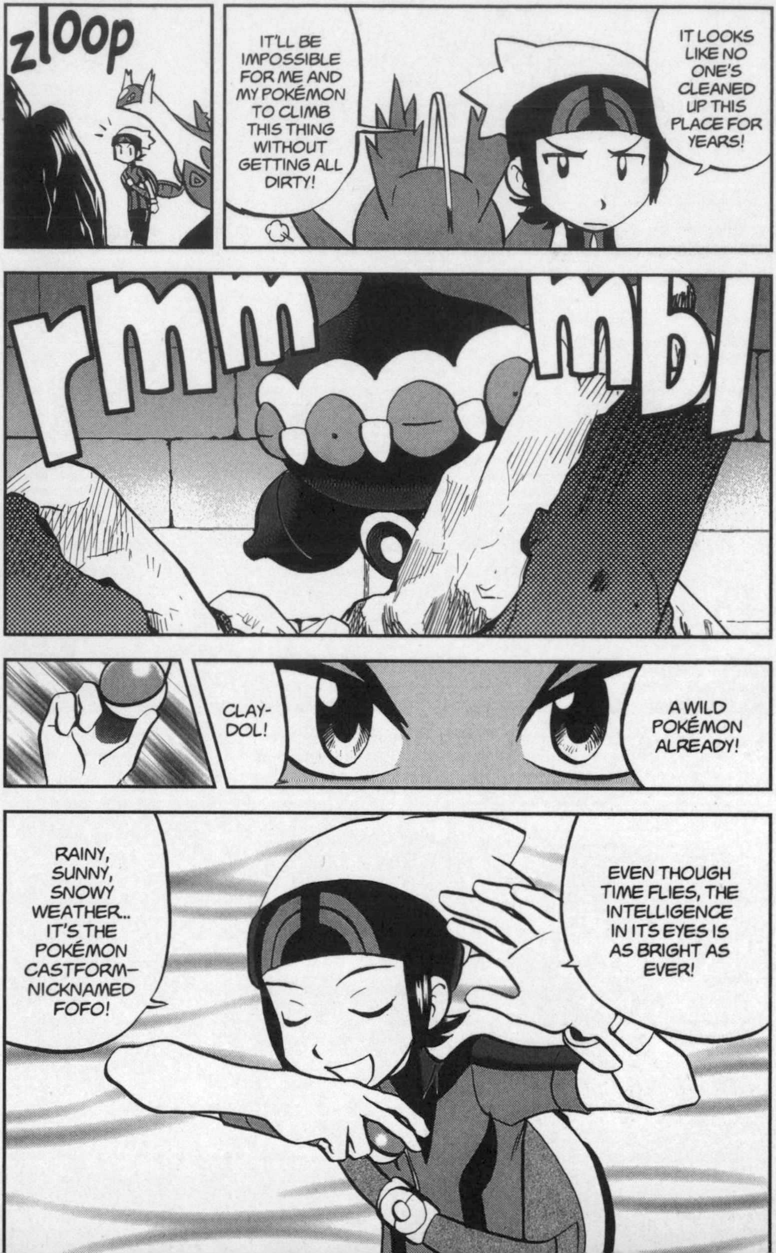
IT LOOKS LIKE NO ONE'S CLEANED UP THIS PLACE FOR YEARS!
IT'LL BE IMPOSSIBLE FOR ME AND MY POKéMON TO CLIMB THIS THING WITHOUT GETTING ALL DIRTY!
zloop
rmm mbl
A WILD POKéMON ALREADY!
CLAY-DOL!
EVEN THOUGH TIME FLIES, THE INTELLIGENCE IN ITS EYES IS AS BRIGHT AS EVER!
RAINY, SUNNY, SNOWY WEATHER... IT'S THE POKéMON CASTFORM—NICKNAMED FOFO!

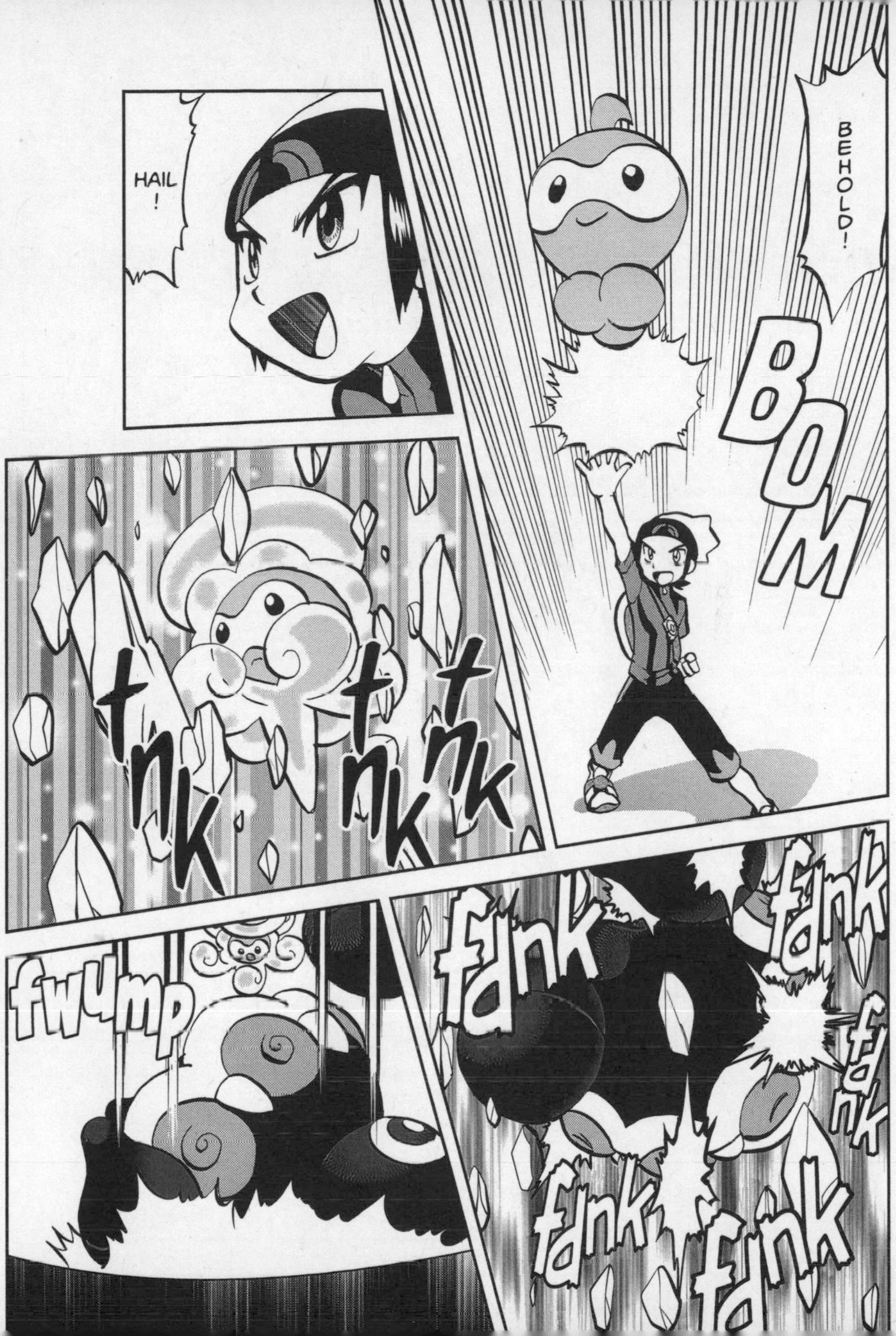
BEHOLD!
BOOM
HAIL!
tnk
tnk
tnk
fdnk
fdnk
fdnk
fdnk
fdnk
fdnk
fwump

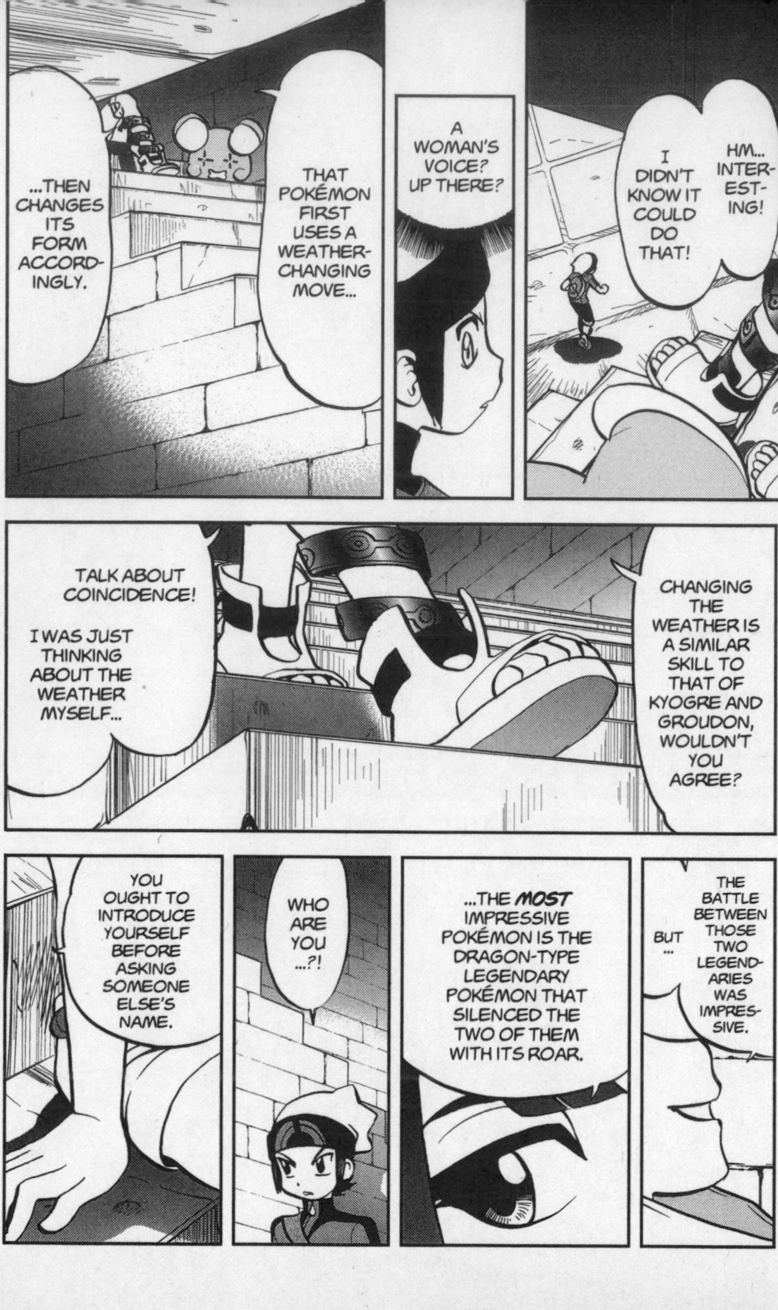
HM... INTERESTING!
I DIDN'T KNOW IT COULD DO THAT!
A WOMAN'S VOICE? UP THERE?
THAT POKÉMON FIRST USES A WEATHER-CHANGING MOVE...
...THEN CHANGES ITS FORM ACCORDINGLY.
CHANGING THE WEATHER IS A SIMILAR SKILL TO THAT OF KYOGRE AND GROUDON, WOULDN'T YOU AGREE?
TALK ABOUT COINCIDENCE!
I WAS JUST THINKING ABOUT THE WEATHER MYSELF...
THE BATTLE BETWEEN THOSE TWO LEGENDARIES WAS IMPRESSIVE.
BUT...
...THE ***MOST*** IMPRESSIVE POKÉMON IS THE DRAGON-TYPE LEGENDARY POKÉMON THAT SILENCED THE TWO OF THEM WITH ITS ROAR.
WHO ARE YOU...?!
YOU OUGHT TO INTRODUCE YOURSELF BEFORE ASKING SOMEONE ELSE'S NAME.

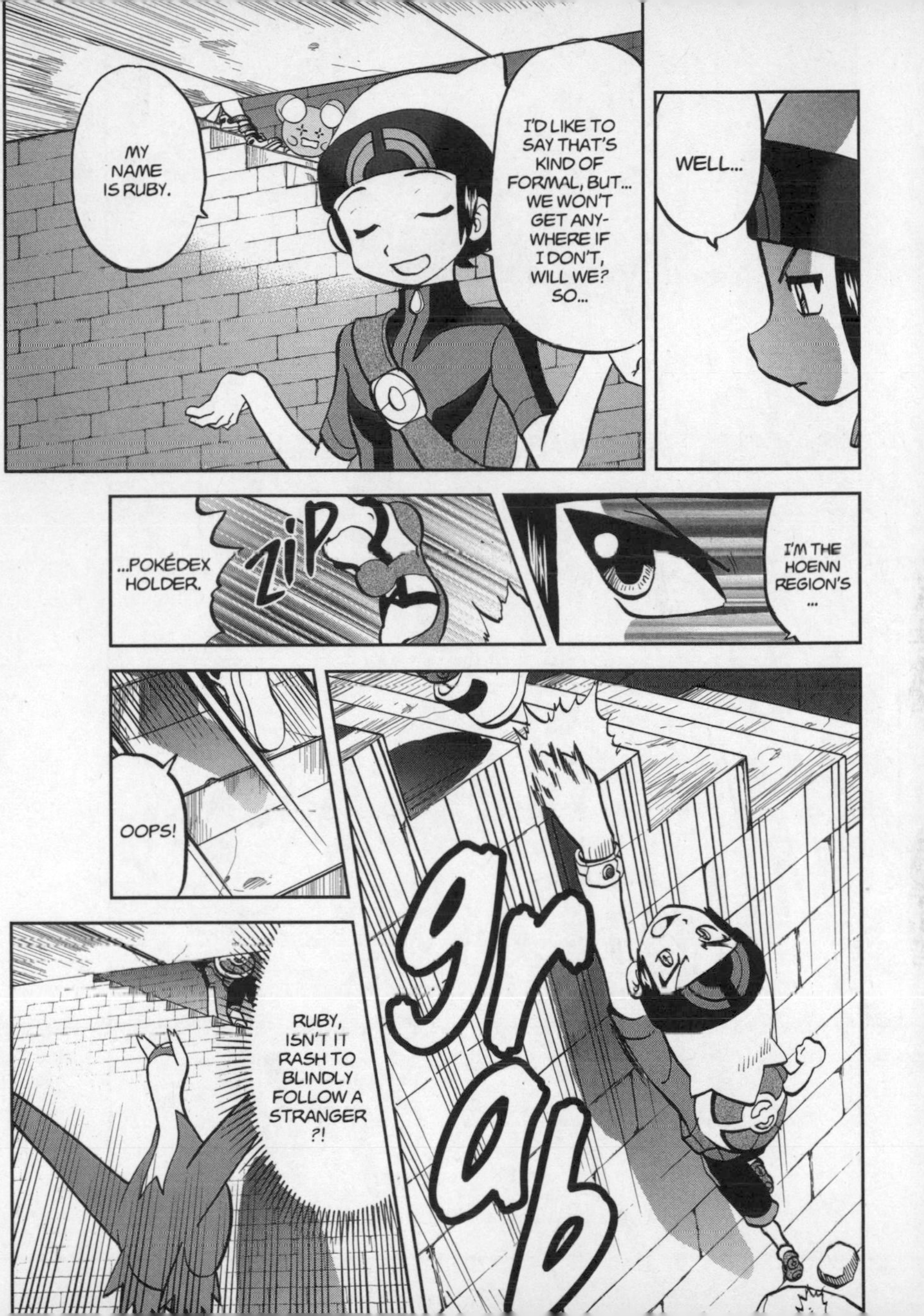
WELL...
I'D LIKE TO SAY THAT'S KIND OF FORMAL, BUT... WE WON'T GET ANY-WHERE IF I DON'T, WILL WE? SO...
MY NAME IS RUBY.
I'M THE HOENN REGION'S ...
ZIP
...POKÉDEX HOLDER.
grab
OOPS!
RUBY, ISN'T IT RASH TO BLINDLY FOLLOW A STRANGER ?!

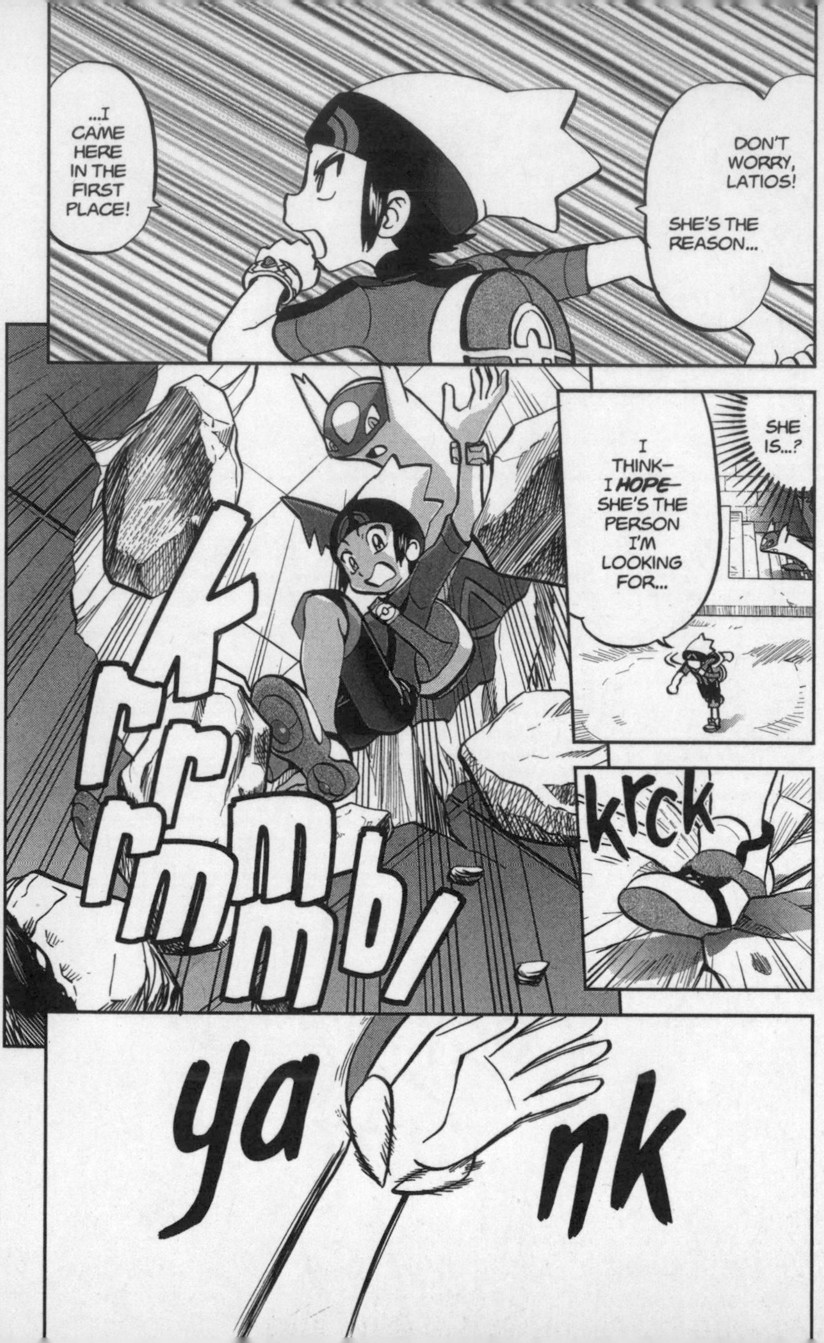
DON'T WORRY, LATIOS!
SHE'S THE REASON...
...I CAME HERE IN THE FIRST PLACE!
SHE IS...?
I THINK— I HOPE— SHE'S THE PERSON I'M LOOKING FOR...
krck
yank

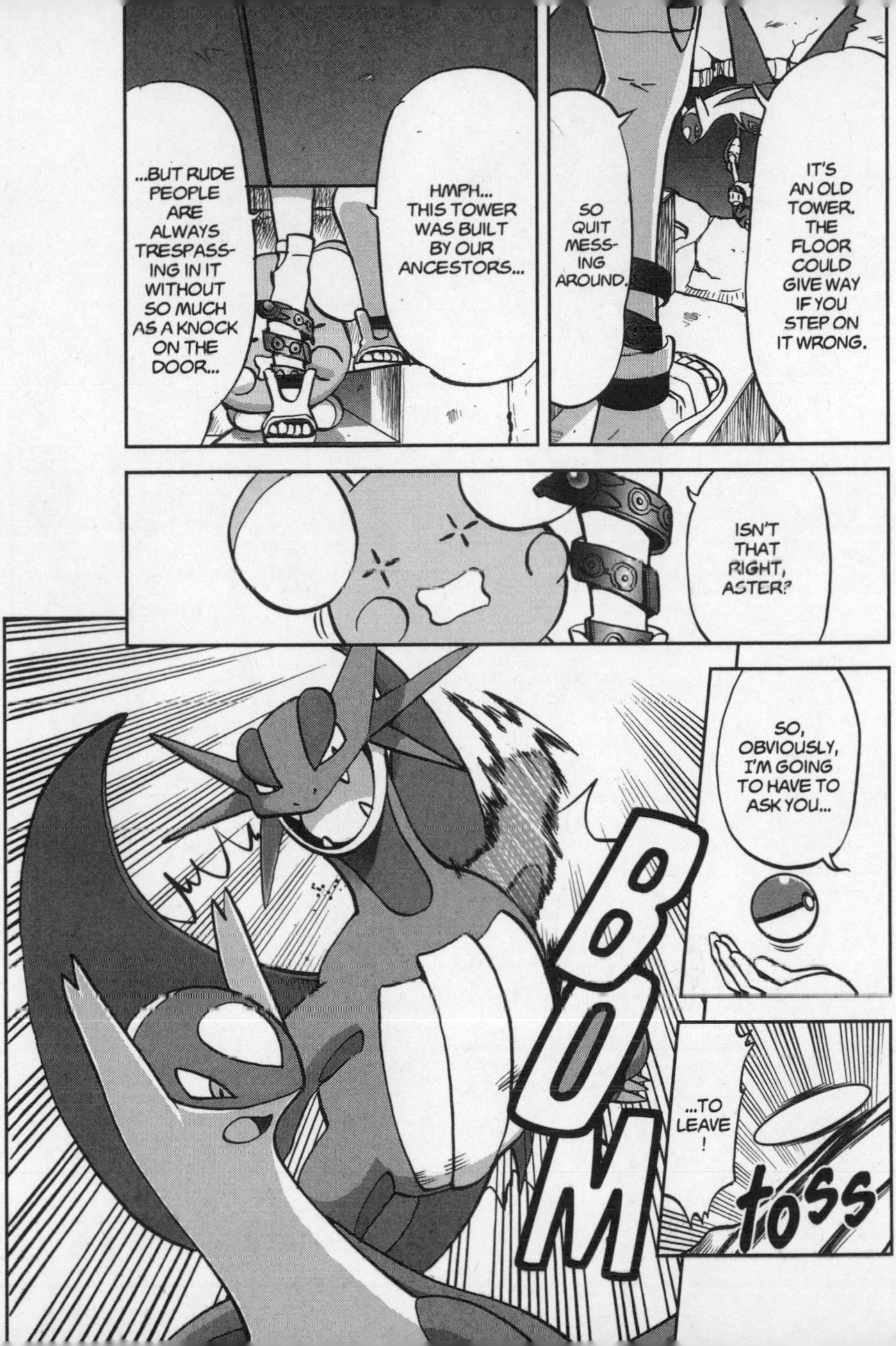
IT'S AN OLD TOWER. THE FLOOR COULD GIVE WAY IF YOU STEP ON IT WRONG.
SO QUIT MESSING AROUND.
HMPH... THIS TOWER WAS BUILT BY OUR ANCESTORS...
...BUT RUDE PEOPLE ARE ALWAYS TRESPASSING IN IT WITHOUT SO MUCH AS A KNOCK ON THE DOOR...
ISN'T THAT RIGHT, ASTER?
SO, OBVIOUSLY, I'M GOING TO HAVE TO ASK YOU...
...TO LEAVE!
toss
BOOM

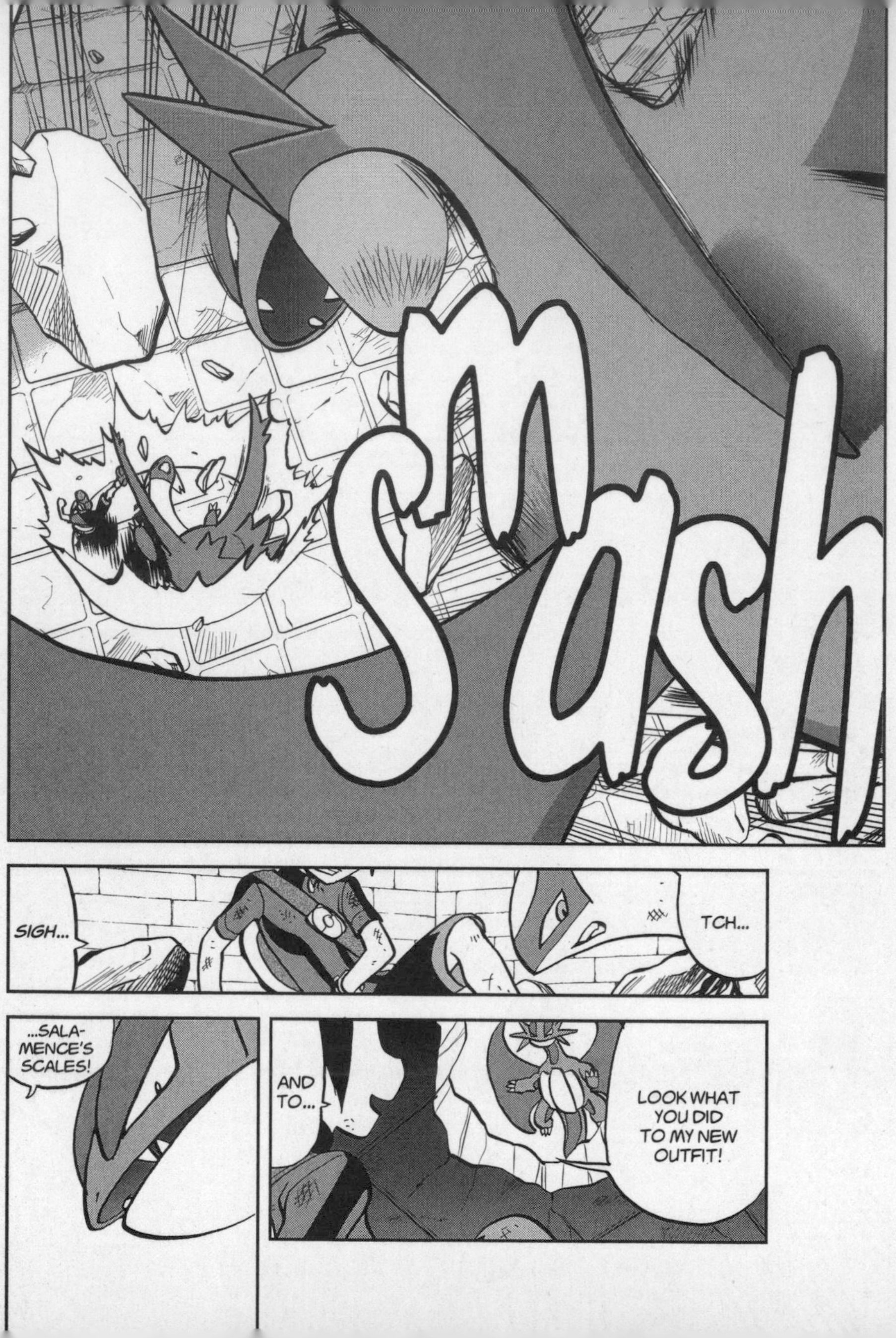
SMASH
TCH...
SIGH...
LOOK WHAT YOU DID TO MY NEW OUTFIT!
AND TO...
...SALAMENCE'S SCALES!

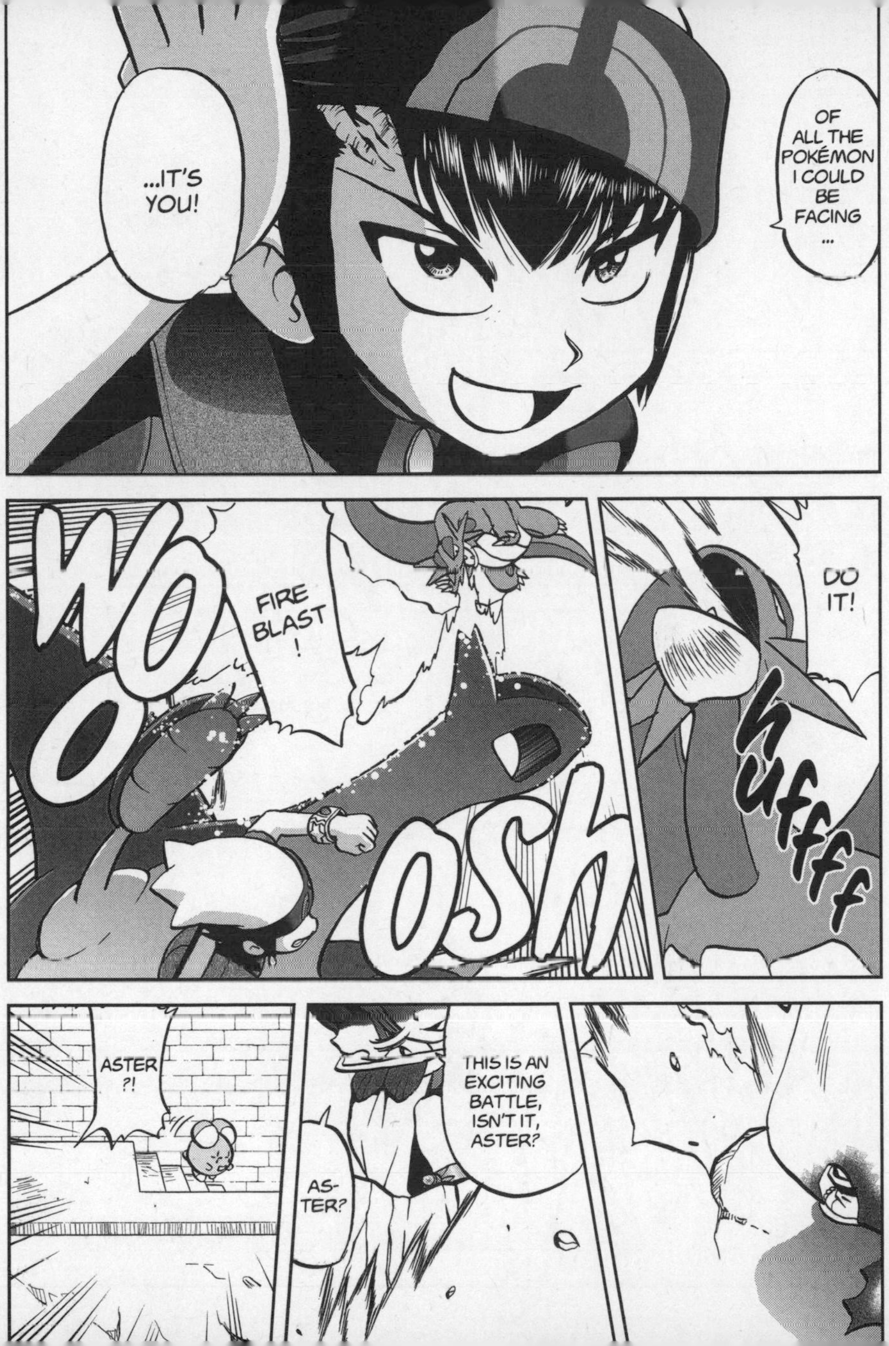

OF ALL THE POKÉMON I COULD BE FACING ...
...IT'S YOU!
DO IT!
huffff
FIRE BLAST!
WOOOSH
THIS IS AN EXCITING BATTLE, ISN'T IT, ASTER?
AS-TER?
ASTER?!

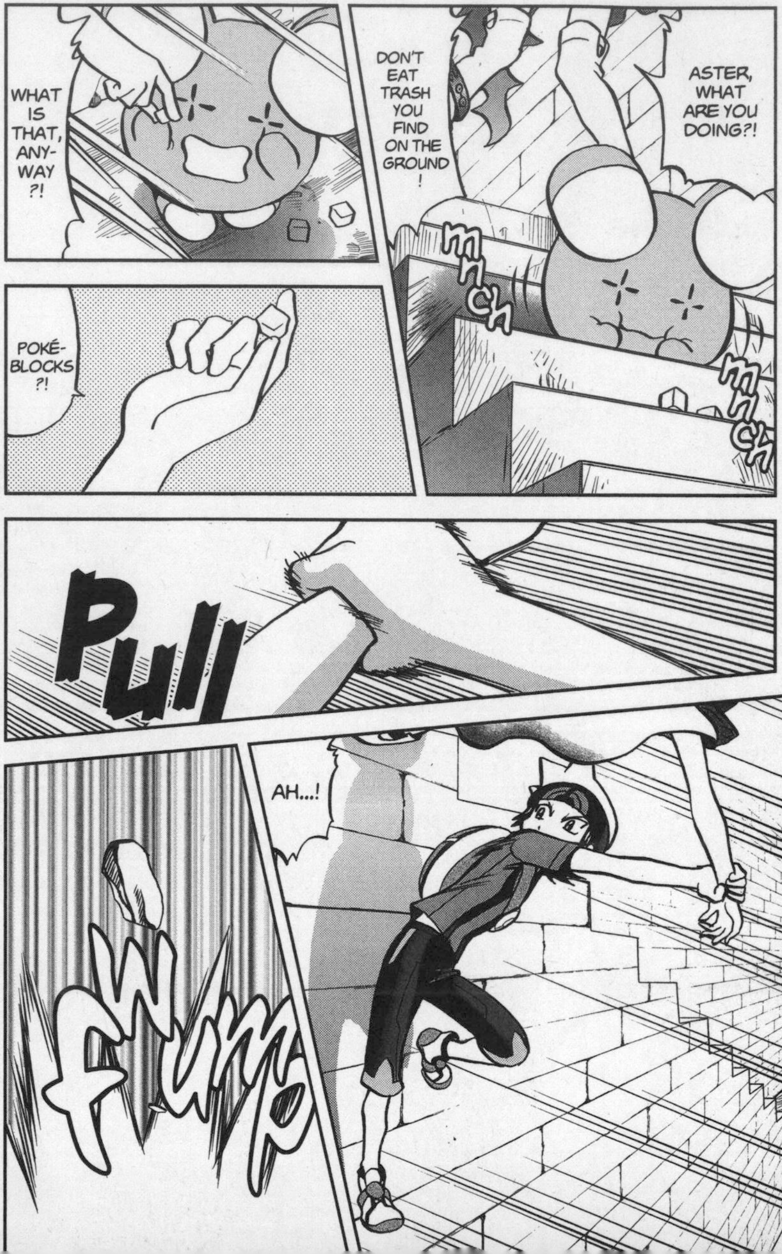
ASTER, WHAT ARE YOU DOING?!
DON'T EAT TRASH YOU FIND ON THE GROUND!
MNCH
MNCH
WHAT IS THAT, ANYWAY?!
POKÉBLOCKS?!
PULL
AH...!
FWUMP

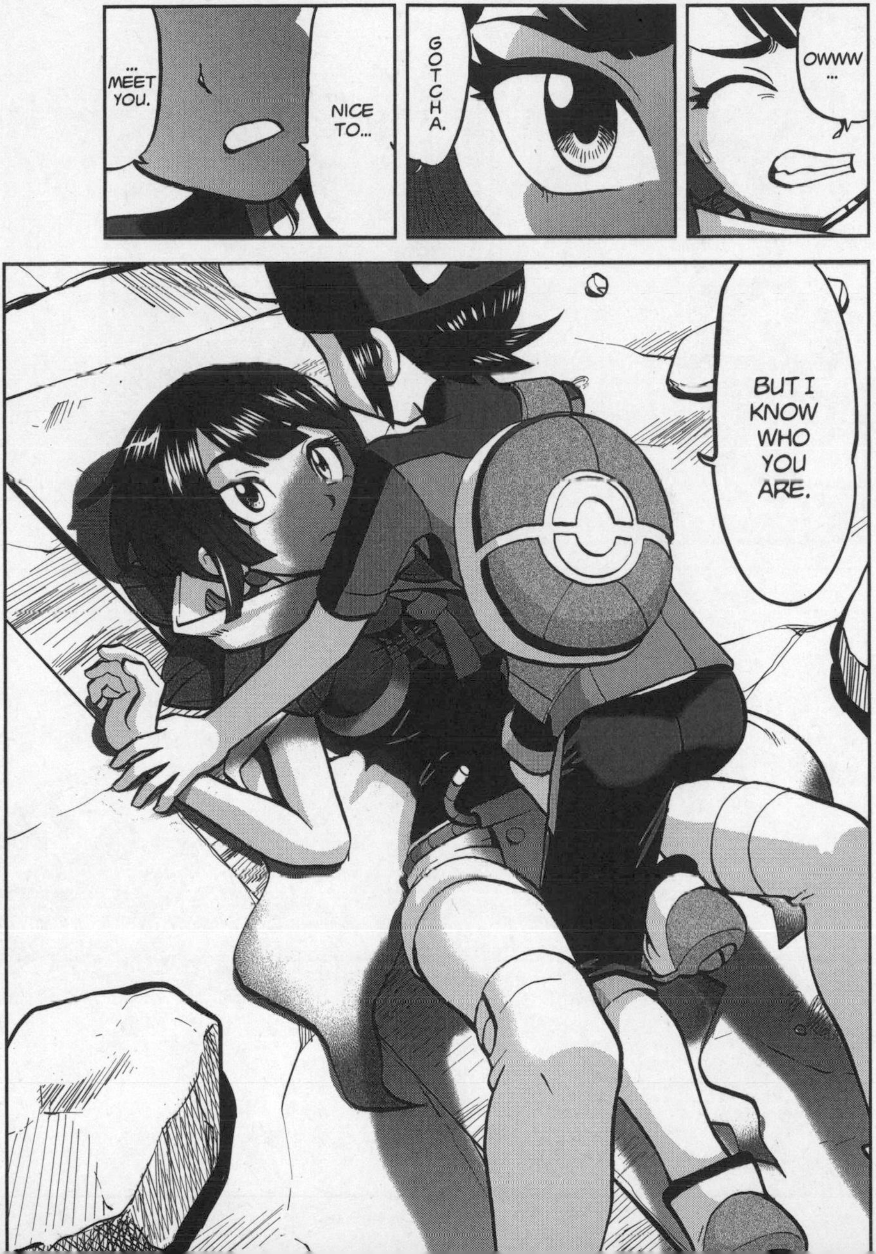
OWWW ...
GOTCHA.
NICE TO...
... MEET YOU.
BUT I KNOW WHO YOU ARE.

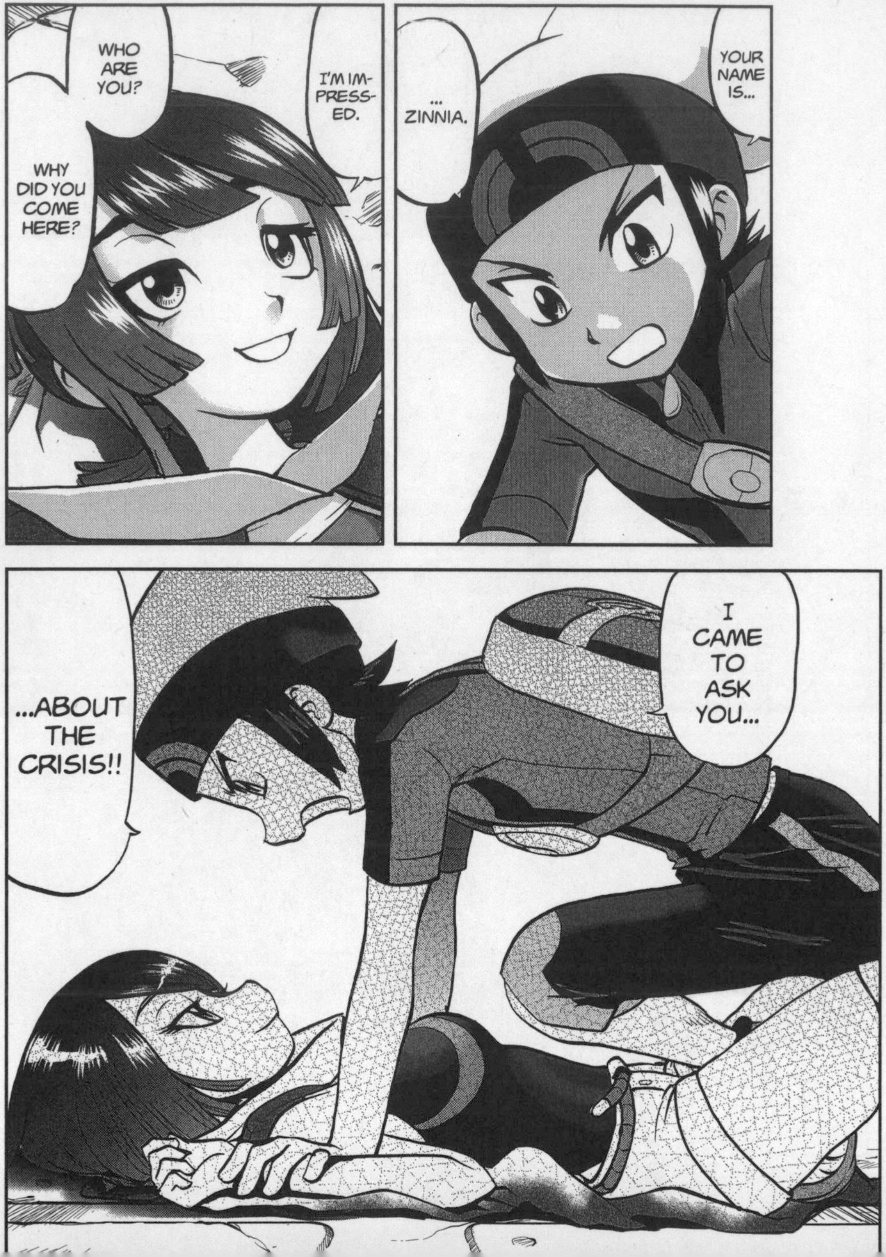
YOUR NAME IS...
... ZINNIA.
I'M IMPRESSED.
WHO ARE YOU?
WHY DID YOU COME HERE?
I CAME TO ASK YOU...
...ABOUT THE CRISIS!!

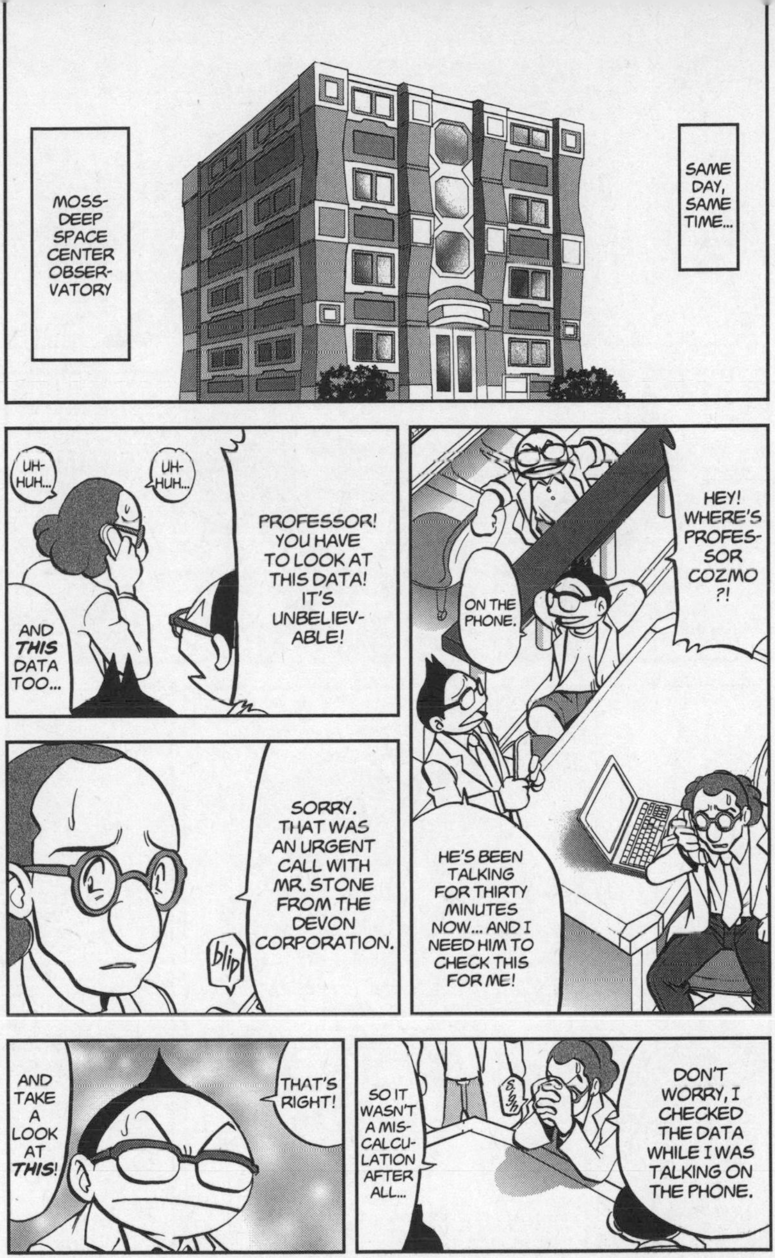
SAME DAY, SAME TIME...
MOSSDEEP SPACE CENTER OBSERVATORY
HEY! WHERE'S PROFESSOR COZMO?!
ON THE PHONE.
HE'S BEEN TALKING FOR THIRTY MINUTES NOW... AND I NEED HIM TO CHECK THIS FOR ME!
PROFESSOR! YOU HAVE TO LOOK AT THIS DATA! IT'S UNBELIEVABLE!
UH-HUH...
UH-HUH...
AND **THIS** DATA TOO...
SORRY. THAT WAS AN URGENT CALL WITH MR. STONE FROM THE DEVON CORPORATION.
blip
DON'T WORRY, I CHECKED THE DATA WHILE I WAS TALKING ON THE PHONE.
SO IT WASN'T A MISCALCULATION AFTER ALL...
THAT'S RIGHT!
AND TAKE A LOOK AT **THIS**!

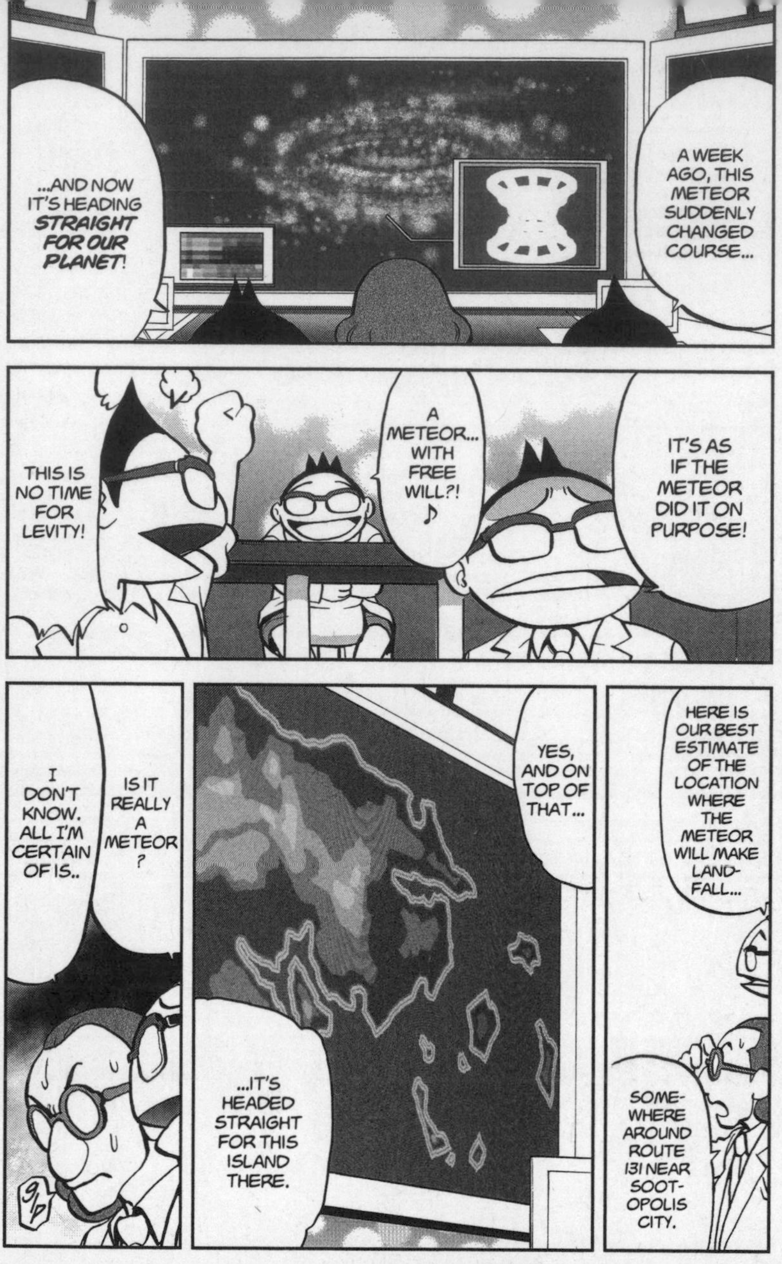
A WEEK AGO, THIS METEOR SUDDENLY CHANGED COURSE...
...AND NOW IT'S HEADING *STRAIGHT FOR OUR PLANET*!
IT'S AS IF THE METEOR DID IT ON PURPOSE!
A METEOR... WITH FREE WILL?! ♪
THIS IS NO TIME FOR LEVITY!
HERE IS OUR BEST ESTIMATE OF THE LOCATION WHERE THE METEOR WILL MAKE LAND-FALL...
SOME-WHERE AROUND ROUTE 131 NEAR SOOT-OPOLIS CITY.
YES, AND ON TOP OF THAT...
...IT'S HEADED STRAIGHT FOR THIS ISLAND THERE.
IS IT REALLY A METEOR?
I DON'T KNOW. ALL I'M CERTAIN OF IS..

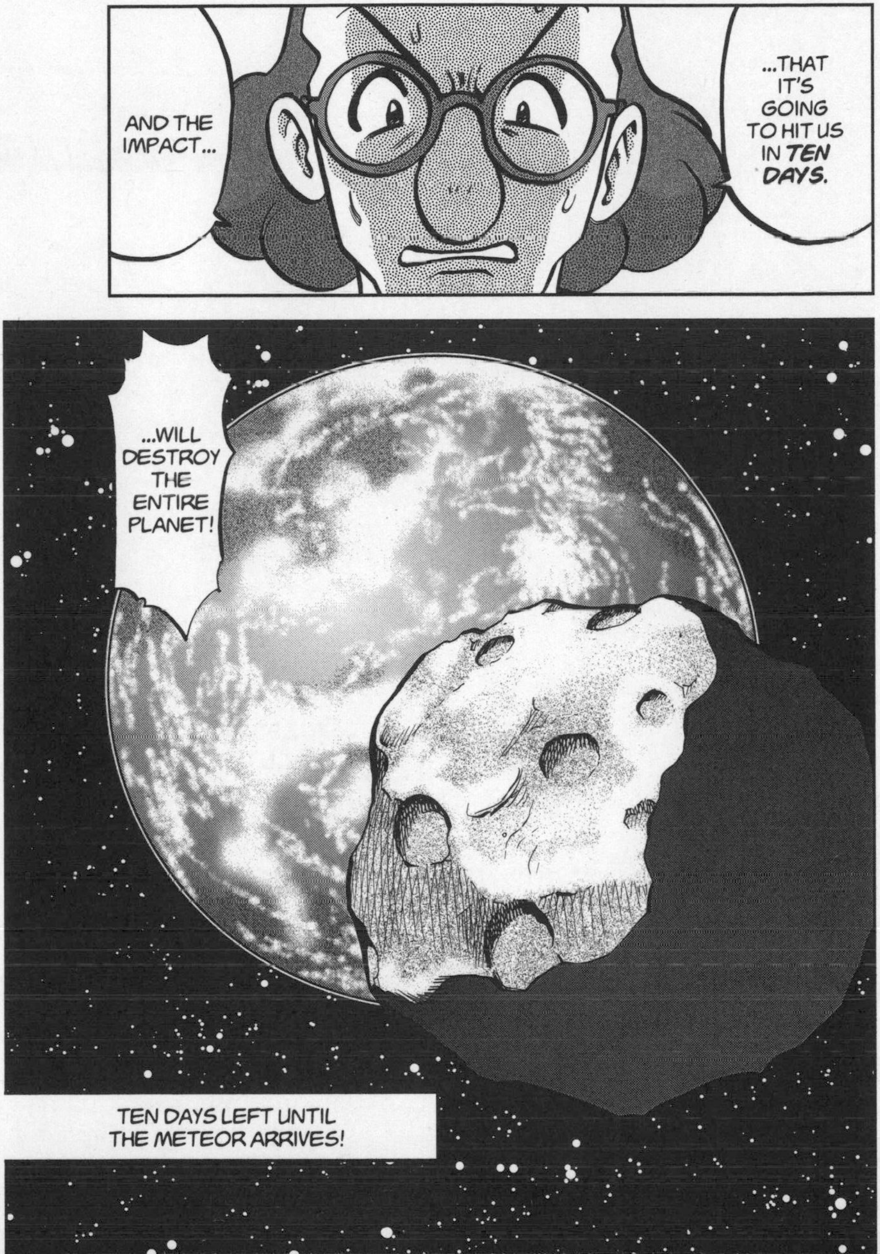
...THAT IT'S GOING TO HIT US IN *TEN DAYS*.
AND THE IMPACT...
...WILL DESTROY THE ENTIRE PLANET!
TEN DAYS LEFT UNTIL THE METEOR ARRIVES!

SKY PILLAR

A soaring tower located in-between Sootopolis City and Pacifidlog Town. It is so high that it looks as if it reaches up to the sky. The tower is filled with traps to drive away intruders. Legend has it that the edifice was built by an ancient tribe.

WEATHER INSTITUTE

An institute that specializes in meteorological research. Some of Hoenn's Legendary Pokémon are deeply connected to the weather, so the data gathered at this institution is also used for research on them.

MOSSDEEP SPACE CENTER

Located in Mossdeep City, this space center is a key institution for rocket development. The rockets launched here are fueled by a special form of energy provided and co-developed by the Devon Corporation. Professor Cozmo, the world's leading specialist in meteors, has been invited to work here.

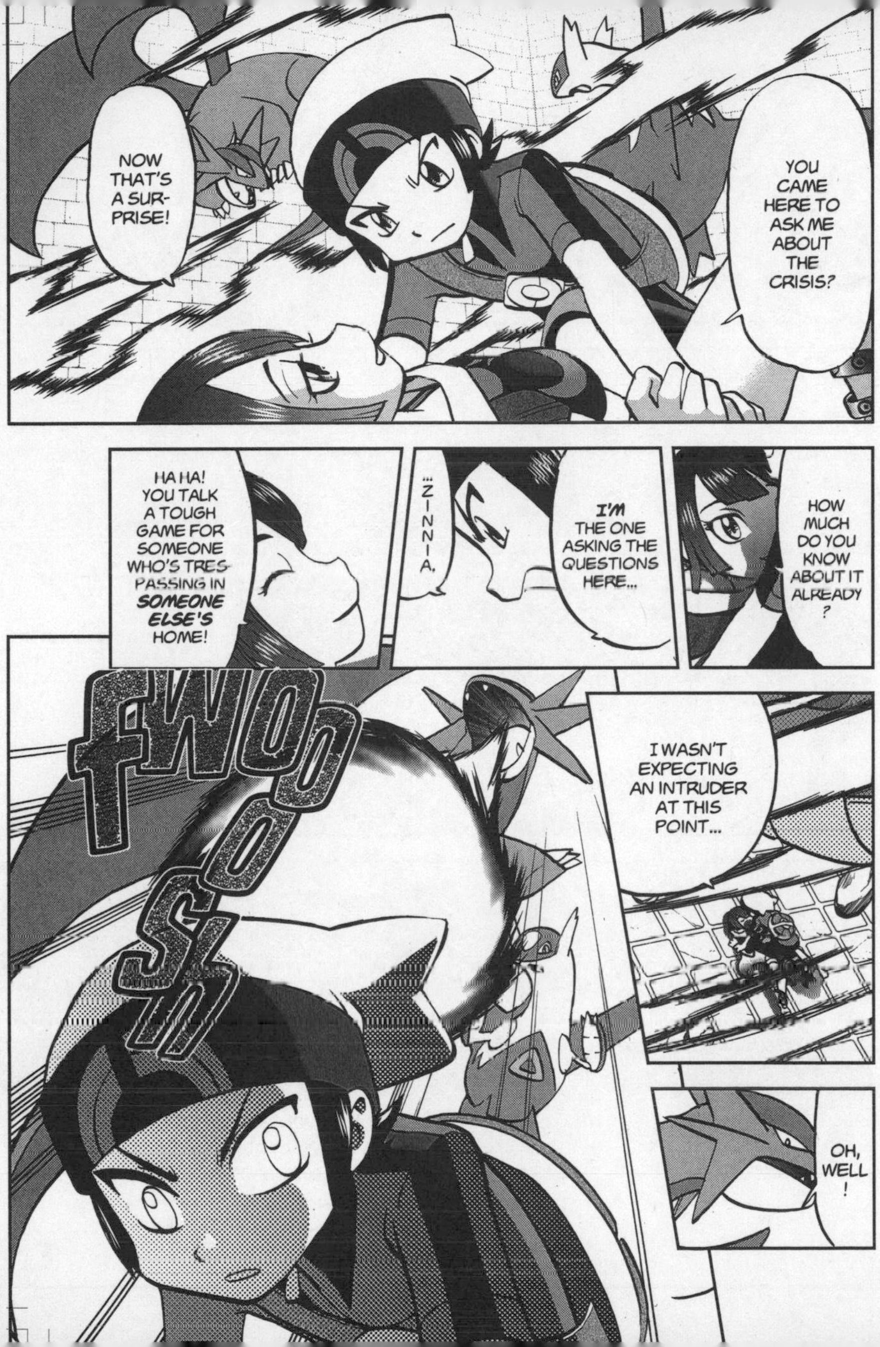
YOU CAME HERE TO ASK ME ABOUT THE CRISIS?
NOW THAT'S A SUR-PRISE!
HOW MUCH DO YOU KNOW ABOUT IT ALREADY?
I'M THE ONE ASKING THE QUESTIONS HERE...
...ZINNIA.
HA HA! YOU TALK A TOUGH GAME FOR SOMEONE WHO'S TRES-PASSING IN SOMEONE ELSE'S HOME!
I WASN'T EXPECTING AN INTRUDER AT THIS POINT...
OH, WELL!
FWOOOSH

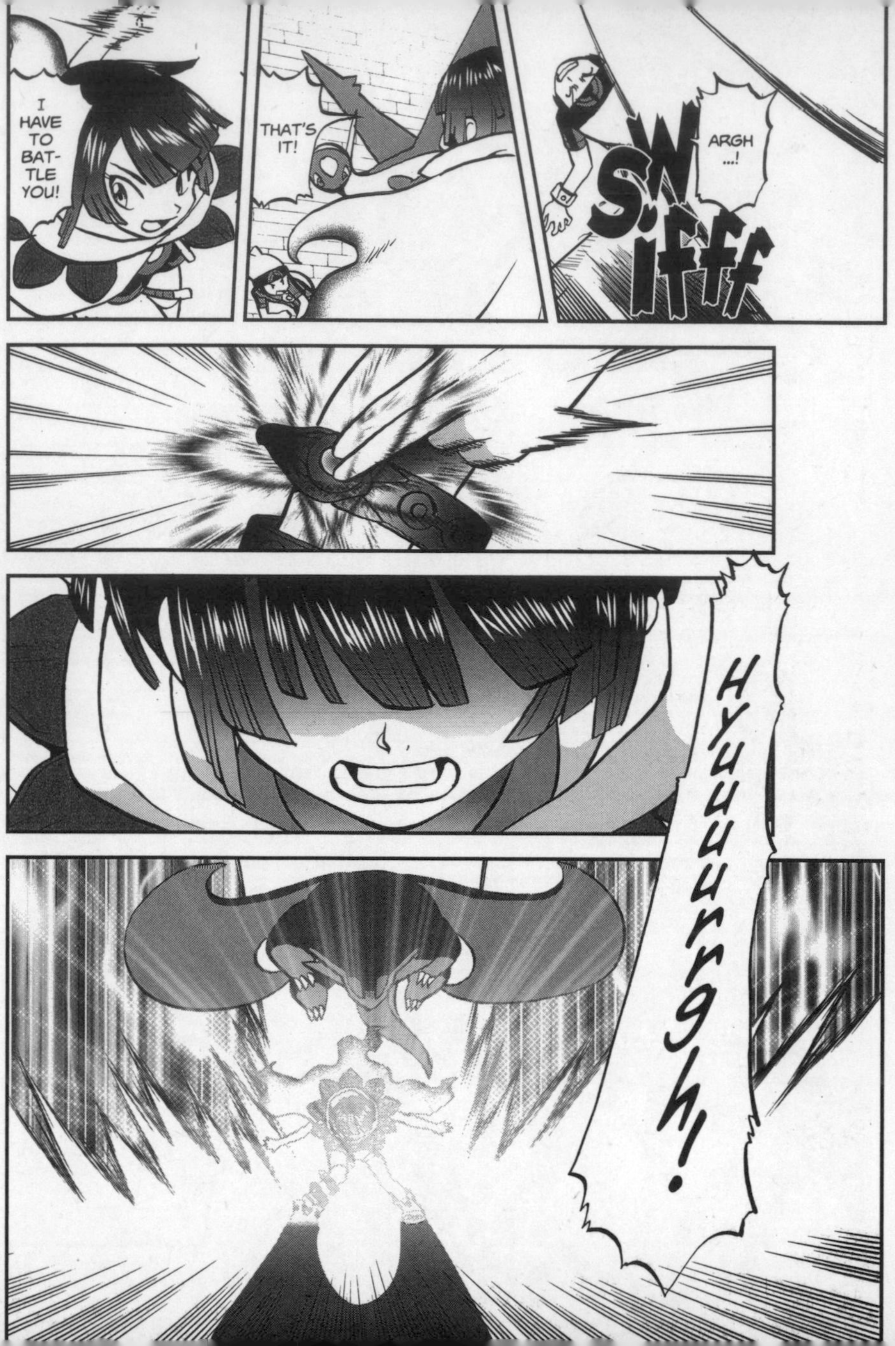
ARGH...!
SWIFFF
THAT'S IT!
I HAVE TO BATTLE YOU!
HYUUUURRGH!

Omega Alpha Adventure 3

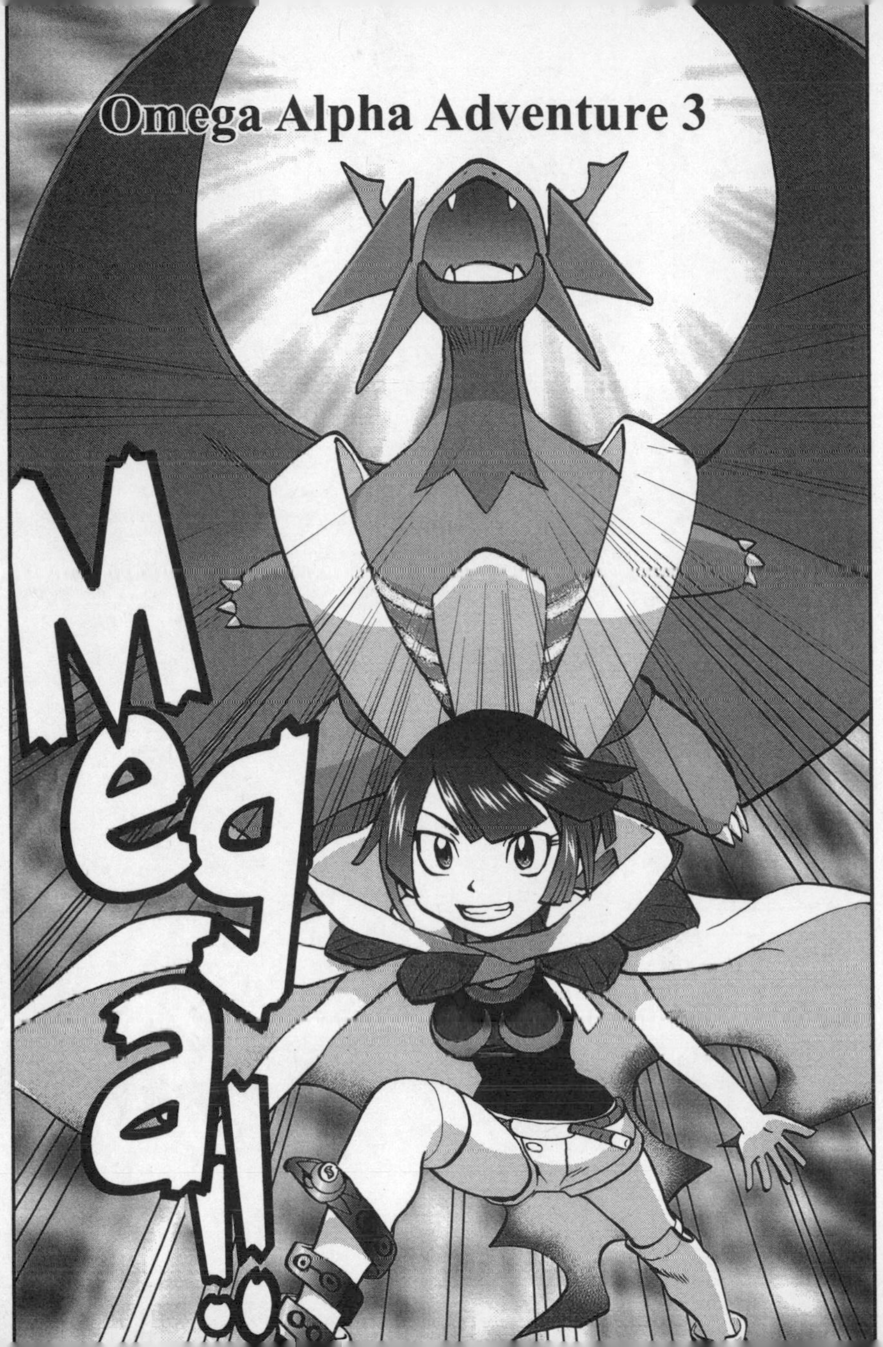
Mega!!

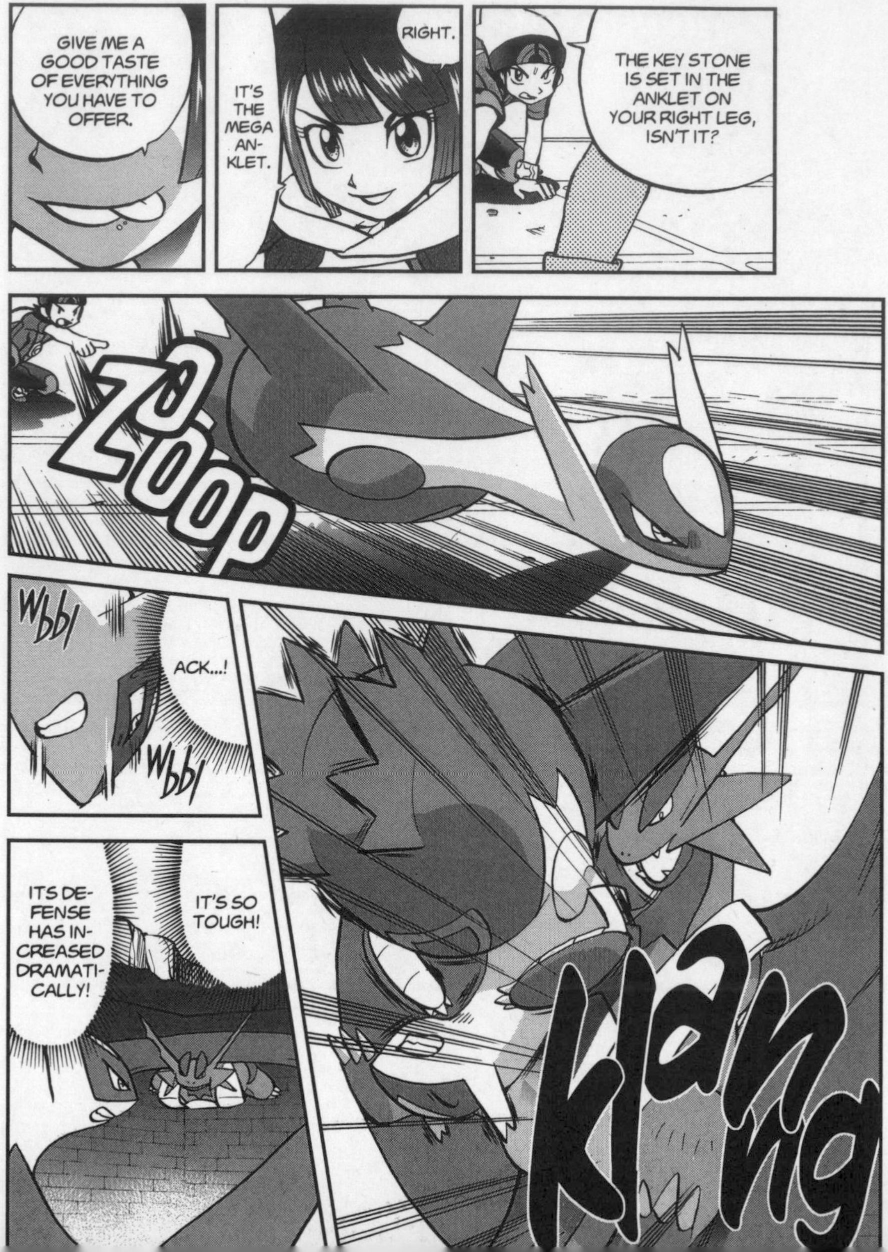
THE KEY STONE IS SET IN THE ANKLET ON YOUR RIGHT LEG, ISN'T IT?
RIGHT.
IT'S THE MEGA AN-KLET.
GIVE ME A GOOD TASTE OF EVERYTHING YOU HAVE TO OFFER.
ZOOOP
KLANNG
WBBL
ACK...!
WBBL
IT'S SO TOUGH!
ITS DE-FENSE HAS IN-CREASED DRAMATI-CALLY!

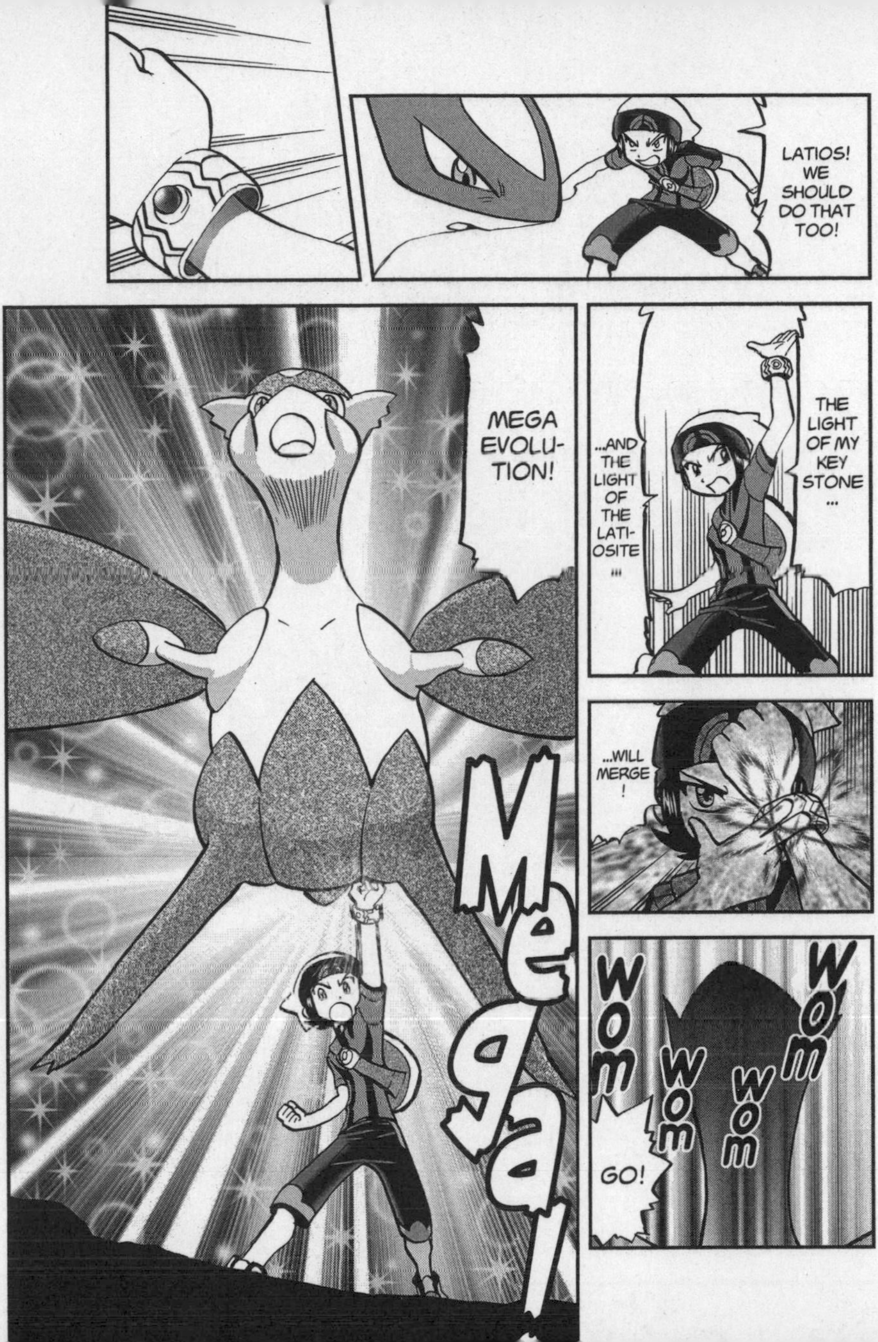
LATIOS! WE SHOULD DO THAT TOO!
THE LIGHT OF MY KEY STONE ...
...AND THE LIGHT OF THE LATIOSITE ...
...WILL MERGE!
wom wom
wom wom
wom wom
wom wom
GO!
MEGA EVOLUTION!
Mega!

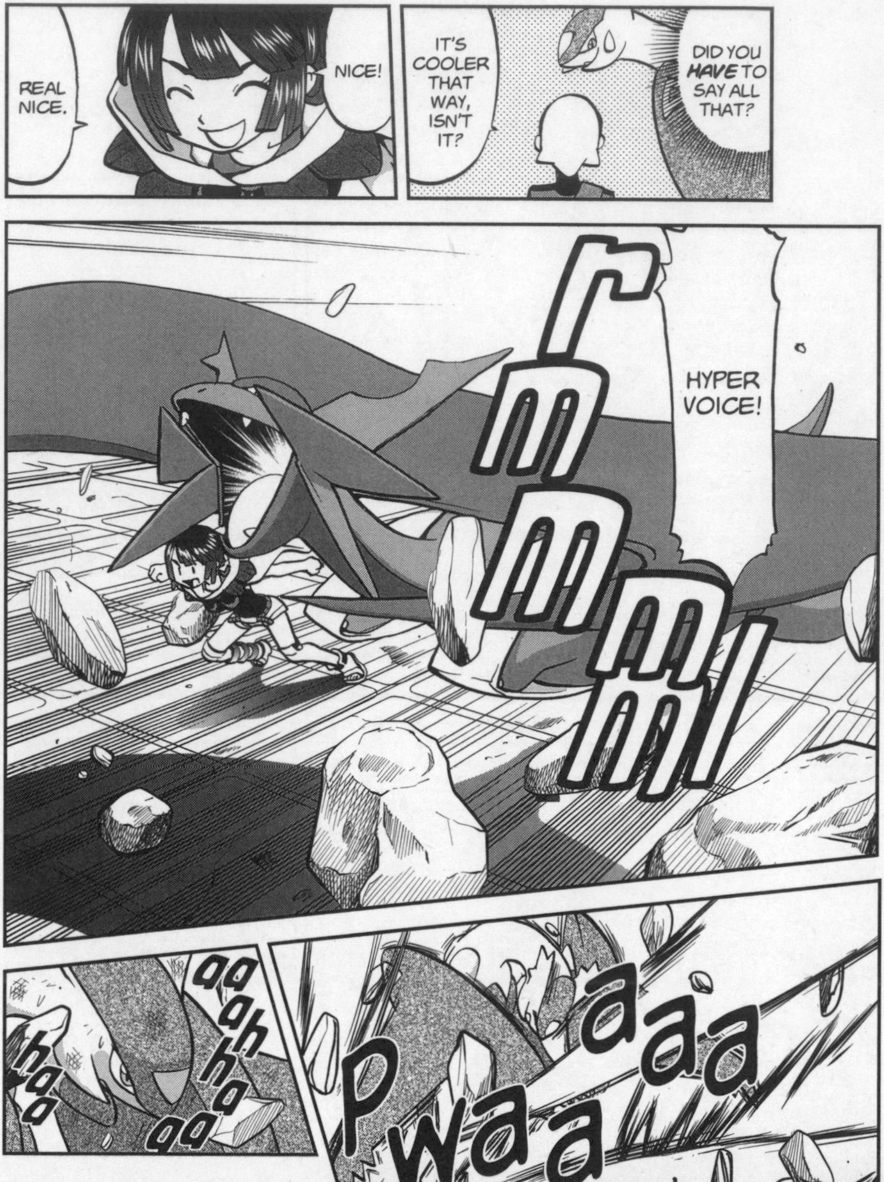
DID YOU HAVE TO SAY ALL THAT?
IT'S COOLER THAT WAY, ISN'T IT?
NICE!
REAL NICE.
HYPER VOICE!

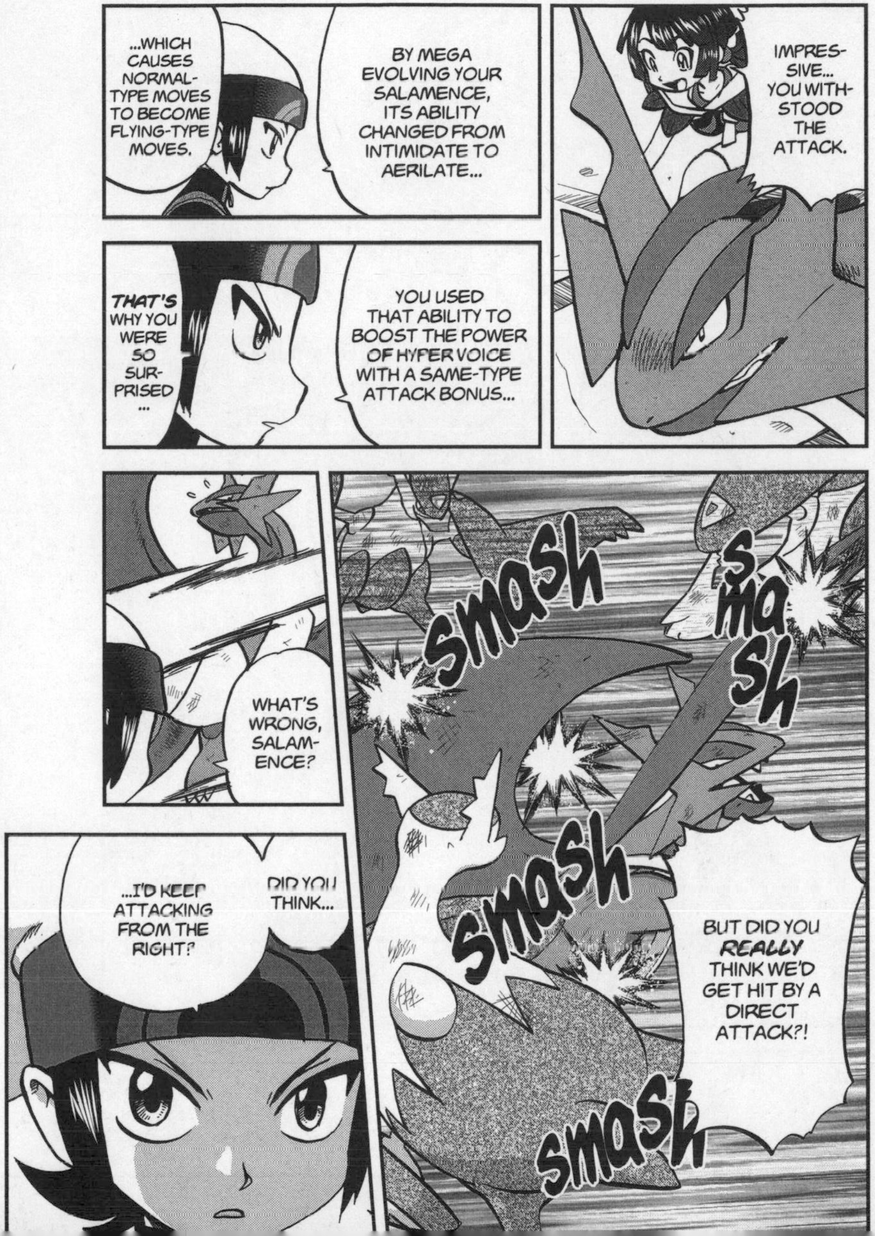
IMPRESSIVE... YOU WITHSTOOD THE ATTACK.
BY MEGA EVOLVING YOUR SALAMENCE, ITS ABILITY CHANGED FROM INTIMIDATE TO AERILATE...
...WHICH CAUSES NORMAL-TYPE MOVES TO BECOME FLYING-TYPE MOVES.
YOU USED THAT ABILITY TO BOOST THE POWER OF HYPER VOICE WITH A SAME-TYPE ATTACK BONUS...
THAT'S WHY YOU WERE SO SURPRISED...
SMASH
SMASH
SMASH
SMASH
SMASH
BUT DID YOU *REALLY* THINK WE'D GET HIT BY A DIRECT ATTACK?!
WHAT'S WRONG, SALAMENCE?
DID YOU THINK...
...I'D KEEP ATTACKING FROM THE RIGHT?

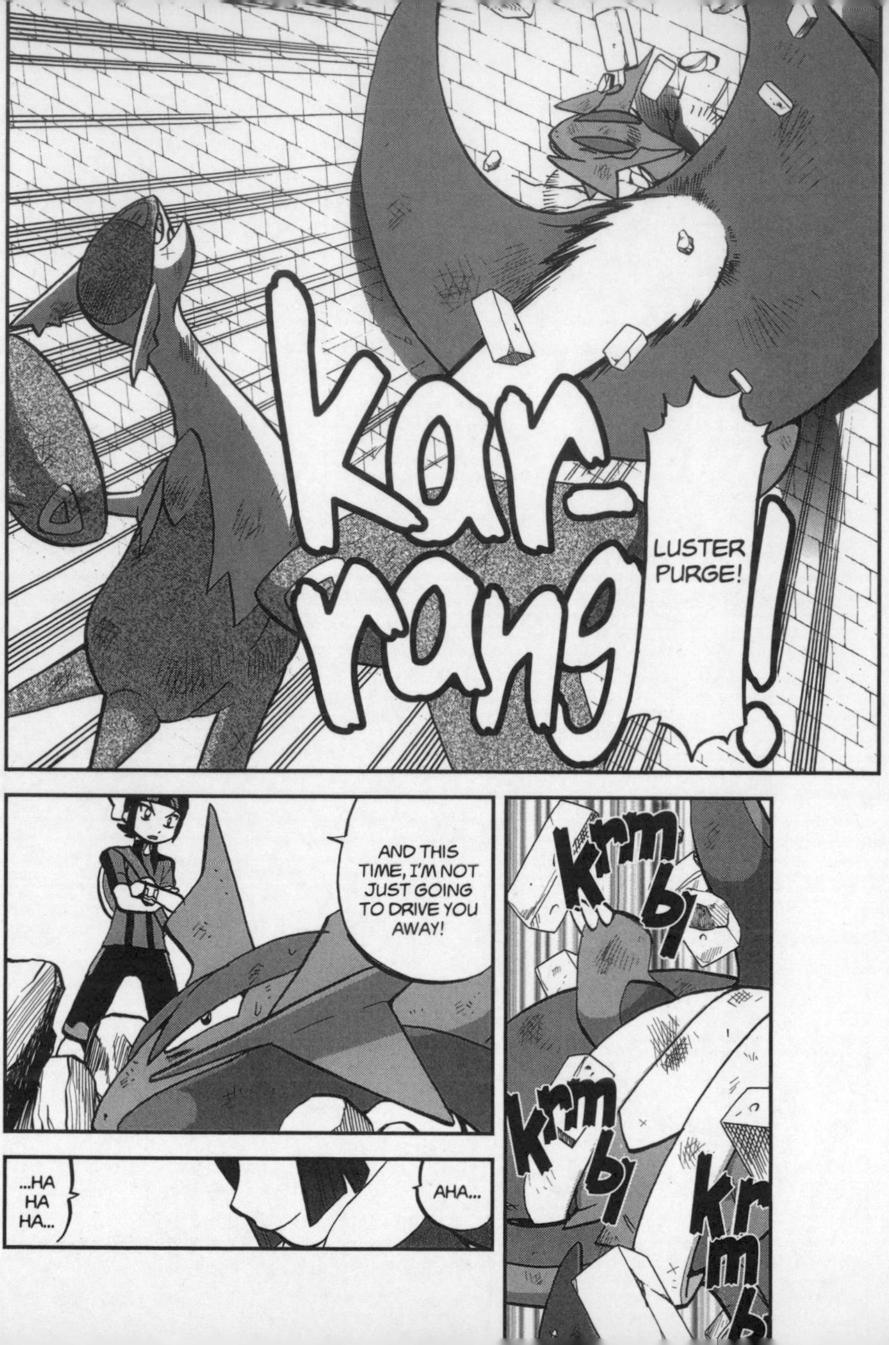
kar-rang!
LUSTER PURGE!
Krmbl
Krmbl
Krmb
AND THIS TIME, I'M NOT JUST GOING TO DRIVE YOU AWAY!
AHA...
...HA HA HA...

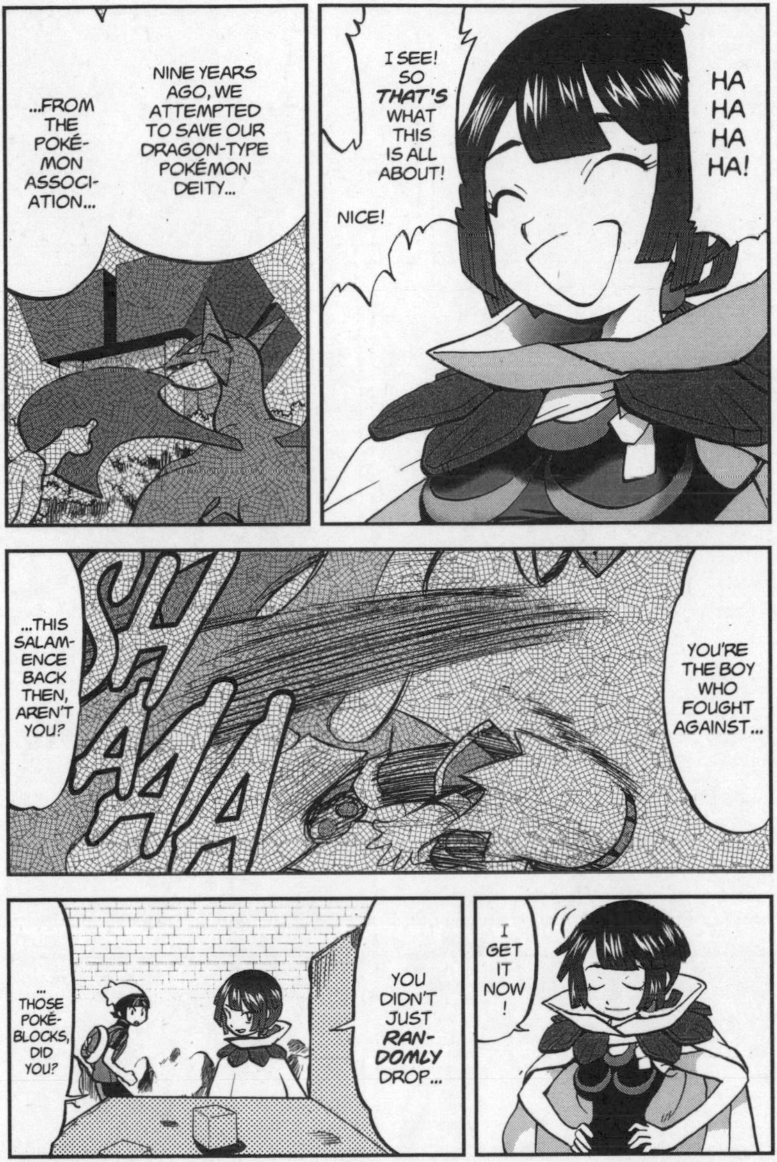
HA HA HA HA!
I SEE! SO THAT'S WHAT THIS IS ALL ABOUT!
NICE!
NINE YEARS AGO, WE ATTEMPTED TO SAVE OUR DRAGON-TYPE POKÉMON DEITY...
...FROM THE POKÉMON ASSOCIATION...
YOU'RE THE BOY WHO FOUGHT AGAINST...
SHAAA
...THIS SALAMENCE BACK THEN, AREN'T YOU?
I GET IT NOW!
YOU DIDN'T JUST RANDOMLY DROP...
...THOSE POKÉBLOCKS, DID YOU?

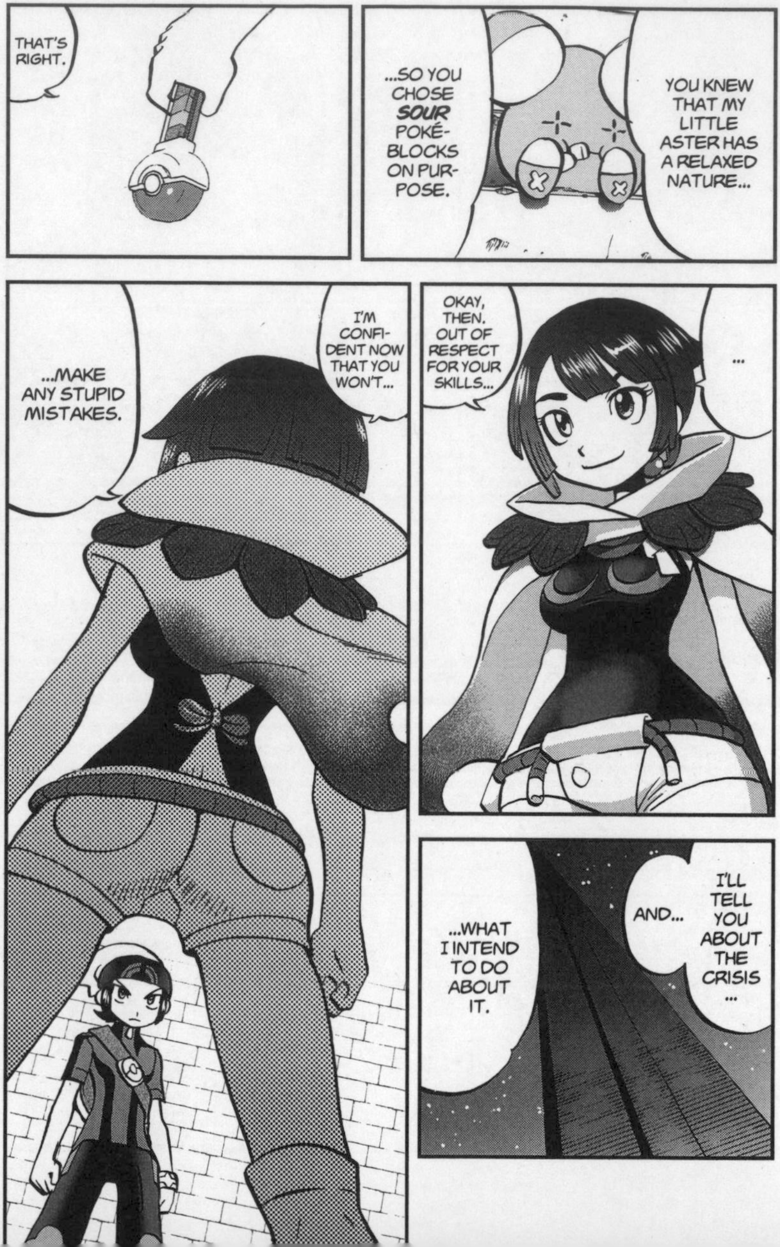
YOU KNEW THAT MY LITTLE ASTER HAS A RELAXED NATURE...
...SO YOU CHOSE **SOUR** POKÉBLOCKS ON PURPOSE.
THAT'S RIGHT.
...
OKAY, THEN. OUT OF RESPECT FOR YOUR SKILLS...
I'LL TELL YOU ABOUT THE CRISIS...
AND...
...WHAT I INTEND TO DO ABOUT IT.
I'M CONFIDENT NOW THAT YOU WON'T...
...MAKE ANY STUPID MISTAKES.

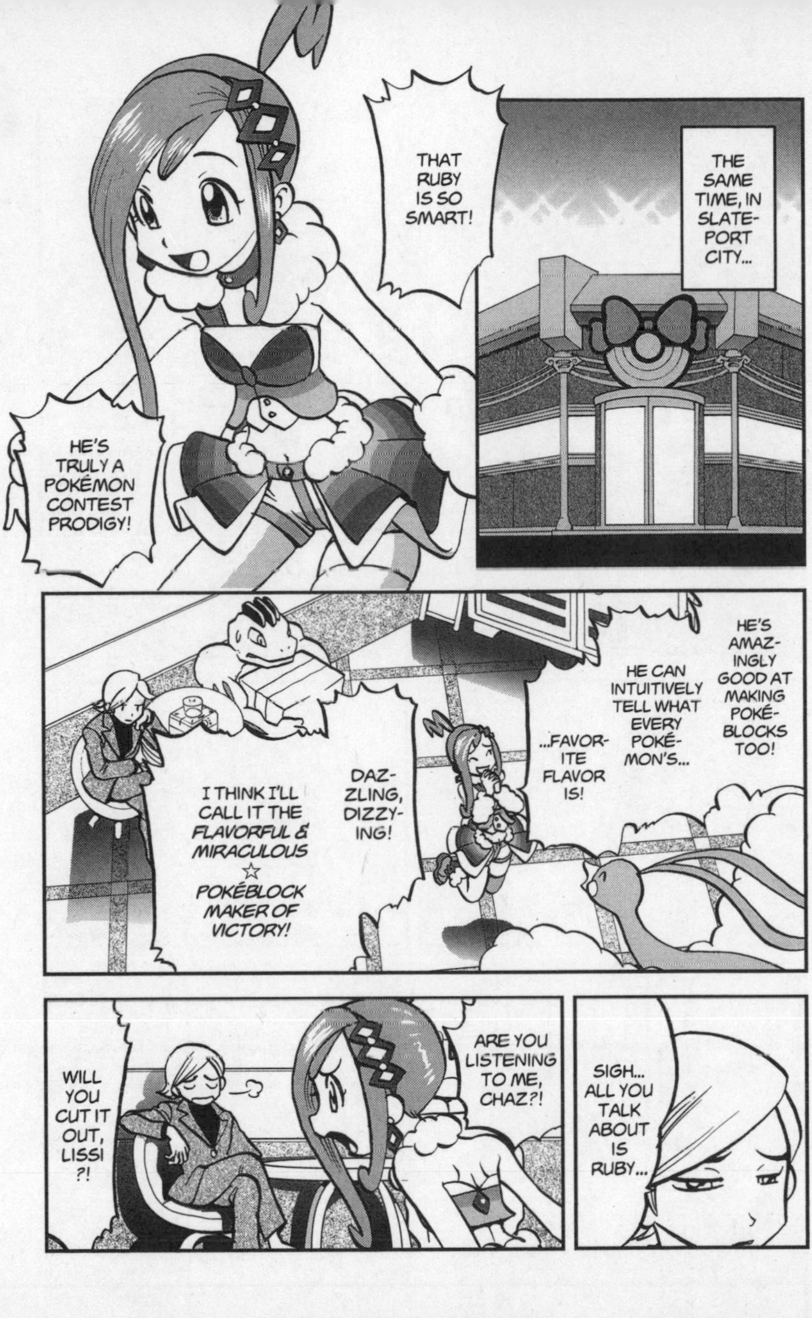
THE SAME TIME, IN SLATEPORT CITY...
THAT RUBY IS SO SMART!
HE'S TRULY A POKÉMON CONTEST PRODIGY!
HE'S AMAZINGLY GOOD AT MAKING POKÉBLOCKS TOO!
HE CAN INTUITIVELY TELL WHAT EVERY POKÉMON'S...
...FAVORITE FLAVOR IS!
DAZZLING, DIZZYING!
I THINK I'LL CALL IT THE *FLAVORFUL & MIRACULOUS ☆ POKÉBLOCK MAKER OF VICTORY!*
SIGH... ALL YOU TALK ABOUT IS RUBY...
ARE YOU LISTENING TO ME, CHAZ?!
WILL YOU CUT IT OUT, LISSI?!

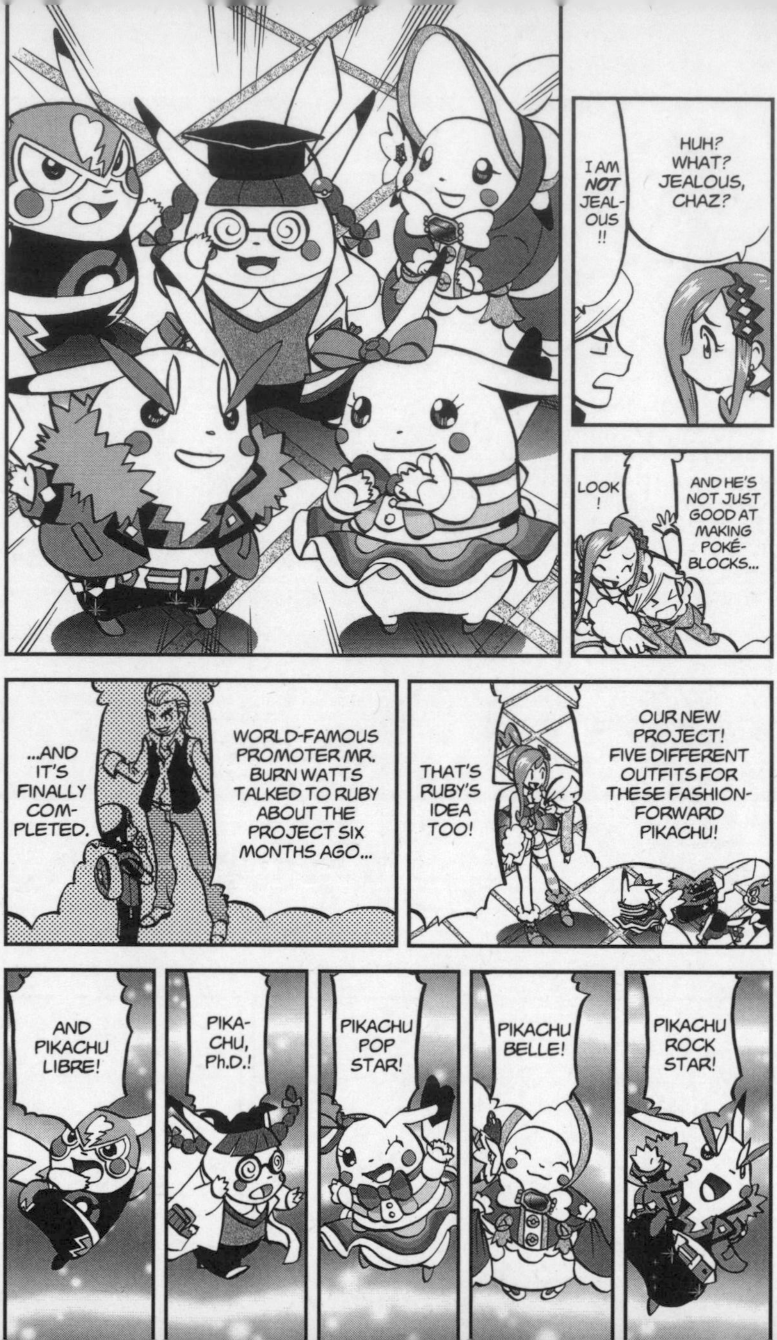
HUH? WHAT? JEALOUS, CHAZ?
I AM NOT JEALOUS!!
AND HE'S NOT JUST GOOD AT MAKING POKÉBLOCKS...
LOOK!
OUR NEW PROJECT! FIVE DIFFERENT OUTFITS FOR THESE FASHION-FORWARD PIKACHU!
THAT'S RUBY'S IDEA TOO!
WORLD-FAMOUS PROMOTER MR. BURN WATTS TALKED TO RUBY ABOUT THE PROJECT SIX MONTHS AGO...
...AND IT'S FINALLY COMPLETED.
PIKACHU ROCK STAR!
PIKACHU BELLE!
PIKACHU POP STAR!
PIKACHU, Ph.D.!
AND PIKACHU LIBRE!

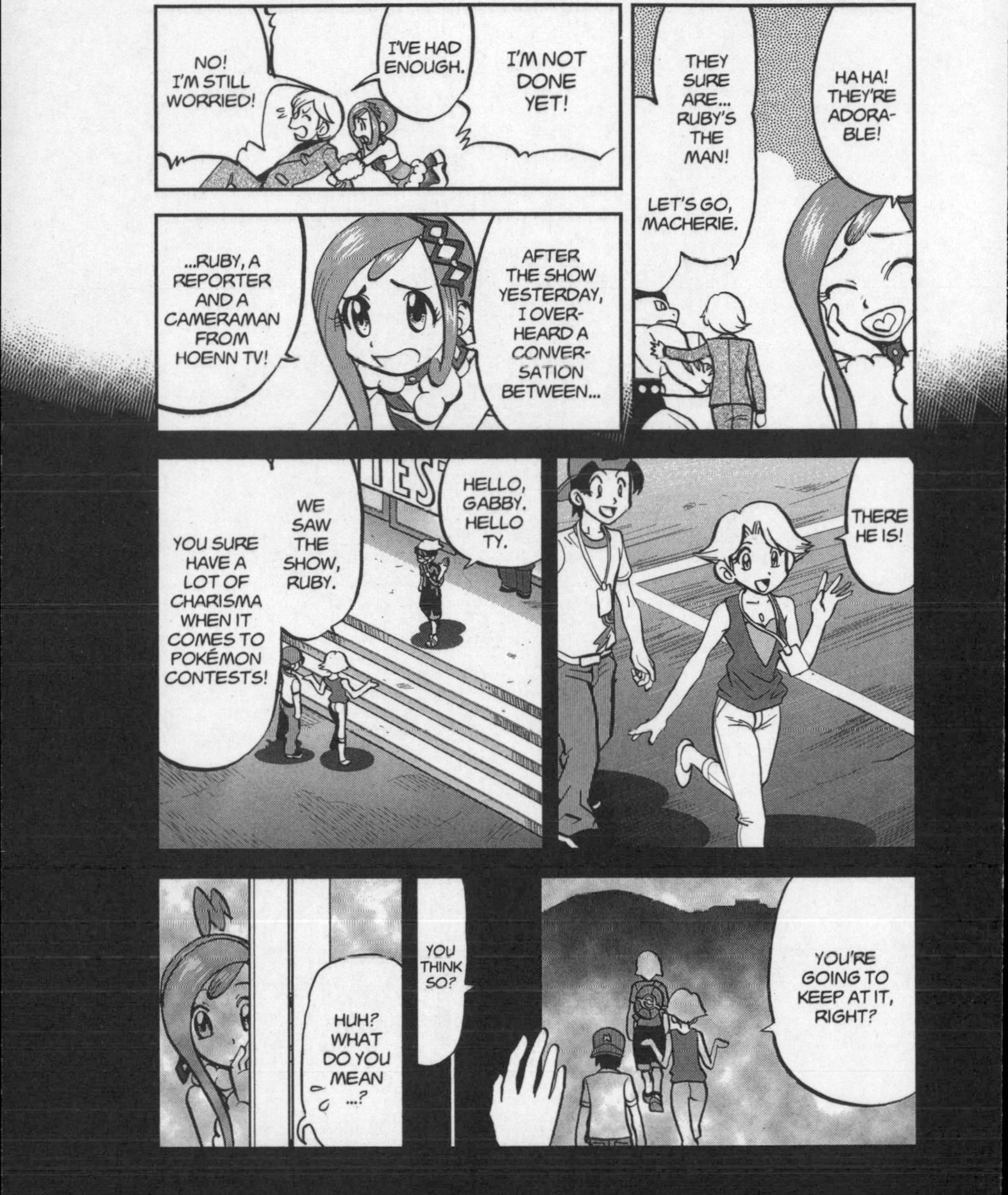
HA HA! THEY'RE ADORABLE!
THEY SURE ARE... RUBY'S THE MAN!
LET'S GO, MACHERIE.
I'M NOT DONE YET!
I'VE HAD ENOUGH.
NO! I'M STILL WORRIED!
AFTER THE SHOW YESTERDAY, I OVERHEARD A CONVERSATION BETWEEN...
...RUBY, A REPORTER AND A CAMERAMAN FROM HOENN TV!
THERE HE IS!
HELLO, GABBY. HELLO TY.
WE SAW THE SHOW, RUBY.
YOU SURE HAVE A LOT OF CHARISMA WHEN IT COMES TO POKÉMON CONTESTS!
YOU'RE GOING TO KEEP AT IT, RIGHT?
YOU THINK SO?
HUH? WHAT DO YOU MEAN ...?

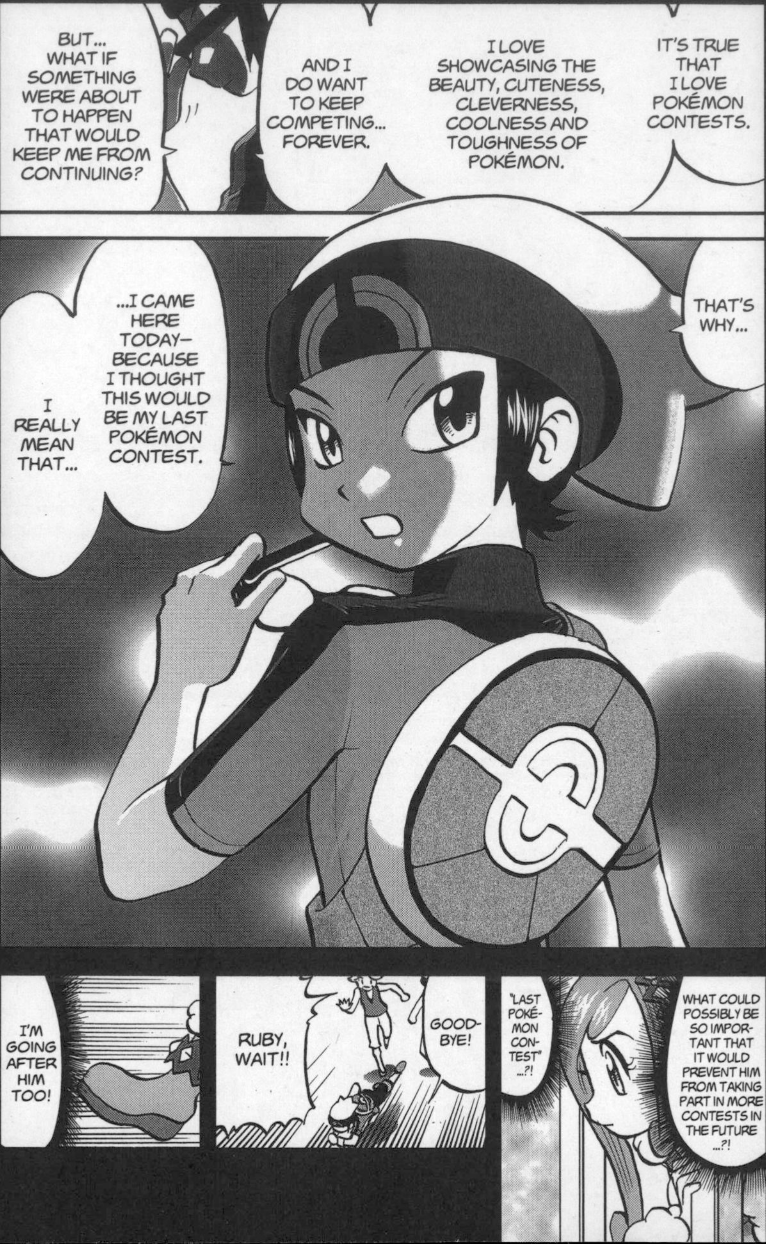
IT'S TRUE THAT I LOVE POKÉMON CONTESTS.
I LOVE SHOWCASING THE BEAUTY, CUTENESS, CLEVERNESS, COOLNESS AND TOUGHNESS OF POKÉMON.
AND I DO WANT TO KEEP COMPETING... FOREVER.
BUT... WHAT IF SOMETHING WERE ABOUT TO HAPPEN THAT WOULD KEEP ME FROM CONTINUING?
THAT'S WHY...
...I CAME HERE TODAY— BECAUSE I THOUGHT THIS WOULD BE MY LAST POKÉMON CONTEST.
I REALLY MEAN THAT...
WHAT COULD POSSIBLY BE SO IMPORTANT THAT IT WOULD PREVENT HIM FROM TAKING PART IN MORE CONTESTS IN THE FUTURE ...?!
"LAST POKÉMON CONTEST" ...?!
GOOD-BYE!
RUBY, WAIT!!
I'M GOING AFTER HIM TOO!

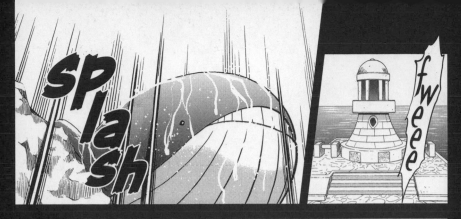

fweee
splash
f-dmp
LORRY, TO THE SOUTHERN ISLAND!
I SEE. IT'S THAT SIMPLE, IS IT?
HOW DO YOU MEAN?
HE MUST HAVE FOUND SOMETHING MORE ENJOYABLE THAN POKÉMON CONTESTS IN ANOTHER REGION AND WANTS TO SPEND TIME ON THAT FROM NOW ON...
WHAT?! THAT'S IMPOSSIBLE!

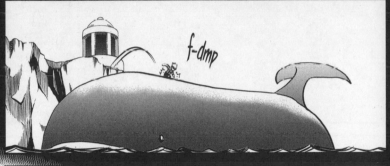

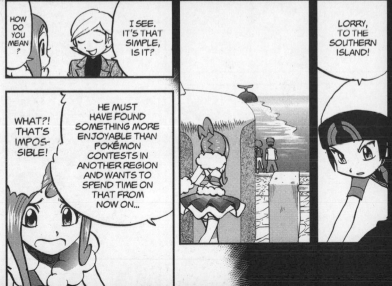

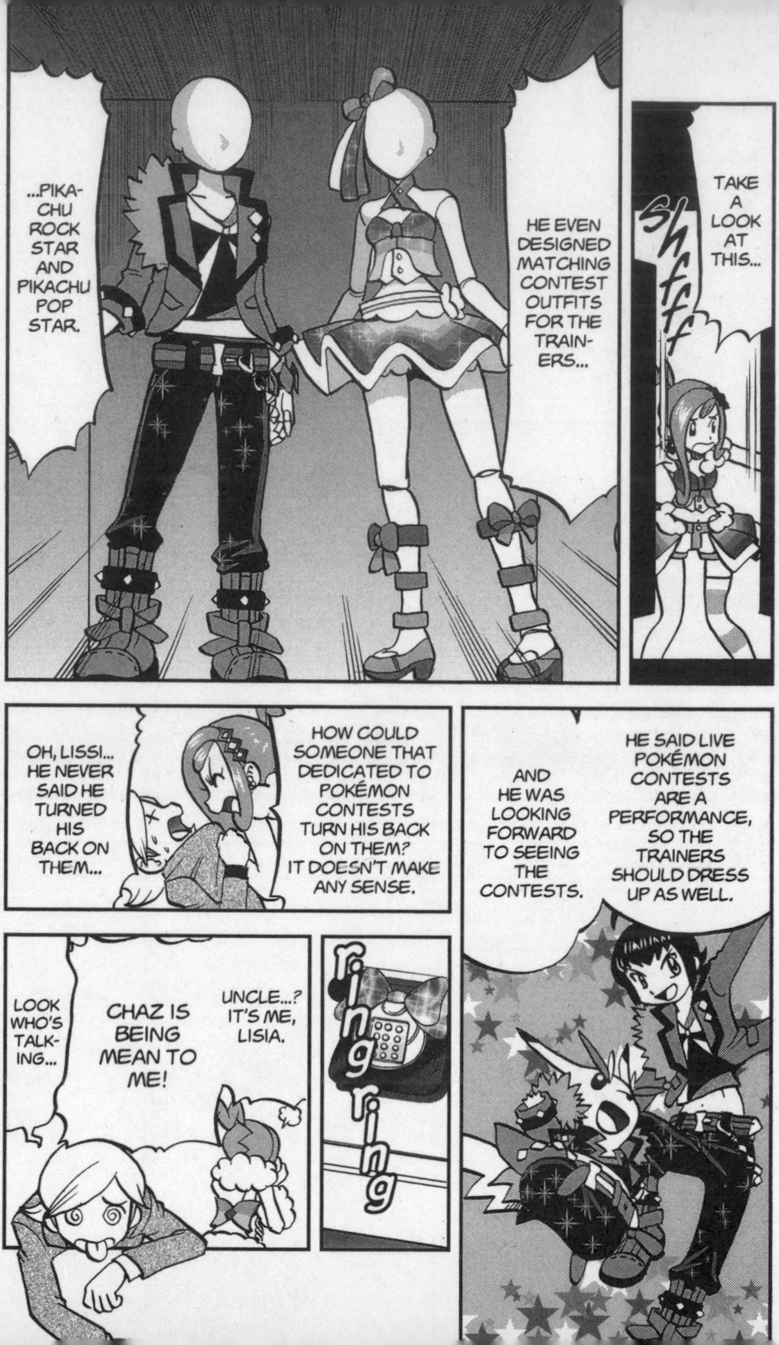
TAKE A LOOK AT THIS...
SHFFF
HE EVEN DESIGNED MATCHING CONTEST OUTFITS FOR THE TRAIN-ERS...
...PIKA-CHU ROCK STAR AND PIKACHU POP STAR.
HE SAID LIVE POKÉMON CONTESTS ARE A PERFORMANCE, SO THE TRAINERS SHOULD DRESS UP AS WELL.
AND HE WAS LOOKING FORWARD TO SEEING THE CONTESTS.
HOW COULD SOMEONE THAT DEDICATED TO POKÉMON CONTESTS TURN HIS BACK ON THEM? IT DOESN'T MAKE ANY SENSE.
OH, LISSI... HE NEVER SAID HE TURNED HIS BACK ON THEM...
RING RING
UNCLE...? IT'S ME, LISIA.
CHAZ IS BEING MEAN TO ME!
LOOK WHO'S TALK-ING...

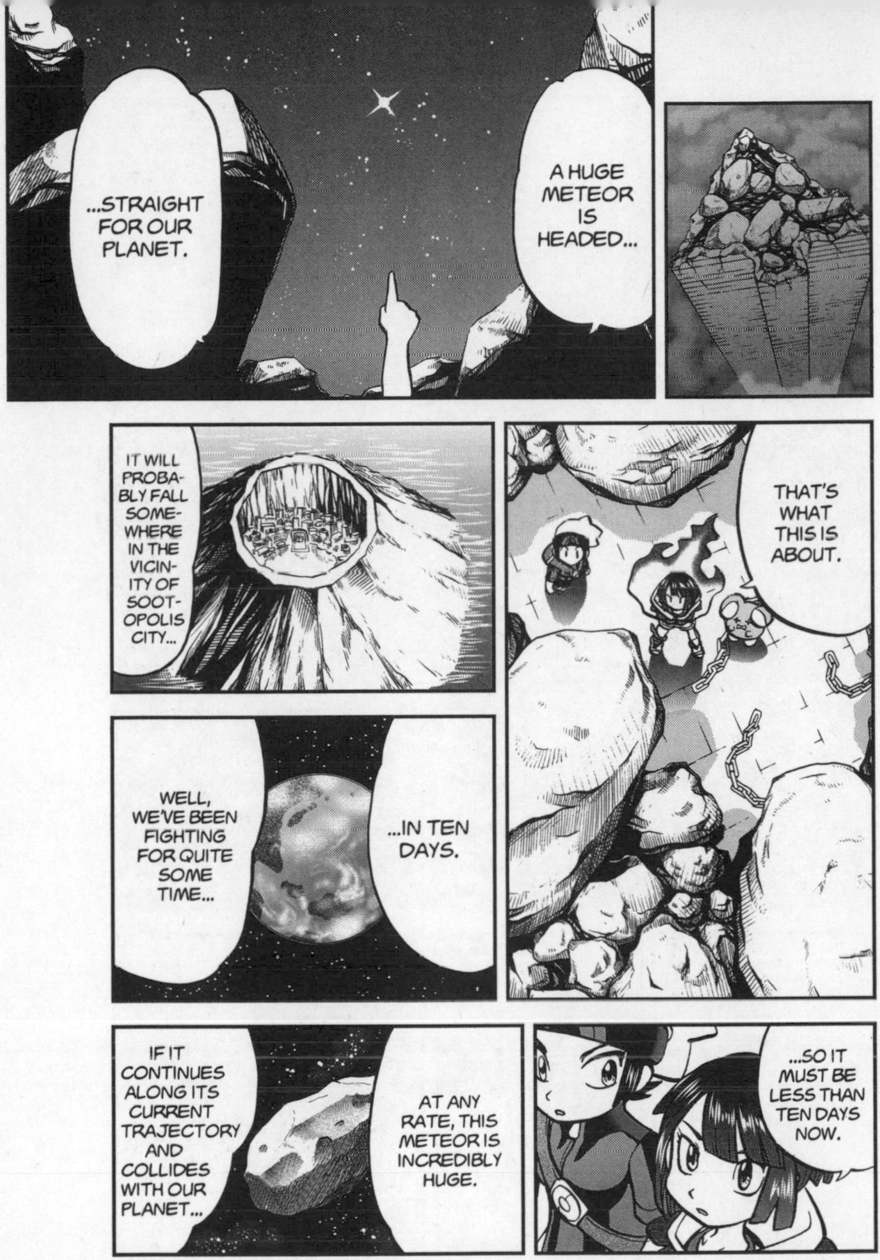
A HUGE METEOR IS HEADED...
...STRAIGHT FOR OUR PLANET.
THAT'S WHAT THIS IS ABOUT.
IT WILL PROBA-BLY FALL SOME-WHERE IN THE VICIN-ITY OF SOOT-OPOLIS CITY...
...IN TEN DAYS.
WELL, WE'VE BEEN FIGHTING FOR QUITE SOME TIME...
...SO IT MUST BE LESS THAN TEN DAYS NOW.
AT ANY RATE, THIS METEOR IS INCREDIBLY HUGE.
IF IT CONTINUES ALONG ITS CURRENT TRAJECTORY AND COLLIDES WITH OUR PLANET...

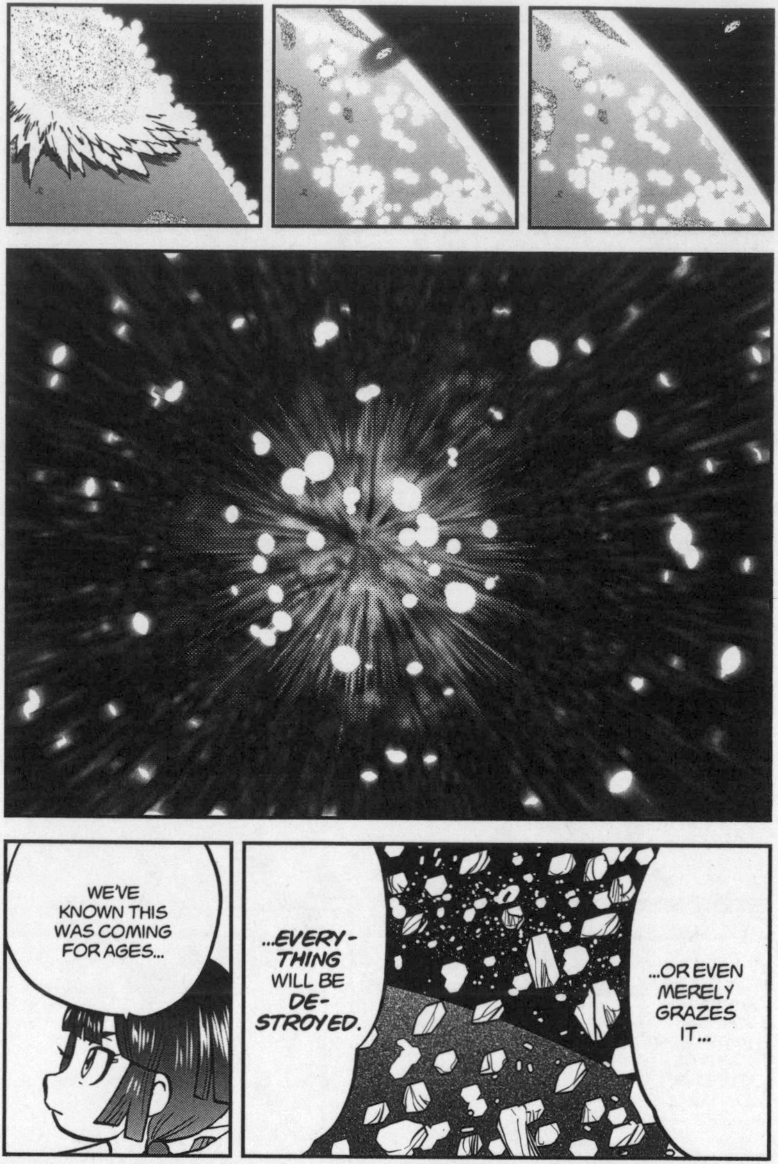
...OR EVEN MERELY GRAZES IT...
...EVERY-THING WILL BE DE-STROYED.
WE'VE KNOWN THIS WAS COMING FOR AGES...

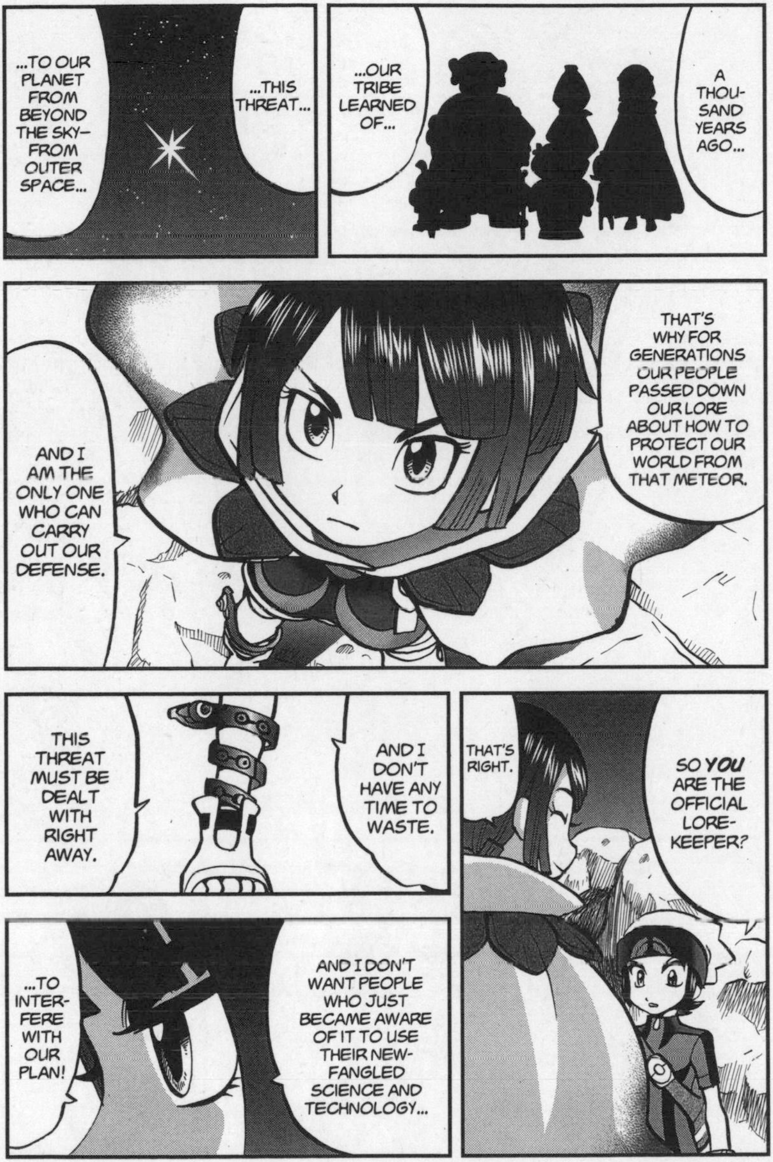
A THOUSAND YEARS AGO...
...OUR TRIBE LEARNED OF...
...THIS THREAT...
...TO OUR PLANET FROM BEYOND THE SKY—FROM OUTER SPACE...
THAT'S WHY FOR GENERATIONS OUR PEOPLE PASSED DOWN OUR LORE ABOUT HOW TO PROTECT OUR WORLD FROM THAT METEOR.
AND I AM THE ONLY ONE WHO CAN CARRY OUT OUR DEFENSE.
SO *YOU* ARE THE OFFICIAL LORE-KEEPER?
THAT'S RIGHT.
AND I DON'T HAVE ANY TIME TO WASTE.
THIS THREAT MUST BE DEALT WITH RIGHT AWAY.
AND I DON'T WANT PEOPLE WHO JUST BECAME AWARE OF IT TO USE THEIR NEW-FANGLED SCIENCE AND TECHNOLOGY...
...TO INTERFERE WITH OUR PLAN!

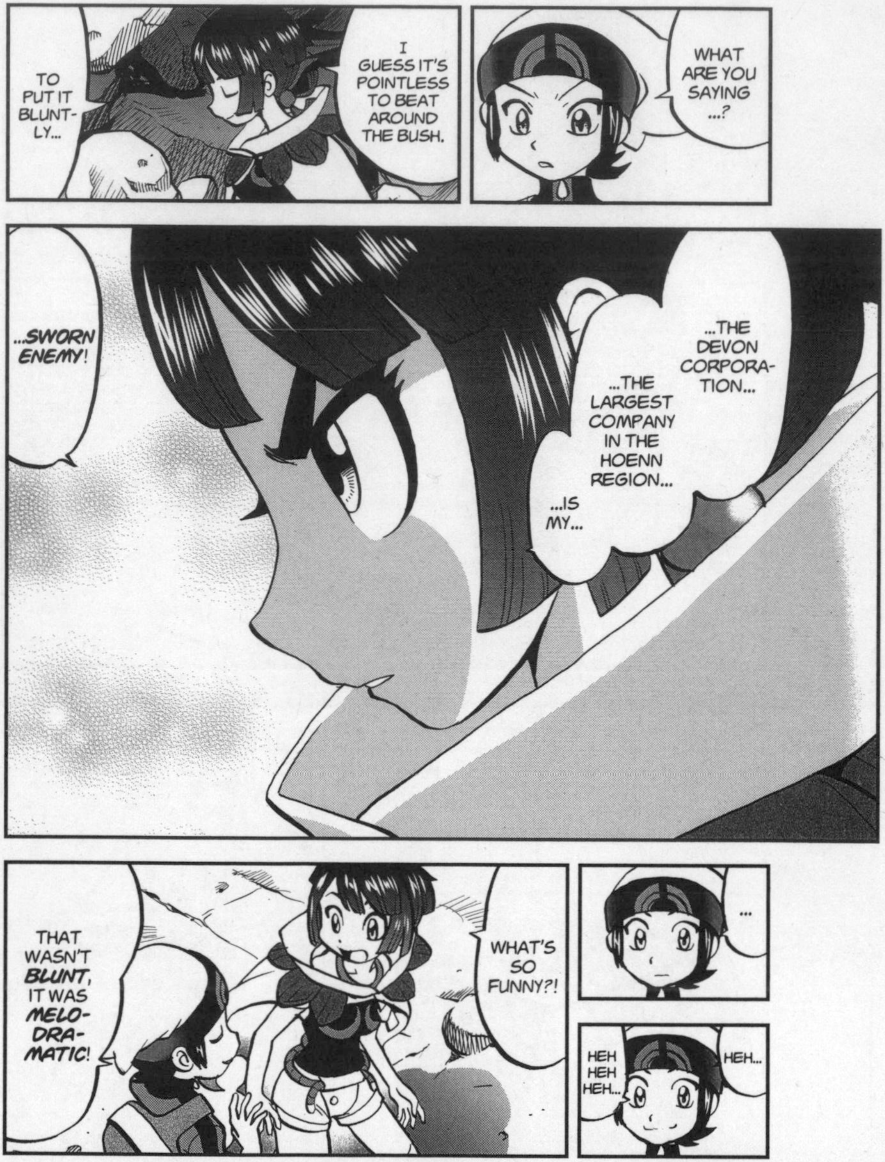
WHAT ARE YOU SAYING ...?
I GUESS IT'S POINTLESS TO BEAT AROUND THE BUSH.
TO PUT IT BLUNT-LY...
...THE DEVON CORPORA-TION...
...THE LARGEST COMPANY IN THE HOENN REGION...
...IS MY...
...SWORN ENEMY!
...
HEH...
HEH HEH HEH...
WHAT'S SO FUNNY?!
THAT WASN'T BLUNT, IT WAS MELO-DRA-MATIC!

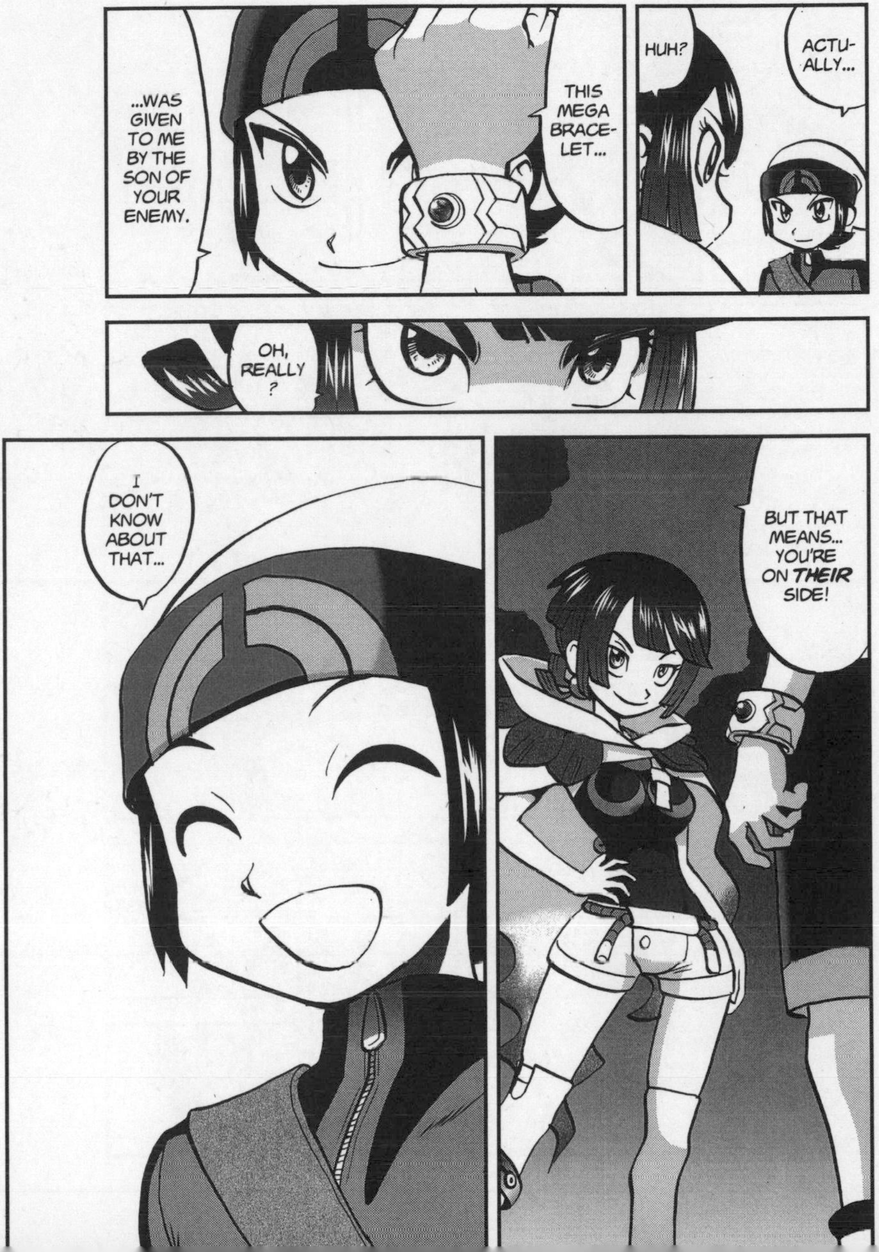
ACTU-ALLY...
HUH?
THIS MEGA BRACE-LET...
...WAS GIVEN TO ME BY THE SON OF YOUR ENEMY.
OH, REALLY?
BUT THAT MEANS... YOU'RE ON *THEIR* SIDE!
I DON'T KNOW ABOUT THAT...

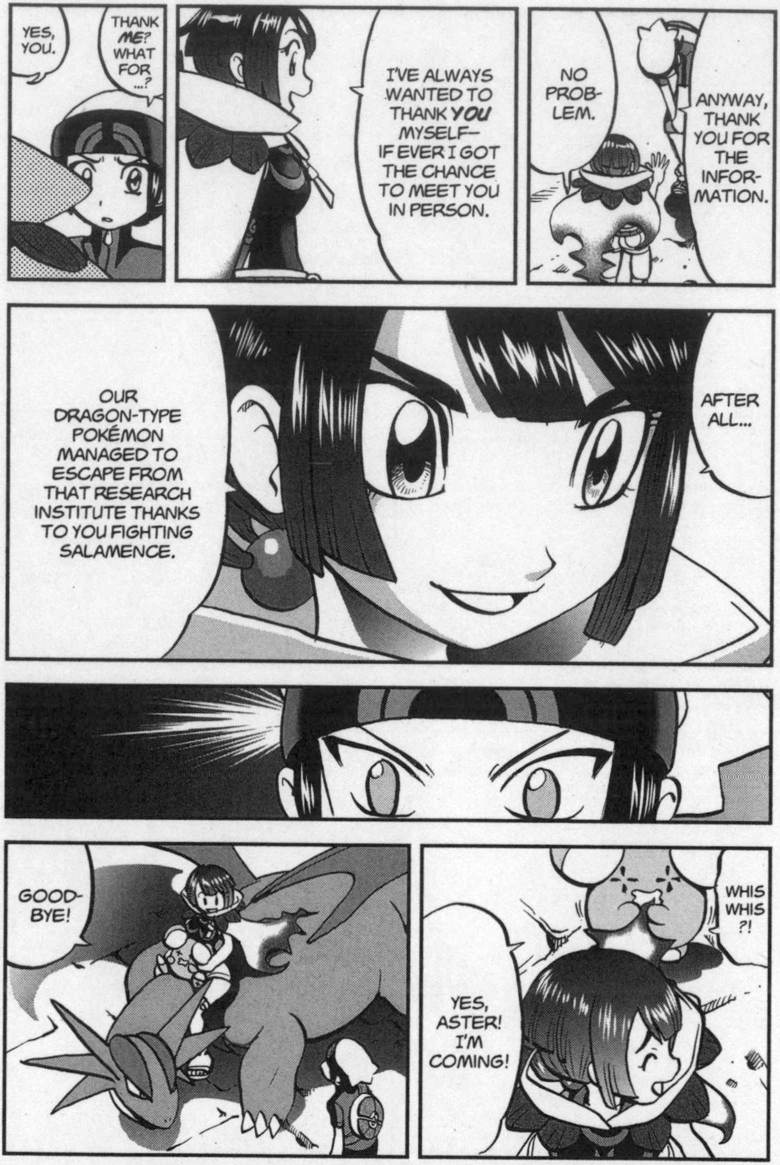

ANYWAY, THANK YOU FOR THE INFORMATION.
NO PROB-LEM.
I'VE ALWAYS WANTED TO THANK **YOU** MYSELF— IF EVER I GOT THE CHANCE TO MEET YOU IN PERSON.
THANK **ME**? WHAT FOR ...?
YES, YOU.
AFTER ALL...
OUR DRAGON-TYPE POKÉMON MANAGED TO ESCAPE FROM THAT RESEARCH INSTITUTE THANKS TO YOU FIGHTING SALAMENCE.
WHIS WHIS ?!
YES, ASTER! I'M COMING!
GOOD-BYE!

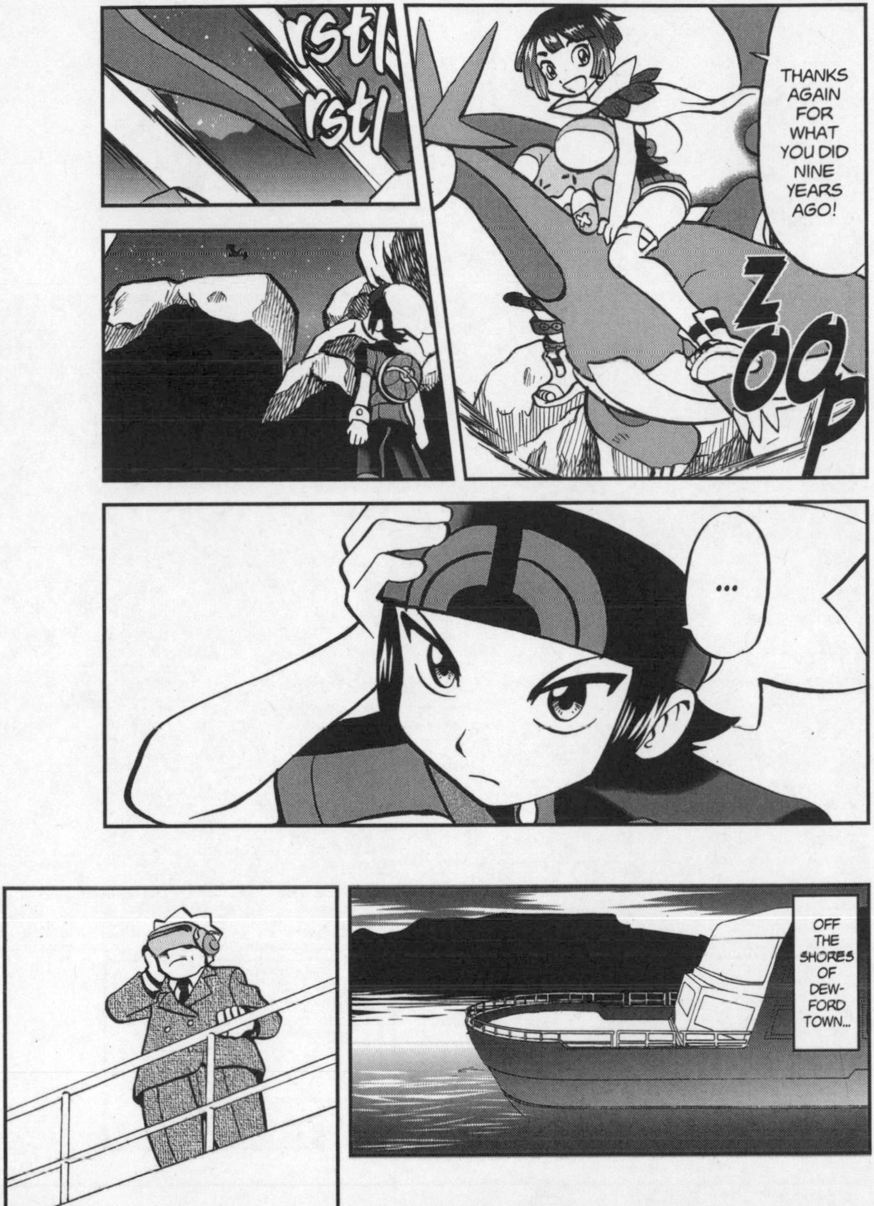
THANKS AGAIN FOR WHAT YOU DID NINE YEARS AGO!
ZOOOP
rstl rstl
...
OFF THE SHORES OF DEW-FORD TOWN...

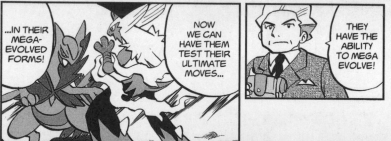

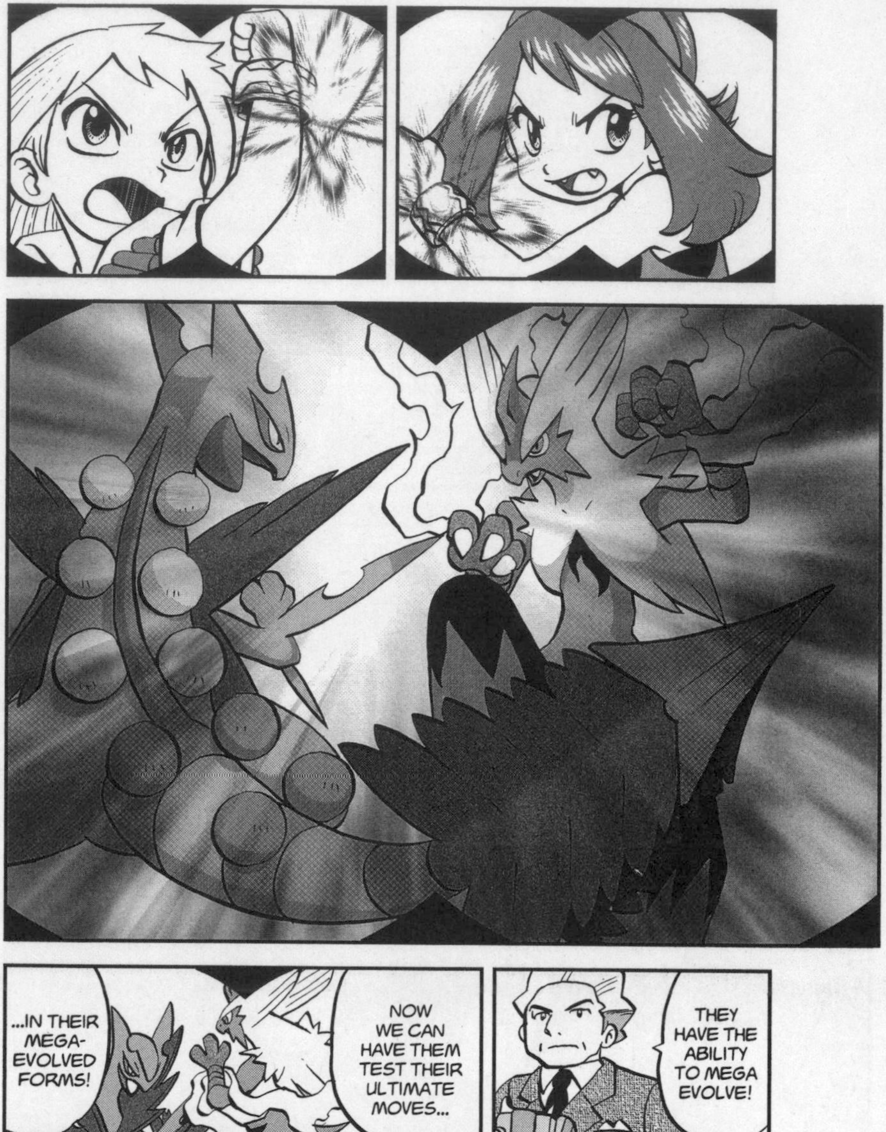
THEY HAVE THE ABILITY TO MEGA EVOLVE!
NOW WE CAN HAVE THEM TEST THEIR ULTIMATE MOVES...
...IN THEIR MEGA-EVOLVED FORMS!

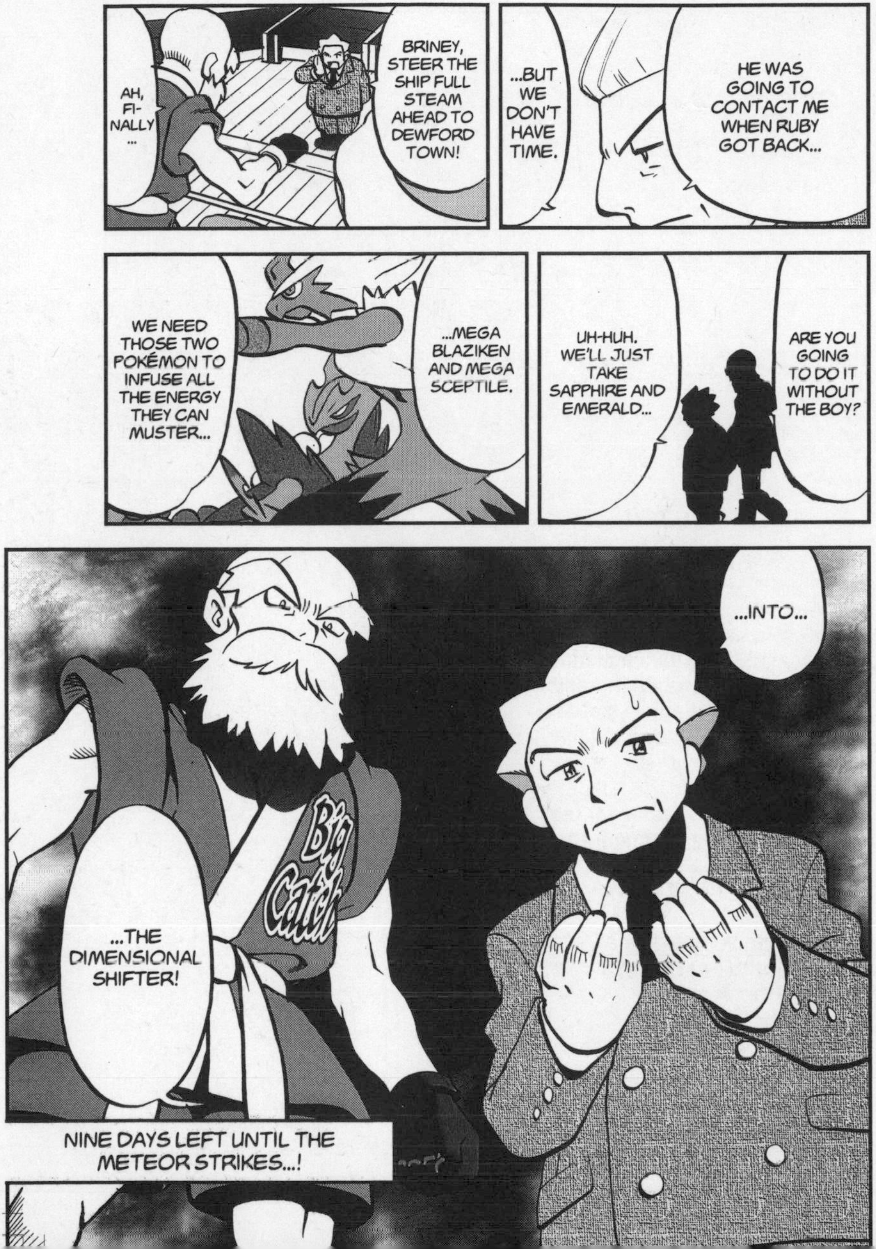
HE WAS GOING TO CONTACT ME WHEN RUBY GOT BACK...
...BUT WE DON'T HAVE TIME.
BRINEY, STEER THE SHIP FULL STEAM AHEAD TO DEWFORD TOWN!
AH, FI-NALLY...
ARE YOU GOING TO DO IT WITHOUT THE BOY?
UH-HUH. WE'LL JUST TAKE SAPPHIRE AND EMERALD...
...MEGA BLAZIKEN AND MEGA SCEPTILE.
WE NEED THOSE TWO POKÉMON TO INFUSE ALL THE ENERGY THEY CAN MUSTER...
...INTO...
Big Catch
...THE DIMENSIONAL SHIFTER!
NINE DAYS LEFT UNTIL THE METEOR STRIKES...!

MEGA EVOLUTION

A super evolution that can only be used in situations when incredible power is needed, such as battles and long-distance travel at high altitudes. On top of that, both the Trainer and the Pokémon require a particular stone for the Mega Evolution to succeed. The bond between the Pokémon and the Trainer is critical as well.

It can be shocking to see a Pokémon who has finished evolving transform into yet another form, but the transformation is not permanent. After a momentary boost in power, the Pokémon returns to its usual final form. The origin of Mega Evolution is still unknown.

Pokémon ΩRuby • αSapphire
Volume 1
VIZ Media Edition

Story by HIDENORI KUSAKA
Art by SATOSHI YAMAMOTO

©2016 The Pokémon Company International.
©1995–2016 Nintendo/Creatures Inc./GAME FREAK inc.
TM, ®, and character names are trademarks of Nintendo.
POCKET MONSTERS SPECIAL ΩRUBY • αSAPPHIRE Vol. 1
by Hidenori KUSAKA, Satoshi YAMAMOTO
© 2015 Hidenori KUSAKA, Satoshi YAMAMOTO
All rights reserved.
Original Japanese edition published by SHOGAKUKAN.
English translation rights in the United States of America, Canada, the United
Kingdom, Ireland, Australia and New Zealand arranged with SHOGAKUKAN.

Translation—Tetsuichiro Miyaki
English Adaptation—Bryant Turnage
Touch-Up & Lettering—Annaliese Christman
Design—Shawn Carrico
Editor—Annette Roman

Printed in the U.S.A.

Published by
VIZ Media, LLC
P.O. Box 77010
San Francisco, CA 94107

10 9 8 7 6 5 4 3 2 1
First printing, September 2016

www.viz.com

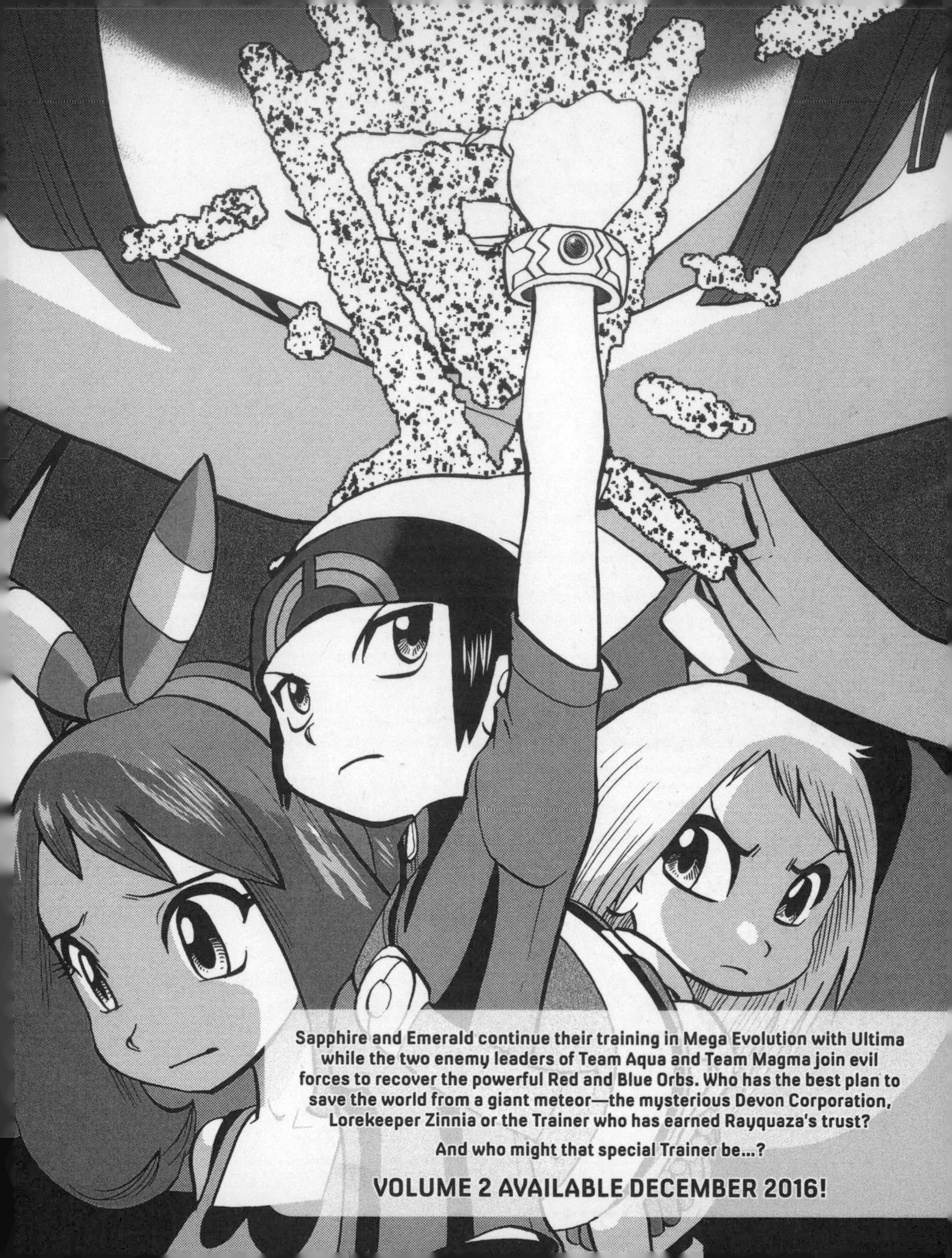
Sapphire and Emerald continue their training in Mega Evolution with Ultima while the two enemy leaders of Team Aqua and Team Magma join evil forces to recover the powerful Red and Blue Orbs. Who has the best plan to save the world from a giant meteor—the mysterious Devon Corporation, Lorekeeper Zinnia or the Trainer who has earned Rayquaza's trust?
And who might that special Trainer be...?
VOLUME 2 AVAILABLE DECEMBER 2016!

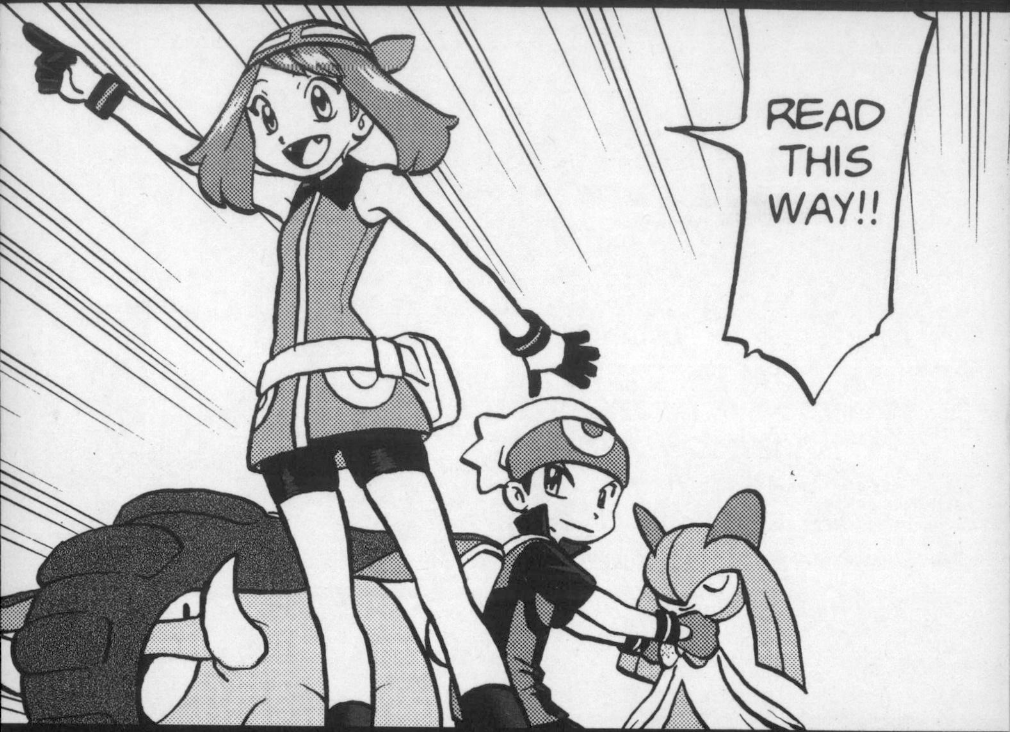
READ THIS WAY!!

THIS IS THE END OF THIS GRAPHIC NOVEL!

To properly enjoy this VIZ Media graphic novel, please turn it around and begin reading from right to left.

This book has been printed in the original Japanese format in order to preserve the orientation of the original artwork. Have fun with it!

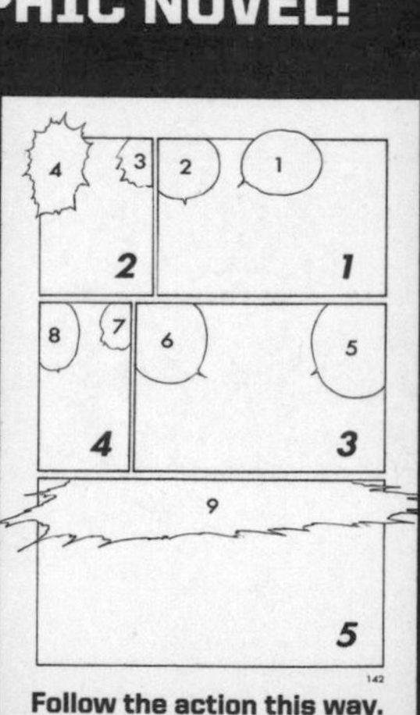
1
2
1
3
4
2
5
6
3
7
8
4
9
5

Follow the action this way.